PREY FOR ME

PREY FOR ME

A Psycho-Sexual Thriller

John Casti

The X Press

Prey for Me is a work of fiction. All the characters are products of the author's imagination and should not be construed as real, and any resemblance to actual persons living or dead is entirely coincidental. Neither the publisher nor the author can be held liable for any third-party material referenced in the book.

First printing 2020

Published by The X-Press, Orlando, FL and Vienna, Austria

ISBN 978-0-9972557-7-5 paperback
ISBN 978-0-9972557-8-2 e-book

To those who understand the difference between need *and* want*—*
and are not afraid to act upon it

Prologue

Five Years Earlier

London

The lecture hall at the London School of Economics was filling fast as she made her way to a seat in the first row. Wearing a pair of sheer black stockings with a short skirt, she wanted to attract the attention of the professor, whom she'd been seeing in a secret relationship for a few weeks now.

She thought to herself that coming from New Zealand to the LSE was the best decision she'd ever made. Her course of study was Behavioral Psychology and Finance, the two sides of which she hoped would shed light on what had happened to her in her past, as well as what could happen with her life in the future.

The professor entered the room and moved to the podium, which was directly across from where she was sitting. As he started shuffling his notes to begin the lecture, she sat up straight, crossed her legs to attract his attention and showed him a coquettish smile.

She thought he was extremely attractive: a tall, dark, Italian-appearing man in his early forties, slightly graying hair and very dark brown, sensuous eyes. She liked everything from his appearance and behavior to his slight accent that mimicked her own Kiwi twang. It was that common geographical background that had brought them together in the first place, she recalled. And for dinner tonight they would revisit the scene of their first meeting, the Radio Rooftop Bar.

*

Radio Rooftop is one of London's most iconic venues, situated on the 10th Floor of ME London, one of the most luxurious hotels in London with striking views across the River Thames and London's impressive skyline. They took a table outside on the terrace to enjoy the changing views of the capital as the sun set, stretching from the Shard and St. Paul's downstream, to the London Eye and Big Ben.

"This place is so special," she told him. "I'm sure you remember when we began our time together here, five weeks ago and counting. I'm very happy you chose it tonight."

"Yes," he replied, "it seems a fitting location for a conversation about the lovely time we've spent together and where dame fortune may be leading us."

She looked across the table with an almost predatory gaze, which then softened into a welcoming smile as she told him, "I'm enjoying you so much. I hope we can continue to develop our relationship into something very, very special. Maybe even into a permanent partnership. How would you feel about that?"

"I think I'd be very happy about such a future with you. But we're getting ahead of ourselves. First you have to finish your studies here, then turn that new-found knowledge into a good job in The City. That should all be completed by the end of the year. Let's talk about escalating our life together then. Meanwhile, we should just enjoy what we have now and be thankful for it."

"I'm so happy since I asked you to be my mentor," she said, knowing it would please him. Then, deliberately trying to mimic his slightly formal way of speaking, she continued: "Here we are now already speaking about a lifetime partnership. I would never have believed that I'd have such amazing luck."

Lifting his glass to hers, he said, "Let's have a nice dinner and talk about that mentoring and luck just a bit more. Okay?"

"Perfect," she said, opening the menu.

In the end, they decided to share a Mediterranean Tapas Board for their main course. While going through the olives, beef meatballs, padron peppers and guacamole, he described in a bit more detail the type of mentoring he could offer to accelerate the development of her career.

He told her he would provide consultations on various questions that came up as she made her way from the LSE lecture halls to the trading floors in The City. He would also open doors for her at various financial firms and offer letters of recommendation to influential managers at those firms. Taken together, these actions should suffice to have a good job waiting for her immediately upon graduation, he assured her, "but only if you work hard and graduate with honors."

"That's exactly what I have in mind," she told him.

"I will do all those things with pleasure," he confirmed. "Maybe we can get started on it as early as next week. What do you think?"

She agreed and they moved on to the dessert course, a bowl of coconut and vanilla rice pudding for her, a chocolate crumble for him.

He looked around and then said, "The restaurant is getting a bit crowded and is really too noisy for a serious conversation. If you're agreeable, perhaps we could talk more comfortably about the future together over a nightcap at my place. As you know, I live rather near here so we can stretch our legs a bit on the way."

"That sounds lovely."

*

A couple of weeks later, she came to the professor's office, closed the door and said to him, "We never seem to go out any more.

Unless I'm very much mistaken, you appear to be doing all you can to distance yourself from me. What's going on?"

"Nothing is 'going on'," he replied. "I'm just overwhelmed with work now that the term is nearing an end. It's the usual stuff. Student consultations, preparation of final exams, faculty meetings, et al."

"I see," she replied, not seeing anything at all.

She paused for a moment, then jumped up from her chair, "I have an idea. Let's go for an excursion outside London on Saturday. Just a day trip to someplace nice and interesting. What do you think?"

"That sounds very appealing," he replied. "Where do you want to go?"

"It will be a surprise. We can stay at your flat Friday evening and then get an early start on Saturday. I'll take you to one of my favorite places."

"Which would be ... ?"

"A secret until we get there. I said it would be a *surprise*."

"Well, alright." he consented. "Why don't you come around five on Friday? I'll be right here working, and we'll go to dinner."

"That sounds perfect."

*

As they left the professor's flat on Saturday morning, he couldn't hold back his curiosity any longer, and pressed her to tell him where they were going. Finally, she said, "We're going to get a train at Victoria Station that will take us to Lewes, where we'll change for a train to Seaford. From there we'll walk a bit and enjoy the day visiting the Seven Sisters."

"Oh what a wonderful idea," he said. The Seven Sisters comprised a magnificent series of white chalk cliffs lining the coast of the Sussex South Downs, with grass as green as a golf course and magnificent sea views. "Friends have often told me how lovely they are. But I've never taken the time to go out to see them in person. I'm looking forward to doing that today—with *you* as my special guide."

On the train to Lewes, they had a compartment to themselves and were able to relax, enjoy the scenery and talk about their past, present, and especially their future. At one point, the conversation waned for a few minutes. She thought this would be a good time to ask him yet once again about something that had been bothering her.

"Why have you been ignoring me?" she asked. "I've barely seen you at all recently, and even then only in your flat. Are you embarrassed by being with me or something?"

"No, I'm not at all embarrassed. Just the opposite. But I have a potential problem—and an opportunity—brewing with my colleagues that bears upon us."

"What kind of problem?" she inquired.

"A few weeks ago, one of my colleagues told me that I will be evaluated for promotion at the faculty meeting at the end of the semester. As a result, I have a huge amount of work facing me in the coming weeks, preparing the material for the committee to use in their evaluation. There will certainly be very little free time for us to meet like this again. In view of this development, I think we should not see each other personally after today, at least not until the semester has ended."

She sat back, silently digesting this development, as he wondered what was really going through her mind. Finally, she leaned toward him, took his hands in hers and said, "I understand. Such a chance doesn't come very often to get an endowed professorship at such a prestigious university as the LSE. You can't afford to bet your job that it will ever come around again."

He leaned back, looking at her lovingly, and told her, "We have a couple of months until you graduate. During that time, I will still support you as a mentor and help introduce you to people in The City. But for your sake and mine, I think the best course of action is not to see each other privately until the term is over. It's only a matter of a few weeks, and then the coast will be clear for us to move forward together. My promotion will have been settled, you will have graduated, and then we can do whatever we want. There's just no time for us to do that in the immediate future. That's all."

He went on to point out that this period was crucial for her life, too. "The personal and professional decisions you'll make in the coming months will impact your life for many years, perhaps longer. I feel you need as many degrees of freedom as possible to make these decisions, unencumbered by a relationship whose future is problematic, at best."

"Why do you think it's problematic?" she asked, almost too sweetly.

"Primarily because we're each making decisions in this period that will send our lives along different trajectories from where they are today. Who can really say whether those new trajectories will still be moving in parallel or will begin to diverge?"

She sat silently digesting this metaphor. Finally, she nodded her head in agreement and turned to look out the window.

I think he's trying to get rid of me, she thought quietly to herself.

*

They exited the train at Seaford, a small town next to the ocean with a lovely esplanade. Leaving the town, they began to walk up the fairly steep footpath along the grassy mounds that led to the top of the cliffs, or 'sisters,' as they're called.

For the next several miles they had nothing but spectacular sea views over an endless ocean stretching out to their right. But they had to be careful, as most of the cliffs were not fenced off for safety, but were left bare and unprotected so their beauty could be appreciated.

He remarked, "There don't seem to be very many people out today. Maybe because it's Saturday, not Sunday, and the weather's a bit cloudy. So much the better for us. But don't get too close to the edge. It's a long way down to the water."

At one point along their walk, she asked him if they could stop for a moment and catch their breath. He agreed and they stood looking out over the sea.

"Spectacular view," he exclaimed. "I will certainly never forget this place. Thanks so much for bringing me here."

She smiled back at him, stepped back a bit and looked over his shoulder at the lighthouse down next to the ocean.

Once they caught their breath, they began walking again, and soon the path leveled off. They were then able to relax as they walked, no longer walking uphill but on flat ground. Finally, they reached the top of the cliffs.

As they were walking along the edge, admiring nature, a seagull landed nearby. He motioned towards it and said longingly, "That bird seems to have more freedom than either of us right now."

She looked sternly at him and replied, "That's not my fault. You're the one who unilaterally took the decision to end our partnership. You say it will be just temporary. But how do I really know? I think it's very selfish of you and I don't like it one little bit."

They walked a bit further and she looked out over the sea to the lighthouse and told him, "Sometimes I feel so let down by people that I'd like to become a lighthouse keeper. The problems in life are other people and their agendas. Out on that lighthouse, I could escape from all that human factor stuff and become pure."

They walked another couple of hundred yards or so in silence, then stopped as he said, "You don't seem to realize that I truly want what's best for both of us. We each have to re-program our lives over the next few months. To do this effectively, we both require as much freedom of action as we can get in order to take decisions that we'll have to live with for many years—perhaps the rest of our lives. Don't you understand that?"

"That sounds nice on the surface. But in fact it's very self-serving. You want what's best for you, and right now I'm just an extra weight you have to carry. Now you want to get rid of the weight and fly like that bird."

She stared at him for several seconds, her face frozen in a manic look. Trying to break the tension, he bent down to retie his shoelace.

He's an unfaithful friend. Like my former husband. I don't want any more unfaithful men. I can find some other advisor to help me get a job. The world must be rid of unfaithful men.

She surveyed the wide-open scenery. There was not another soul in sight. As he stood back up, she spread out her arms, and with an enigmatic smile on her face moved toward him as if to give him a big hug. He spread his arms to welcome her, as well.

When she got close enough to touch him, she moved her arms back and gave him a big push in the chest, sending him over the edge of the cliff! He was so astonished that he didn't even scream out as he fell onto the rocks nearly 300 feet below.

Smiling slightly, she then stepped back and nodded her head in confirmation of her actions. Turning away from the sea, she began to make her way back toward the train station for the return to London.

Episode I

The E-Mail

Santa Fe

The last rays of the setting sun bathed the towering Sangre de Cristo Mountains in the pastel pink-and-blood-red-orange glow that artists make pilgrimages to Santa Fe to experience.

Victor Luigi Safir gazed pensively out of his study window at the reddish hues on the ski area, the colors that gave these majestic mountains their name. Victor swirled the last remnants of the smoky-flavored Lagavulin whisky around in his glass, puzzling yet again over the breakdown three months earlier of his marriage to Karin.

How had it all come apart so quickly, he wondered? One day, she was there as she'd always been, joking, cajoling, laughing, teasing, supporting; then, virtually overnight, she told him that seventeen years of being the junior partner in Victor L. Safir, Inc. was about fifteen years too many, and she wanted to get on with her own life.

On her way out the door, Karin had delivered an even more stinging assessment.

"Couple your privileged upbringing with an inborn sense of entitlement," she said, her two suitcases sitting in the taxicab, "and it's not surprising that you still look at every woman who piques your curiosity. And just like your work in mathematics, you never give up until you've solved the problem. Well, that may work in mathematics and make you a world-renowned person. But let me tell you things simply don't work that way at all in real-life.

I've spent way too many years hoping you'd finally grow up. But it never happened. Now it's someone else's turn to stroke your ego. This Karin has had enough."

Just before Karin left in the taxi for her flight to Sweden, she asked Victor to send her things to her sister's home, telling him her lawyer would be in touch.

Victor knew exactly how it had happened. He had simply refused to accept the consequences that the extended absences in distant time-zones for his work had inevitably brought down upon him. No one, not even someone as selfless as Karin, would or could provide a support system for him indefinitely.

Now Victor couldn't help but recall another observation Karin once made several years earlier when she was confronting him about one of his long absences.

"Victor, you simply don't realize how lucky you've been in your life," she said. "Your genius in mathematics has supplied you with a lifelong support system that few others ever have. First it was your parents, then the university, then a tenured faculty job in Zürich. But not even that was enough."

Victor recalled staring at her and searching himself for a reply or a way to interrupt her.

"Then you became famous for your work, so you were coddled by the system like a small child. In short, you were never forced to grow up. Intellectually, you're off the scale; personally and socially, you're still a spoiled little child."

Recalling all of this, Victor realized that he saw the signs of an impending break. But as always, he simply ignored them.

Like the stresses in an earthquake fault that must be relieved from time-to-time in order to avoid the Big One, the marital stresses had also been building up incident-by-incident, episode-by-episode. Victor knew he'd done nothing to relieve these strains and tensions. So the iron laws of human nature—every bit as relentless and unyielding as all laws of nature—took control and Karin finally snapped.

Goodbye marriage, Victor acknowledged to himself ruefully.

The saddest part came with Karin's final words to him as she got into the taxi taking her to the airport.

"I'll always love you, Victor. And I'm not throwing you away. But I'm pushing fifty, and I can't wait for miracles. With you, 'someday' just never comes. I'm sure you'll soon find another woman to look after you. You're good at that. I hope she'll be able to manage your nature better than I could. I've done my part. Now it's time to start looking after my life, not yours."

Okay.

In the many weeks following Karin's departure, Victor thought he'd simply have to pick himself up off the floor and start over again. It wasn't the first time he'd been laid flat in life. But his optimistic side always hoped it would be the last. In any case, let's have a hard look at the facts, said Victor's analytical mind, as he brought out a sheet of yellow legal paper to record them.

On the physical side of the balance sheet, he was a fifty-two-year-old academic and intellectual, standing just a shade over six feet tall, with a straight back and no signs yet of the paunchy middle-aged spread that had overtaken so many of his colleagues. A bit on the slender side at 170 pounds, he could thank his daily workouts at the gym for his excellent physical condition. His Sicilian genes showed up in the dark complexion and black, wavy hair, now slightly graying around the edges.

Victor's dark-brown eyes were of a type often seen in people with a gift for conceptual thought, although he always felt they were so large they'd look better on a cow than a human. Still, on a number of occasions women had told him that his eyes projected a kind of sensuous melancholia. Victor never thought of cows as being especially sensuous. Given the sad fate of a cow on this earth, a touch of melancholy was perhaps not totally out of place. In any event, he was ready to accept this feminine verdict in the cause of furthering personal relations with the opposite sex.

Turning to the non-physical side of his asset column, Victor was a professor of philosophy and science at the Rio Grande Institute in Santa Fe, New Mexico. He was known in certain circles worldwide for his popular writings on various aspects of man and nature living in that twilight zone where science becomes philosophical and philosophy becomes scientific. This sprang from his curiosity about eternal puzzles like the origin of life, the existence of intelligent extraterrestrials and the importance of nature versus nurture in determining human social behavioral patterns. He had turned this curiosity into an avocation by using questions of this sort as the core material for a series of popular books and lectures that had brought him a wide international following.

His academic research efforts however were directed quite differently. He focused on how to use computers as laboratories for experimenting with systems like business enterprises and road-traffic networks, doing controlled, repeatable experiments of the sort that cannot be performed on those same systems in the real world.

The combination of academic work, writing, lecturing, and consulting brought in a more than comfortable income each year, which together with his extensive foreign travel and wide circle of friends and acquaintances, gave Victor a lifestyle that most people could only dream about. A pretty decent asset side of the balance sheet, he concluded, with a characteristic lack of modesty.

Victor was forced to admit that the liability side was not without its own impressive set of entries. There were now two failed marriages, one short and ill-fated in his early 20s—and now the second—heading the list. No children from either marriage, a fact that his Sicilian nature deeply regretted.

Throw in a self-absorbed nature, prolonged absences from home and family, and a rather dominant, controlling Type A personality, and the formula for marital disaster not-so-magically appears. He wrote all of this down dutifully.

When he was finished and reviewed his document, he wrote at the bottom that he seemed to have an innate inability to understand just what women wanted from him, anyway.

Scrutinizing these pros and cons like a tax accountant trying to ferret out every possible deduction, Victor wondered what it all added up to. No refunds, that's for sure, he sadly concluded.

If one could say anything about Victor's personal relationships from this mass of conflicting signals and confusing data, it was that he would probably be well-advised in the future to stay away from conventional living arrangements like marriage, home, and family. He just didn't seem cut out for that kind of life.

On the other hand, logic told him that every relationship—personal, professional, family, business—has only a finite useful lifetime. Victor believed that the people who prospered in life were those having an innate sense for when a relationship had run its natural course—and were not afraid to make a change, even if there was no ready-made, new relationship waiting in the wings.

Perhaps, he thought, what happened between him and Karin was foreordained, and he just happened to have had the bad luck to be the one that got left.

After all, the *a priori* odds are fifty-fifty that when you enter into a relationship of any kind, you'll be the one that gets left, he reasoned. But that was Victor the mathematician at work and not the man.

Victor wondered whether he could change some of these liabilities. Unfortunately, though, self-knowledge, he ruefully thought, is by no means a universal tool for changing who you are. And he was old enough and experienced enough to know that no relationship, marriage or otherwise, was a reform school.

After several decades of experimentation, he had come to the conclusion that intimate personal relationships were a lot like shopping for shoes. You go to the shoe store and see some design that blows you away. You just have to have it. You try it on and discover that while it looks fantastic, it simply doesn't fit. It's painful to walk in and no amount of stretching or after-market service is going to change that. What to do?

Well, Victor thought, all you can do is forget that shoe and look around for another design that is also attractive—but fits. You buy that one and hope for the best. And for a long time it works just fine. Then like every relationship, even with shoes, eventually another model comes available that is even more attractive and you simply must give it a go.

This shoe-store metaphor seemed to be the story of Victor's life, socially-speaking. Actually, thinking about his marriage to Karin in this context, he was a bit surprised it lasted as long as it did.

*

Consoling himself marginally with this bit of armchair philosophy, Victor leaned back in his desk chair and again stared out at the dying embers of pastel orange and pale pink on the Sangres, as they slowly merged into dark shadows of gray and black across the ski slopes, Night began to fall.

Just as he was about to rouse himself out of this reverie and pour another splash of Lagavulin, one of the two computers beneath his desk pinged softly, like the last gasp of a dying pinball machine, distracting him for a moment from the illusory comforts of the liquor cabinet.

Damn, thought Victor, *I've really got to silence that e-mail notification system.*

Even so, right now it had the salutary effect of drawing his mind away from the destructive channels it had been running in lately, especially at this time of the evening. He looked over to see what part of the world was calling for his attention now.

To his surprise, he saw the message was from England—but not from one of his usual correspondents. Pretty late in the night for someone in Britain to be up sending him anything. That's one of the best things about e-mail. It respects no time zones or national boundaries. How did we ever do without it, Victor idly wondered, as he called the message up onto his screen:

> Dear Professor Safir,
>
> My name is Elisabeth-Alexandra Lynne. I work as a financial analyst for the firm of Merit Capital Management, Ltd. in London, where I'm currently developing models of decision-making in financial markets. I've read of your work on computer modeling of such markets with great interest, and would like to speak with you about it. I'm planning a trip to the Financial Analyst's meeting in Tortola in the British Virgin Islands at the beginning of November. Would it be possible for me to come to Santa Fe afterwards to meet with you? I'm sure you get many requests of this sort. So I hope you will be available to talk with me.
>
> Sincerely yours,
> Elisabeth-Alexandra Lynne

This kind of request was by no means unusual for Victor. His books and media appearances had brought enough international recognition to attract a variety of admirers to Santa Fe to meet with him. If he was in town, Victor was always happy to oblige.

One never knew where such a meeting would lead, and not infrequently it resulted in an interesting professional venture.

Meeting this Ms. Lynne was all part of what was increasingly becoming a new-found—but entirely unanticipated—career as an evangelist for the joys of modern science. And encounters with the financial services industry are the things from which juicy consulting contracts arise.

With the financial demands being made upon him in the last letter from Karin's lawyer still dancing through his head, Victor had the uneasy feeling he'd soon be investing rather heavily in divorce once again.

The lucrative consulting fees on offer nowadays in the financial services sector could soothe that pain considerably. So Victor dashed off his reply:

> Dear Ms. Lynne:
>
> Thanks very much for your message. I'm sorry to possibly spoil a visit to Santa Fe for you, but as it happens I will be speaking at the Financial Analyst's meeting in Tortola mentioned in your message. So perhaps we can arrange to meet there to discuss the issues you want to speak with me about. While I have very limited time in Tortola and several people from firms such as your own to speak with during my visit, I will certainly find time to hear about you and your firm's work. May I suggest that we try to find each other at the 'get-acquainted' cocktail party on Sunday evening before the meeting? We can then see if a follow-up meeting would be of mutual benefit. Thank you again for your interest in my work.
>
> With best wishes,
> VS

In his recent work, Victor was studying how to create what in essence was a computer game based on the stock market. The players were the traders, who would use rules to buy, sell or hold securities.

Since Victor would have control over what each trader was actually doing and would know the kinds of rules they were employing to make their trading decisions, he hoped to use this silicon stock market to uncover patterns in the way the traders shift from one trading strategy to another. His belief was that this would open up the possibility of creating a true science of financial decision-making.

The commercial rewards for the first person to come up with such a theory of how traders act and why had not escaped his attention.

So Victor wasn't one bit surprised to receive Ms. Lynne's message. The presentation he was to give in Tortola in a few weeks time would be the public unveiling of his computer stock market, and he expected a standing-room-only audience to be there to hear it.

Episode II

The Meeting

Tortola (British Virgin Islands)

Blackbeard, Bluebeard, Sir Francis Drake. Victor read the tourist brochure about these great scoundrels and pirates, as the little prop plane dipped low over the azure water on its final approach to the Tortola Airport.

Originally discovered by Christopher Columbus on his second voyage to the New World in 1493, the Virgin Islands were named after the eleven thousand virgin followers of Saint Ursula, who was martyred in the fourth century, along with her followers, in Germany.

If there were ever any saints in Tortola, or virgins either, they are almost surely gone by now, Victor thought to himself, especially during a convention of traders and financial analysts.

Once the British took control of the island in the 17th century, cultivating a profitable sugar industry with imported African slaves, the old pirates' days were numbered. But today, the pirates steal their victim's gold using programmed trading, insider information, shady tax dodges and the Internet.

Upon landing, Victor grabbed his small suitcase at an open-sided shed, its sagging walls and corrugated tin roof looking more like a bicycle storage depot than an airport luggage carousel. He tried to get the attention of the lone taxi driver outside the terminal building, but the man seemed more interested in an impromptu game of craps with his pals.

A small bribe finally convinced the driver that a hot fare in one hand was vastly preferable to a cold pair of dice in the other, and they drove out of the airport into the bright late-afternoon sun along a road circling the dazzling, white-sand beach.

When Victor told the taxi driver he had spent his honeymoon on the island many years before, the driver, no doubt angling for a good tip, said "Ah, yes, Tortola. Very good place for lovers, sir."

The sun goes down in the blink of an eye in the tropics, and by the time Victor checked into The Sugar Mill Hotel it was already edging into dark twilight. This stately resort was set on a slight rise above the beach amid lush, tropical vegetation. The beach was protected by a reef that provided calm waters for the numerous swimmers, surfers, and sunbathers, whose day was already ending with a round of margaritas and planter's punch at the beach bar.

Victor thought about his conversation with the taxi driver about his visit to the island, more than seventeen years earlier for his honeymoon with Karin, spent just up the road at a similar resort that seemed to have disappeared. That was a truly wonderful time. He was forced to acknowledge yet again that it was all gone now.

Victor did recall that The Sugar Mill's restaurant—in the restored ruins of a 365-year-old sugar mill—offered the finest cuisine on the island: a mouth-watering combination of French delicacy and Caribbean spices, betraying not one whit of the island's British heritage and administration. He also noted how improved the place seemed to be today, giving him high hopes that at least this part of his trip would measure up to his happy memories.

He'd have to hurry if he wanted to get to the evening's cocktail party reception. He had barely enough time to unpack, grab a quick shower, register for the meeting, and get down to the terrace bar to meet the finance types he'd promised to see—where there might also be the inquisitive Ms. Lynne.

As Victor joined the party, the early-bird conference participants were already gathered around the horseshoe-shaped beach bar, swapping lies about financial coups in distant time zones and the unhappy state of the world's markets. Quickly grabbing an unidentifiable tropical drink from the tray of a passing waiter, he gazed around the gathering, wishing not for the first time that he could somehow avoid rituals such as cocktail parties.

Lately they had become as much a part of his life as airports and banquet speeches. Perhaps we really do get the kind of life we deserve, he said to himself, as he moved into the midst of the crowd and looked around for a familiar face. Before he could complete his scan of the terrace though, a hard slap on the back nearly caused him to spill his drink over the man standing next to him.

"Victor, long time, no hear," came a loud, British-tainted bellow from over his left shoulder.

It was Jack Carleton, a former colleague of Victor's in Zürich. Jack had abandoned academia several years earlier for the high-flying world of financial derivatives—and a several-fold increase in his income—at a large trading house in the City of London, and he'd never looked back. By now Jack had acquired almost legendary status as one of the world's cleverest and most successful manipulators of these arcane instruments of financial magic.

"At a gathering of predators like this, I knew you'd be somewhere close by," Victor said. "How are the sharks treating you in The City nowadays, Jack?"

"Wrong question, Vic, old son. The right question is how are they going to treat *you* tomorrow when you roll-out your stock-market simulation program," Jack said. "Rumor has it that it's close enough to the real thing that the computer almost has the printer spitting out actual dollars, pounds and Euros. This kind of tool might put some of us 'hands-on' professionals out to pasture. You wouldn't want to do that to an old friend like me. Or would you?"

"Jack, there's no one I'd rather put out to pasture than you. But don't hold your breath waiting for it to happen. We academics are a merciful lot. And we're still as far away as ever from the real money on the floor of the exchanges and the trading rooms of the Street. Incidentally, I heard you would be moving on to bigger and better things in New York soon. When will that be?"

The very moment these words left Victor's mouth, he saw Jack's attention drift away, his eyes staring off into the distance somewhere over Victor's shoulder. Turning to see what had drawn Jack away from discussing money, his all-time favorite topic, Victor spotted a statuesque, dark-haired woman with even darker-looking eyes who had come on to the terrace.

She was dressed elegantly, but simply, in a black silken sheath dress. Victor's gaze was captured by a liquid silver necklace draped over a figure that took his breath away. Conversations underway on the terrace and around the bar all seemed to drop their decibel level to a hushed murmur, as she caught the eye of virtually every man in the place. The waiter made a beeline for her, offering a glass of champagne.

Accepting it graciously, she looked out over the group much as a queen might survey her subjects.

"Who is that lovely creature?" asked Jim Maloney, one of the New York traders, who had joined Victor and Jack.

"That's Elisabeth-Alexandra Lynne," answered Jack. "Every trader in The City has a thing for her. She's an analyst at Merit, the asset management firm. By all accounts she has a brain as sharp as her body is beautiful."

This is *going to be interesting,* thought Victor.

"Excuse me a moment, Jack. I'll catch up with you later," Victor said, as he left the group and started across the terrace.

Noting the familiar gleam in Victor's eye, Jack simply shook his head.

Grabbing a frozen margarita from the bar, Victor kept his eye on Ms. Lynne as she moved around the room, greeting an acquaintance here, smiling to another there, her attention drifting from group to group. When she spotted Victor, her gaze fixed upon him like the radar of an F–16 fighter locking onto an anti-aircraft site.

"Ms. Elisabeth-Alexandra Lynne, I presume?" said Victor in his most disarming tone of voice, as he approached her, noticing that her eyes were very dark-green, not brown as he'd thought earlier from a distance.

"Professor Safir. How nice to meet you. I recognize you from the dust jacket of your last book," she replied.

Her voice was an indescribable, impossible combination of the breathless, little-girl tone of Marilyn Monroe and the dulcet, husky tones of a sultry torch singer. His first thought was that it must be the most seductive voice he'd ever heard. He could listen to that voice whispering in his ear all day—and night.

"When people call me Professor Safir, I start looking around for my grandfather," he said jokingly. "Please call me Victor," he told her, hoping she didn't notice how difficult it seemed for him to take his eyes off her.

Seen up close, her features were not quite as perfect as Victor had imagined: eyes just a bit too close together, nose slightly askew, a tooth slightly out of alignment. Strangely, though, these imperfections made her seem even sexier and more alluring—perhaps because they made her a real person, not a Madison Avenue image of a goddess. Odd how endearing it is to live in an imperfect world, Victor reflected, as she spoke.

"Only if you'll call me Alex. All my friends do," she responded with a sort of shy smile. "I've really been looking forward to our meeting. It was extremely kind of you to agree to see me. I do hope we'll find some time to talk."

She was doubtlessly one of the most stunning women Victor had seen in years: lovely, leggy, and to be descriptive without all the words, 'built.' Alex's oval face and porcelain-smooth complexion was framed in long, nearly black hair, pulled back and drawn up in a bun that reminded Victor of the librarian at his grammar school, the leading lady of many of his most erotic pubescent dreams.

This woman was definitely no librarian. And the dress that might have looked hopelessly old-fashioned on someone less striking, looked stunningly modern, even post-chic, on her. As she spoke to him, Victor was drawn in by her intelligent look and her deep-green eyes.

Alex's light tan suggested someone who spent holidays in the south of France, Victor imagined. She wore no rings on her well-manicured fingers, but there was something about the way she lightly touched his forearm when she spoke and the glint in her eye that felt somehow ... predatory. Victor had sensed this before in unmarried women, something he termed 'the hunting instinct'—and not always with single women, either.

"Please tell me a bit more about your interest in stock market simulations. I gather your firm is doing something in this area," he said to open their conversation.

"We're thinking about building a computer model of the dynamics of the trading floor along the lines of what you seem to be doing already. So I'm extremely interested in your talk tomorrow.

I'd like to discuss how we might make use of some of your ideas in our own work," she told him.

"I'm not yet committed tonight," Victor said to her. "Perhaps if you're free for dinner we could talk then?" As he spoke, Victor felt sure that Jack Carleton would understand if he were forced to cancel their dinner engagement tonight for the sake of such a good cause as Alex. She nodded her agreement.

"Excellent. Shall we meet in the lobby then at, say, 8 o'clock? Meanwhile, I'll book a table for us on the veranda."

"That sounds just fine. I'll see you later then," Alex smiled, as she shook Victor's hand and began moving away to join a colleague from her firm.

Watching her walk away, Victor couldn't help but admire the fluid, cat-like grace with which she moved and the tantalizing motions going on beneath that silk dress. Watch yourself, cautioned his rational side. He remembered what his Sicilian grandmother always said: When things look too good to be true, they usually are.

Smiling to himself at this snippet of folk wisdom, Victor moved to the bar to refill his glass and contemplate just a bit more the delectable Elisabeth-Alexandra Lynne.

*

The soft glow of a pair of candles, their flames flickering in the gentle breeze blowing in from the sea, coupled with the relaxing sound of the waves breaking just below the wall of the terrace, created just the right ambience. Victor was glad he was able to arrange a table far removed from the hustle and bustle of the main dining room.

Alex had changed into a stunning diaphanous peach-colored dress, with a dramatically plunging neckline. As she stared at him dreamily, Victor explained the logic of the stockmarket simulation he'd built, managing somehow to keep his eyes above the level of her shoulders.

"But enough about business, Alex," Victor said. "Given a chance, we professors can go on forever. So tell me something about yourself," as the waiter began clearing away the remnants of their meal.

Leaning back, Victor took a sip of the rich Jamaican Blue Mountain coffee that had been set before him and looked over at her expectantly.

"There's not all that much to say, really. I'm just a farm girl from New Zealand, who came to the big city to find out about life."

"New Zealand!" Victor exclaimed. "That's a surprise. I never would have pegged you as a Kiwi. All the New Zealanders I've ever met spoke with a twang you could hear halfway across the Pacific. You sound more like a refined Brit to my untutored ear."

"Lots of people tell me that. Perhaps it's the drama lessons I had as a child. Maybe it's my having lived in London for several years. I don't know. I am a bit of a linguistic chameleon though, so if you were to see me back in Christchurch you'd hear—and see—a very different person, I can assure you."

"How do you like living in London? Given your background in New Zealand, I imagine you find it very exciting."

"Well, I was lucky to get a very nice apartment just near Harrod's, in a building housing the Colombian Embassy. The house is well-maintained and the other tenants are quiet and mind their own business. As for excitement, I do go to the theatre occasionally, as well as to art galleries and the cinema. But most of my excitement comes from my job at Merit."

As they continued this idle chit-chat probing each other's backgrounds, Victor and Alex eyed each other with the same thought in mind: here's a solution to a problem. For Alex, an older man, an intellectual who took her seriously as a professional, a companion, a lover. Victor, on the other hand, saw a ravishingly beautiful, young woman, who was smart, good company, and who would fill the empty space in his life left by Karin's abrupt departure.

"Alex, You don't impress me as much of a farm girl," Victor said. "You're not joking now, are you?"

As he said this, Victor wondered if he might be losing his touch 'reading' women. He'd certainly missed some crucial signs about Alex already.

"No, truly. I spent my first seventeen years growing up on a sheep ranch outside Christchurch. My parents then divorced, and I moved to the city with my mother, brother and sister."

"What then?"

"I went to Canterbury University in Christchurch and did an undergraduate degree in psychology, jumped into a disastrous marriage that lasted only a year, and after the divorce went to London to get as far away from New Zealand as I possibly could."

"You studied finance in London?" asked Victor, now rather intrigued by Alex's background and her readiness to tell him about it.

"I was always interested in the competitive aspect of trading. I did a master's degree at the London School of Economics, where I got interested in the psychology of decision-making. It was a natural step from there to study the psychology of traders in financial markets, since ultimately that's what drives price movements. The people at Merit saw my thesis and made me an offer. That was a few years ago. And now here I am."

"What do you love about this work?" Victor asked.

“When I first started, I was actually a trader at Merit, not an analyst. As you probably know, this is mostly a man’s game. A lot of the other traders made special efforts to humiliate me by maneuvering me into taking losing positions. But I learned quickly how to turn the tables on them, and found that I had a real talent for buying-and-selling. The best part for me was crushing the egos of those hotshot traders.”

Victor couldn’t help but notice the glee with which she said the word ‘crush.’

Alex paused before she continued:

“I liked to watch them squirm, as the manipulators got manipulated by me, just a poor, little girl from the countryside of New Zealand.”

As she told Victor of these successes, Alex’s eyes took on a far-away look and her voice dropped into an even lower register than normal.

Victor noticed this change and felt almost as if someone were walking over his grave. Maybe, just maybe, he thought, Alex’s cocktail-party façade had slipped a little, giving him a glimpse of an entirely different Alex lurking just below her innocent-appearing surface. *Perhaps she was as much a predator as a prey,* he thought.

Victor decided to turn the conversation back to more personal matters.

“Surely there’s more than just price movements and the warped psychology of traders in your life?” he enquired casually, glancing down at the bare ring finger on both her hands. Noting the direction of his glance, she stated softly—and directly—looking him straight in the eye,

“If you mean boyfriends or a husband, there’s no one I’d care to talk about.”

“Just as simple as that, eh?” responded Victor.

"Yes, as simple as that," she said in the same direct, flat tone as his query.

The challenge in her voice warned Victor that there was a will of iron and a brain as quick as a computer lurking beneath this angelic-looking face. He would have to do better than let his brain run on autopilot if he was hoping to get anywhere near the bedroom with this woman.

As they spoke, she seemed to be staring at Victor with laser-like focus that gave him a vaguely hunted feeling. Recalling her unsettling remark about crushing the egos of hotshot traders, made him wonder about her motives for such emotional feelings.

"What about yourself?" she asked with a seductive smile, as she looked up at him over the edge of her wine glass and sat back in her chair.

Victor went through a fast-forward of his life, a little of which Alex already knew from her reading of the dust jacket bios from his books and what she'd gleaned from his profile on the Institute's web page.

He finished by telling her of his recent 'divorce,' thinking that that sounded more definite than a separation with the divorce still pending. He wondered why he even bothered recounting this unhappy episode, unless he wanted to reassure himself that he could still attract a woman like Alex, a quarter of a century his junior.

After pouring her another glass of the rather fine Montrachet they had shared with the meal, Victor shifted gears and put the ball back into her court.

"Now, Alex, what can I do to help you with your project at Merit?"

"At the moment our group has an *idea* about how we might be able to use your methods to study the way traders change their minds as market conditions change. And we'd like to see if we can implement our thinking about this in a market simulation of the type you've built. But we don't know enough about the innards of these kinds of simulations to feel confident that we can actually do it. Or even if it will work if we did manage to put it together."

Smelling not only a generous consulting contract waiting in the wings, but also the very welcome opportunity to be in contact with Alex on a regular basis, Victor mentioned that the wind was picking up and suggested that they move inside for more discussion of this matter.

Taking her hand as she rose from the table, Victor reached out to give her a gentlemanly handshake and then impulsively planted a small kiss on each cheek, European-style. Alex blushed slightly at this gesture of spontaneous intimacy, then smiled up at Victor as they walked out of the restaurant.

"Where should we go, Victor? I see the bar is pretty raucous and not at all the place for a private chat. Any ideas?"

Looking around the hotel lobby, Victor spied a nice little table for two over in the corner, partially hidden behind a large palm plant.

"How about over by that palm?" he said, pointing to the table.

Alex agreed, and they made their way through the lobby and sat down. After receiving the drinks they'd ordered from the waiter, they got down to business. Victor gave Alex the floor with a small wave of his hand. She smiled softly at this gesture, then asked about the possibility of his visiting their firm for a day or two when he came to Europe.

"At dinner, you'll recall I mentioned that I'm headed to Europe right after this conference. I have to leave right after lunch tomorrow. I'm really here just to give the opening presentation and to meet old colleagues, as well as one special new one—you! But I'm sure I can budget a bit of time to drop by London for a day. We could have a meeting then with your colleagues to talk about your project."

"I was just about to say how wonderful it would be if you could come next week to London. We'd be happy to pay for your trip and your time."

"Wouldn't think of it," said Victor magnanimously, putting on his most disarming smile, but already thinking about how he would maneuver things at that meeting to create an irresistible need for his services in the minds of her firm's management.

"The first consultation is always on the house. I'll check my calendar and send you an email later tonight with a couple of possibilities. After you speak with your colleagues, just pick one of those open slots and send me a message, and we'll do it."

"I'm sure almost any day will be fine," said Alex. "I'll double-check with my colleagues and confirm it by the end of the day tomorrow," she said. They then clinked their glasses to seal the agreement, thus ending the meeting.

Victor signaled the waiter for the bill, and they headed for the elevator to go back up to the rooms. In the elevator, Victor told her how much he enjoyed their evening together and hoped they could have an encore when he came to London.

She looked longingly at him for a moment, seemingly in another world, before coming back to life and agreeing with his suggestion. She repeated that they would correspond by email to fix details of the meeting. After another European-style hug and air kisses outside the elevator door, they walked down the hallway in opposite directions to their rooms.

*

Victor watched her for a moment as she was going to her room. He caught the faint smell of her Chanel perfume lingering in the air, making him think of other ladies in other hotels in other countries who used that very same perfume, ones that held many good memories for him.

On the way to his room, he again recalled that small moment when Alex mentioned her pleasure at watching her fellow traders squirm. He wondered once again whether getting more involved with her might entail something much deeper than he'd normally care to get caught up in.

Well, he shrugged, *there's no virtue in timidity. And whatever game is being played, Tortola is just the beginning—if indeed there is any game at all.*

Entering his room, Victor took off his jacket and shoes and thought that perhaps a small nightcap wouldn't go amiss. Opening the door to the mini bar, he dug around a bit until he found one of those splits of hotel mini bar wine that didn't look too poisonous and poured himself a glass.

Just as he sat down on the sofa and was taking his first sip, he heard a quiet knock on his door. He got up from the sofa, put down the glass and crossed the room to the door.

Opening the door, Victor expected to see someone from the hotel staff and instead was surprised to see Alex standing there. As he went to take her hand and invite her in, she rushed forward, flung her arms around him and planted a very real, very long and very sexy kiss on his lips.

As cool as ever, Victor immediately reciprocated and pulled her into the room, quickly closing the door. He turned back to suggest sharing a glass of the wine, but before he could say a word, she was again all over him with more hugs and kisses.

"I just couldn't stay away," Alex said. "I so much wanted to have you in my arms tonight. I had to come here to see if you felt the same."

Victor didn't bother with a verbal reply but stood back for a moment to admire an even sexier-looking, half-transparent dress than the one she'd worn to dinner. He then picked her up in his arms, and began stroking her in all the sensitive places that he knew from experience were the *right* places.

They came back together in what could only be termed an urgent, sexual embrace on the sofa. Their hands, tongues and lips explored each other with passionate hugging and stroking, followed by even more urgent kisses.

Victor came up for air only long enough to say, "I want you so much too, Alex. Let's move next door to the bedroom."

"Yes," she said breathlessly, already beginning to unfasten her necklace while Victor was undoing her dress.

By the time the necklace was off, so was most of the dress, not to mention Victor's shirt with his pants unbuttoned and hanging at half mast as they stumbled toward the bedroom, Alex encumbered by a dress she didn't want and Victor tripping over a pair of trousers that were not quite off but not quite on either.

All that changed by the time they got into the bedroom was that the clothing had disappeared in the blink of an eye as they fell into the bed feeling each other as they'd hoped to do since the moment they'd first met.

"I want to feel you inside me, Victor, top and bottom" Alex cried almost immediately.

Victor moved her on top of him to fulfill the first request. Next she rolled off leaving him on top to take care of his own most urgent needs as well.

When they had each had their itches scratched by the other, Alex jumped up from the bed and went into the living room to get her dress and other clothing.

Still laying in bed in a post-coital daze, Victor didn't really understand what she was doing as he was actually counting on a quick encore. No such luck. By the time he came to his senses and realized that she wasn't coming back, Alex was already dressed and just fixing her hair in the living room mirror. He got himself out of bed and joined her.

"What's going on, Alex? I thought we'd at least be together a bit more before you went back to your room."

"Victor, you need to speak in the morning. You need your rest. I do, too. Let me thank you very much for the lovely fucking. I'll see you in the morning after your talk. Let's speak more about your visit to Merit then."

With that, she opened the door and left Victor standing there rather bemused.

Wow, he thought, as he watched her walk down the hall toward her room. *Could it really be this easy?*

At least his glass of wine was still on the table, and while he finished it off, he tried to understand the situation with Alex. From what he'd seen, this lady was really a puzzle, and almost surely a handful. Yet figuring her out was definitely now high on his agenda.

Victor wondered if it would really be worth it. In any case it wouldn't be boring. He supposed that the game was afoot. What was totally unclear was exactly what *kind* of game they were playing.

When he went down for breakfast the next morning, Victor looked around for Alex but didn't see her.

Well, he thought, *there are probably a couple of hundred people here. Maybe she came earlier or I just missed her. I'll see her at my talk at 10 o'clock, so I can say my farewells to her after that.*

When he didn't see Alex in the audience for his talk, Victor started wondering whether she was all right. Once he escaped from the questioners and other hangers-on following his presentation, he went to the hotel desk and asked them to connect him with her room. The receptionist said, "Ms. Lynne checked out earlier this morning and didn't leave any forwarding address or phone number."

Victor was now more puzzled than concerned. *What the hell happened to her?*

They'd had a nice bit of sex, not more than twelve hours ago, and she said she would see him at his talk. Then she walked down the hall to her room—and now she's gone.

Who knows, Victor thought. *Maybe it's for the best.*

Alex was exciting all right. But she also appeared erratic, to say the least. That wasn't what he needed right now.

Victor wondered if he would get the email they discussed about the visit to her firm next week. Or even if she was really associated with that firm, Merit.

As Churchill said of Russia, he could not forecast her actions. She was a riddle, wrapped in a mystery, inside an enigma.

Episode III

The Project

London

Much of the London Docklands area has been almost magically transformed from the worst kind of waterfront slum into high-class office facilities and apartments for the rich and famous. St. Katherine's Docks, a region just west of the Tower of London, is one such area. That's where Victor found himself on Monday afternoon headed to a brick-fronted, modern three-story building.

The offices of Merit Capital Asset Management, Ltd. were indistinguishable from the many other financial firms Victor had visited in money centers around the world. When he got off the elevator, he spotted a reception desk of battleship proportions. Seated behind the desk was a beautiful, fashion-model-type woman with a smile dazzling enough to melt the coldest of hearts and open the tightest of wallets. Behind her and slightly to the right were rows of offices for junior account executives, which other than their wood paneling and soft carpeting, looked much like the hallways and rooms of an elegant psychiatric hospital for the bewildered.

People with concerned looks on their faces rushed back-and-forth along the hallways, carrying stacks of papers, mumbling mysteriously to themselves about put options on the Japanese yen, commodity straddles on pork bellies or the Fed's bias on interest rates. To Victor, it was all so stylized and routine he had a hard time for a moment distinguishing whether he was in London, New York, Hong Kong, Paris, or Tokyo.

Smiling in Victor's direction, the receptionist asked if she could help. Victor told her he had an appointment with Ms. Lynne.

While she called and arranged for Alex to collect him, Victor gazed absently at the various plaques, trophies, mounted newspaper and magazine articles and other promotional paraphernalia of the successful corporation on display around the reception area. Even though Merit was not in the first rank of heavy hitters in the financial services world, the firm was still a potent player in the game of moving money from one place to another.

Victor was greatly looking forward to a possible professional challenge to see if his academically-inspired stock market simulator could be brought into congruence with the problems of real investors trying to make a lot of real money.

He was equally intrigued to see how Alex would react when he asked her where she'd gone that night in Tortola—and to finding out what kind of game she was playing, if that's what it was.

"Hello again, Victor. Thank you for coming to see us." Alex's low, throaty, slightly breathless voice brought him out of his reveries.

"Ah, Alex. Nice to be here on your home turf. It's a pleasure to see you again."

What a stupid remark, thought Victor. He'd just bid farewell to her a few days earlier at the door of his hotel room in Tortola.

Suddenly, he changed his mind and decided to make no mention of her surprising disappearance after their tryst the night before his presentation. He simply looked at her with a kind of proprietary gleam in his eye, hinting that there was something between them besides business.

Alex was doing nothing to acknowledge what had happened between them, leaving Victor still puzzled about it.

"Please come on back," Alex said. "I've arranged for Jerome Hall, the supervisor of our computer stock market project, to join us in one of the conference rooms. He's also very interested in your work, and eager to hear more about what you said in your talk last week in Tortola."

"I'm afraid I can't give a hands-on demo of the software I showed there," said Victor, eyeing with approval the stylish cream-colored business suit, light-blue satin blouse, and black high heels she was wearing. "I can certainly tell him about the simulator though, and how I think it might be used to address some of the concerns you told me you have regarding the psychology of traders in these speculative markets."

"Oh, that's all right," she said. "Today I just want to introduce you to Jerome and tell you a bit more about our interest in your work. There will be plenty of time for details and demos later."

*

The conference room was dominated by a large, oak meeting table whose mirror-shine and matching set of eight tufted-leather chairs left little doubt that no real work ever went on in here. The room was designed to impress well-heeled clients—and visiting firemen like Victor—who might offer something to enhance the bottom line of Merit's annual report.

Alex introduced Victor to her boss:

"Victor, this is Jerome Hall. He's the leader of our research group," she said, pointing towards a thin, emaciated-looking, young man with a pasty complexion, nervously looking as if he'd rather be back in his office than in this or any other meeting room.

Alex continued, "Of course, Victor knows my background and interests in the psychology of markets and traders from our discussions in Tortola. What we'd like to do today is ask him to say a bit about his stock market simulation, so we can determine how what he's doing might be used to move our own research forward on understanding how market sentiments shift. Is this okay with you, Victor?"

"Yes that sounds just fine, Alex," he said.

Jerome said nothing. He just nodded, seeming to defer to Alex.

"Basically," Victor started, "inside the computer we have created a toy version of a real stock market. Instead of the three thousand or so firms whose shares are traded on the New York Stock Exchange, in our world there is only a single firm. And instead of the thousands of traders whose decisions move prices on a real exchange, our surrogate world has just sixty traders. What's quite surprising, though, is how realistic the movement of prices in this 'toy world' mirrors the patterns of price changes in a real market like the NYSE."

At that moment, Jerome interrupted by asking, "What question—or questions—are you trying to address with this simulator?"

"Let me give you a graphic image," said Victor. "Think of one of those big message boards in a place like Piccadilly Circus or Times Square. Those boards are composed of thousands of light bulbs, which flash on and off at different times to spell out a message. Suppose each possible trading rule is represented by one of these bulbs. Then at any given moment in our simulator, 60 of the bulbs are on representing the rules that are currently being employed by the traders. All the other bulbs are off.

"You mean those are the rules that are currently not being used?" asked Jerome.

"Precisely," replied Victor.

"At the next trading period, some of those lights go off and others go on, reflecting a change of trading rules on the part of some of the traders. What we want to know is whether after a long period of time, the lights that are on tend to cluster in some small region of the message board. Or do lights continue to go on and off all over the board indefinitely? *That's* the question that really interests us."

Victor paused long enough for Alex to interject, "You mean that if you see the lights clustering, it says that there is something predictable about the traders' collective psychology," she asked, "and we might be able to exploit that predictability to get larger-than-average trading profits. Is that it?"

"Precisely," Victor smiled.

As if reading his thoughts, Alex looked over at Jerome and said, "It seems to me that we ought to speak with the higher-ups here at Merit about trying to put together a project aimed at developing this simulator further in the direction of real markets."

Alex then turned to Victor with a smile.

"Would you be available to help us with this, Victor?" she asked. "Assuming, of course, we could get management approval for such a project."

"I'd certainly like to see this idea developed into a working tool," agreed Victor. "And Merit seems to be the type of place to make that happen. So yes, I would be ready to help." He could see the next step of his two-fold strategy falling into place.

"Okay. Jerome and I will discuss this further and we'll get back to you on it within the next few days," she said, getting up from the table, indicating that the meeting was over.

Jerome left the room as quietly as he had entered it, barely giving Victor a chance to say goodbye. Alex was straightening out her papers on the table and getting ready to escort Victor back down to reception. As soon as they were alone, she turned to him with a knowing smile.

"It was very clever of you, Victor, to give Jerome just a glimpse of what you're really doing but not enough to let him see what's behind the smoke-and-mirrors. What *I* want is to get beneath the surface of Victor Safir, Inc. I want to know what makes your program tick."

It was an abrupt shift, and Victor could see the Alex who had come to his hotel-room door at the beginning of their recent night together in Tortola. He moved toward her and put his arms around her very affectionately. As if hit by a jolt of electricity, she immediately jumped back, seemingly surprised at his behavior.

"What do you think you're doing, Victor? I definitely want to work with you on this simulator. But that doesn't extend to hugs and kisses in the office. Okay?"

"Well, Alex, somehow I thought what happened between us in Tortola had certainly extended to that at least, and I thought it was very nice, and quite beyond 'just business.' "

"I'm sorry, Victor. I really don't know what you're talking about," she replied. "I am eager to have you work together with us here and hope we can make that happen. But I don't have any ideas that go beyond that."

"Yes, our conversation today puts Merit right at the top of my list of potential partners for the simulator development, and our discussion with Jerome cemented that. We should both definitely be thinking about how to realize that relationship."

"I agree," Alex replied. "You'll hear from me about our internal discussions soon. Now I have to run to another meeting. I'm sure you can find your own way back to the reception."

*

As Victor made his way out of Merit and started back to his hotel, he was now even more puzzled by Alex.

How could she not acknowledge in any way their intimacies just a few days earlier in Tortola. It was hard to believe that she couldn't remember such an encounter, unless she was having some serious memory loss or other psychopathic condition that had caused her to block it out.

Her disappearance the next day was a clear indicator that she did recall coming to Victor like that and wanted to avoid seeing him the next morning.

Victor had to wonder then if this was all a kind of game Alex was playing with him, by acting as if she remembered nothing about their passionate encounter in Tortola.

Once you've tasted the forbidden fruit, it's the reptilian brain that's in control and you only want more, Victor thought. And he definitely wanted more. Time had come to figure out how to get it.

On the way to his hotel, Victor went through the entire interaction this morning with Alex from the moment they met in the reception to when she ushered him out the door. He couldn't help but interpret this sequence of events as her playing a game with him.

Victor had a more than passing interest in the theory of games, which had originally been developed by the legendary mathematician John von Neumann and his colleague Oskar Morgenstern at the Institute for Advanced Study in Princeton. Their focus was on the simplest type of game, what's called a two-person, zero-sum game.

Here there are two players, who each make a decision. The outcome is a payoff to one player and an equal loss to the other. So the net payoff is zero: What I win, you lose, and vice-versa.

A key element in the two-person, zero-sum game is that each play of the game has a winner and a loser.

From what Victor had seen so far, he wasn't sure whether that was the kind of game Alex was playing. In their game, if each of them *trusted* the other it should be possible for both of them to come out winners.

Yet he knew he should be on the lookout for a chance to have the upper hand.

Victor knew also that Alex had studied game theory at the London School of Economics, so neither he nor she were what would commonly be termed 'game players.' They were more like 'game theorists,' each looking for the right strategy for the game they were individually playing.

Victor saw Alex possibly playing a zero-sum game.

On the other hand, he was definitely playing a sequence of 'prisoner's dilemma' games, in which both players can benefit—but only if they trust each other.

Somehow, Victor had to figure out a way to get Alex to shift from a zero-sum mentality to a game of mutual trust.

Episode IV

The Rapprochement

London

The day after Victor's meeting at Merit turned out to be bright and sunny, so he decided to take a walk in Hyde Park and reflect on the situation with Alex.

Was it possible that Alex really did not remember that they'd had sex in Tortola? She was even the one who initiated it. What kind of game is she playing? Victor was never one to judge without all the facts, so he decided to contact her again and propose they get together outside the halls of Merit. He just needed to figure out how to invite her, in a gentlemanly, even romantic, fashion.

Leaving Hyde Park at Queen's Gate, Victor thought he'd drop by the Natural History Museum and see what exhibit was being featured that day. Strolling along Queen's Gate to the Museum, he was still pondering the question of how best to contact Alex.

Just before he reached the Museum, he passed a rather posh-looking flower shop and saw his solution. He would send Alex a lovely arrangement of flowers accompanied by a card inviting her to meet. He entered the shop and examined a number of different types of flower arrangements and how they might be used to convey an emotional message to Alex that he really wanted to see her.

Finally, he defaulted to the standard solution of a dozen long-stem red roses, hoping to express his passion for her in a traditionally stylish manner. But he didn't think it would be appropriate to send this message to her at the office.

Luckily though, he remembered from their dinner in Tortola that Alex had mentioned she lived in a building where the Colombian Embassy was housed. From that Victor could easily find the street address for her and that should be enough to ensure delivery of the flowers and his invitation.

He asked the clerk at the shop if he could use their phone book for a moment to look up the address, then he made his order for the flowers. He told the clerk he'd like to include a card with the flowers, and chose one from a nice selection available at the counter.

> Dear Alex,
>
> I will be in London for a couple more days and would very much like to see you again on a social basis, not at the office. I find it difficult to imagine that you don't recall our lovely evening together in Tortola, and I would like to develop the feelings we have for each other beyond the confines of a simple business relationship.
>
> As it happens, I will be doing a radio interview with the BBC tomorrow evening. I'd be honored if you would care to attend. We might then discuss over dinner afterwards how our time together might be best spent, both professionally and personally. The interview will be at Bush House at 7pm tomorrow. So please let me know by email or otherwise if you will be able to attend.
>
> With warm personal regards,
> Victor

The next morning Victor received a message at his hotel.

"Why not?" Alex wrote. "Actually, I wouldn't mind tagging along to the radio interview if that's all right with you. An opportunity to see Victor L. Safir in action. I can hardly wait to see you in your element. I missed your talk in Tortola. Now I can try to make up for that. It's already been too long."

Bingo, thought Victor, as he immediately replied to her message suggesting they meet in front of Bush House shortly before 7 o'clock and take things from there. He also noted to himself that he was still wondering why she wasn't at his talk in Tortola and wanted to find out why she left the hotel instead.

Maybe he could work those questions into their dinner conversation tonight, as well.

*

In 1919, the London County Council agreed to lease a site at the intersection of the Strand and Aldwych to the Bush Terminal Company of New York for 99 years at a rent of $55,000 per year! Irving Bush, president of the New York firm hired architect Harvey Corbett to develop a building on the site where buyers could meet and purchase goods under one roof, a kind of forerunner to the modern shopping mall.

By 1924 the Centre Block of the structure was completed and Bush House was born, and in 1929 it was declared 'the most expensive building in the world,' having cost $10 million to build. Since 1938 it has been home to the BBC World Service, which transmits the news from there to much of the civilized world.

Victor stood on the front steps of this rather imposing monstrosity, braving a brisk autumn wind shortly before 7 o'clock, worrying if Alex would arrive in time for his live interview. Just as he was about to give up on her and go inside, a taxi braked sharply in front of him and she elegantly stepped out.

Casually paying the driver, Alex seemed oblivious to the time and that the interview was scheduled to begin in just six minutes.

After settling her fare with the driver, she turned to greet Victor with a wave and a smile. Almost a fanatic for punctuality, Victor was once again thinking that he was going to have his hands full with this lady.

"Am I late?" she asked ingenuously.

“Almost,” growled Victor, trying to keep his impatience under control. “Let’s go inside and try to find the studio for the show.”

Fortunately, the producer of the show had just sent his assistant to the lobby to look for Victor. They were immediately ushered down one of the many labyrinthine hallways of Bush House and into a back elevator that took them to the studio, where the show’s moderator had already begun introducing Victor to his audience.

Luckily the program was a science special, devoted to the uses of mathematics in everyday life, a topic on which Victor had pontificated many times in the past. Almost as soon as Victor sat down at the microphone, the moderator began asking him about his new book on great theorems and theories of 20th-century mathematics and why they mattered in everyday life.

Alex took a seat in the studio, directly across from Victor, where the combination of her short, cream-colored skirt, sheer, black-tinted silk stockings, and crossed legs posed the serious danger of taking his mind far, far away from the delicacies of Morse’s Theorem and the subtleties of the Simplex Method.

Seasoned campaigner that he was, Victor managed to gamely choke his way through the interview—by carefully avoiding any more glances in Alex’s direction—with enough coherence that he hoped listeners would be left with the impression that he really had written a book from which they could painlessly learn a bit of why modern mathematics is interesting—and not just for mathematicians.

*

“Well, that’s enough to give anyone an appetite,” exclaimed Victor, as he and Alex left Bush House following the interview. “Let’s get some dinner. What kind of food would you like?”

"I don't really know this area very well," she said. "Why don't you choose?" Then she added, teasingly, "After all, you're the star tonight. You should get to decide."

"Do you like Japanese?" he asked.

"I've never actually been to a Japanese restaurant," she confessed.

Amazing, thought Victor. There's this whole other world out there, inhabited by people like Alex, who can live in a world-class city like London never having gone to a Japanese restaurant. He found this bordering on the inconceivable. He also regarded it as an opportunity.

"Great! Then let me introduce you to a new kind of dining experience. There's a place I know just a few blocks from here over on Shelton Street, where you'll get the best introduction possible to Japanese cuisine outside of Kyoto. Are you up for that?"

"Let's go," answered Alex, a touch of asperity in her voice and aggression in her look, at what she perceived as a subtle putdown by Victor of her provincialism.

Like its namesake district in Tokyo, *Shinjuku* is a funky, avant-garde Japanese restaurant tucked into a side street in Covent Garden. During the short walk through Covent Garden Market from Bush House to the restaurant, Alex expressed her admiration of Victor's ability to explain such difficult mathematical and scientific ideas to a general audience, especially over the radio where he had no visual props or images to help convey the ideas.

As she continued to stroke his ego, Victor's subconscious was working overtime with her strange behavior. He couldn't lose the feeling that he was being manipulated in some hard-to-define way for some even harder-to-define reasons known only to her. And yet he could not pull himself away from this woman.

Put these negative thoughts out of your mind, he told himself. That was his rational mind speaking, probably because the last thing he wanted to believe right now was anything but exactly what she was telling him in her profuse compliments about his radio presentation. But the alarm bells kept ringing quietly at some level deeper than the frontal cortex, and no amount of logical thought seemed able to silence them completely.

They were greeted by a young Japanese hostess—with pink-dyed hair, eleven-inch platform shoes and eye makeup that appeared to have been slapped on with a trowel—who took them to their seats.

Making their way to the table, Victor had a look at the chef whose hair was tied back in a ponytail reminiscent of an ancient samurai. He was busy throwing knives about with seemingly reckless abandon for the amusement of the patrons sitting at the sushi bar. As a long-time patron of *Shinjuku,* Victor got a nod of recognition from the chef, one that did not go unnoticed by Alex as they passed by.

"You seem to be well-known at this place," she remarked. "You'll have to pick out something good for me for my first dining experience in a Japanese restaurant."

"Yes, tonight I'm introducing you to a new experience. If we get our stockmarket project going, I hope you'll be introducing me to some new experiences over the coming months, as well."

"I'm sure there's nothing I could teach you, Victor," she replied, her eyes looking at him like a cat watching a canary.

Victor ordered a combination of yakitori (pieces of chicken in teriyaki sauce grilled on skewers), sashimi (raw fish) and tempura (vegetables and shrimps deep-fried in batter), together with a cup of Japanese sake for Alex. For himself, he asked for a shabu-shabu (thinly-sliced beef cooked at the table in boiling broth), along with a bottle of Japanese beer.

"I hope this will be the first of many Japanese meals we'll have together," he said, looking her straight in the eye and raising his glass to toast her.

As they waited for the appetizers to appear, Victor asked Alex to tell him a bit more about her background and how she saw her life unfolding.

She began by telling him more about her childhood, even though she'd begun this story in Tortola.

"I grew up on a sheep ranch outside Christchurch," she said, "near the picturesque seaside town of Akaroa. Then I moved to the city with my mother and brother and sister after my parents divorced when I was a teenager."

"What did you do there?" asked Victor.

"I studied psychology at Canterbury University, ending up with a First Class degree and no particular idea of where to go or what to do with it."

"So what *did* you do?"

"I think I told you when we were in Tortola that I got married."

"Yes, you did say that. Why?" asked Victor in a mock surprised tone.

"I don't really know," she answered. "Probably mostly to get out of the house and away from my mother. Also, I suppose it was a little bit because I didn't know what else to do. Maybe I even thought I was in love. Who can really say? It's difficult to disentangle these things."

Almost as an afterthought, she said with a shrug, "In any case, the marriage lasted only about a year."

"Why? What happened?" Victor asked.

"Simple. My husband was too boring. He was an accountant, five years older than me. His idea of the good life was a ranch-style house in the suburbs, two dogs, and watching football on the telly after dinner, a can of beer in his hand. I'm not cut out for that kind of life," Alex stated with conviction.

She stared into the distance replaying those bad-old-days in her mind, wondering again why she had to get married to find out these obvious facts about a man she had lived with for over two years while they were students together.

The waitress appeared with their food and a burner at the table in order to prepare Victor's shabu-shabu. The ministrations of the waitress snapped Alex back into the present, and she watched as the pot of broth was brought to a nice simmer. She waited for the waitress to leave before speaking again.

"I don't know why I'm telling you all this. It's not at all interesting and has nothing to do with the person I am today."

"That's debatable," said Victor. "I think we're all the product of our past experiences, and it sounds like you've had quite a few not-so-happy ones in your life already. I may be wrong. So tell me what kind of person you think you are now."

"Maybe you'll find out one of these days," she said enigmatically, a Mona-Lisa-type smile on her face—but not in her eyes. "Now I want to be the interrogator. But before I start dissecting *your* life, show me how to use these chopsticks. I seem to be making a mess of things here."

Victor attempted to show her the best way to hold the chopsticks and wasn't surprised how quickly she mastered it and switched to some rather intense questioning of him.

Her probing led him to a potted version of his academic and personal history, more like a press release than anything that revealed what went on below the surface of his life. Not one to be fobbed off with this kind of canned performance, Alex finally held up her hand:

"Look, Victor," she said. "I like you very much and I'm looking forward to our working together over the coming months. But don't patronize me. If you want to know something about me, fine; but you're going to have to give as good as you get. And you haven't yet told me anything about Victor L. Safir, the person, but only about the public persona. I can—and have—obtained this information from publicly-available sources. Let's agree to either just exchange superficial banalities and let it go at that. Or you can really tell me about yourself. One way or the other. You choose."

Rather sheepishly Victor apologized. "You're absolutely right," he said. I'm so accustomed to running on autopilot when people ask me about myself, that I just load-in the standard program and let my mind go on vacation while my mouth is working overtime. You deserve a whole lot better than that. Let me make it up to you, okay?"

"I'm sorry too, Victor. I didn't mean to jump all over you about this. But I'm so used to men patronizing me, thinking that there can't possibly be a working brain beneath this fancy hairstyle, that I get a bit impatient with it at times. Apologies accepted and no hard feelings."

"I'll tell you what," he said smiling back at her. "Do you like jazz?"

"I like it," she answered.

"Well then, let's walk over to Soho to Ronnie Scott's club and see if we can catch a set. What do you say? It's only a ten-minute walk from here."

"I'd love to," Alex smiled back, reaching across the table to briefly touch the back of his, sealing their truce.

Ronnie Scott's Jazz Club on Frith Street in Soho is without a doubt one of the world's most important live-music clubs. Started in 1959 by sax man Ronnie Scott, it has been the London home of jazz greats ranging from Art Farmer and Dizzy Gillespie to unknowns of every style.

As Victor and Alex approached the club, he could already hear the buzz from the crowd as the five-piece combo was well into their second set of the evening. Glancing over at Alex, he saw the gleam in her eye of a seasoned jazz fanatic, a look that somehow eased his discomfort from the vague, predatory-like stares he thought he'd seen her throwing his way earlier. If you like jazz, then you're all right with me, he thought, as they eased their way through the standing-room only crowd and up to the bar.

Victor finally managed to get a glass of chilled white wine for Alex and a beer for himself, as well as slip the hostess a tenner to find them a table not far from the stage.

The combination of the wailing sax, a pianist who seemed on the verge of challenging the great Thelonius Monk himself, and the bass man from jazz heaven ultimately combined to transport him into some other universe, one where divine chords and magical improvisations took the place of sex, money, greed and power.

He loved this place!

Alex seemed more relaxed than at any moment in their time together, either in Tortola or earlier here in London. Looking over at him with her infinitely deep green eyes as if he were the only man in the world, Alex reached out for his hand and gave it a squeeze. Smiling back at her, Victor slid over a bit on his chair so that their hips and thighs brushed against each other gently, and he put his arm around her shoulder and gave her a squeeze.

Perfect, thought Alex, *just perfect,* turning her attention back to the music.

*

After the music, Alex invited Victor back to her flat for a drink and a chat, an invitation he took up with alacrity. Entering her modest, but very comfortably furnished three-room apartment in the fashionable Knightsbridge section of London, Victor was immediately taken by the marvelous selection of colors, plants and furnishings that Alex had put together transforming a rather ordinary flat into an almost gracious home.

He could see that this was a woman with taste and style, if nothing else.

While she busied herself in the kitchen organizing drinks and arranging snacks, she asked Victor to pick out some nice *romantic* background music from the large collection of CDs on the shelf in the living room.

Returning from the kitchen with a tray of bottles and a bucket of ice, together with a plate of cheese and crackers, Alex motioned to Victor to come sit next to her on the sofa. Almost immediately, she leaned toward him and softly said how much she'd enjoyed his company over the past days, and nuzzled herself up next to him in a very tender, endearing way.

Victor was now even more puzzled about her unpredictable behavior. She seemed able to turn her sexual charm on and off like a light bulb. Yesterday off, today on. He thought of her aloof attitude at the office yesterday, and now she was back on again tonight, or her spontaneous appearance at his hotel room in Tortola, followed by her mysterious disappearing act the next morning.

Perhaps I'll just have to get used to this if I'm going to continue this relationship, Victor thought.

He leaned down and kissed her very gently on the forehead, ears and neck, before taking her head in his hands and giving her a long, lingering kiss on the lips.

Alex reacted with an open-mouthed kiss of her own, followed by the kind of embrace that Victor had previously associated with only the most intimate of his lovers. As one embrace led to another, he realized that Alex was ready to move on to the physical level. But before he could take her hand to lead her to the bedroom, she reached over to undo his tie, took *his* hand, and without a word being spoken motioned for him to follow her.

As Alex slowly undressed before Victor, he was again mesmerized by her exquisite figure and could barely take his eyes off her for long enough to get out of his own clothes. She walked slowly toward the now fully-undressed Victor, wearing only skimpy black thong-type panties. She looked up at him, batting her big green eyes, and asked with a shy, little-girl smile, "Do you still like?"

Barely able to choke out a reply in the face of the dazzling, voluptuous figure bared before him, Victor threw all previous concerns and cautions to the wind, reached out to gently run his hands over her extraordinary body and brought her to him in a tender, yet strong, all-encompassing embrace.

For Victor the love-making that night was of the type one reads about only in the most erotic novels or explores in teenage fantasies. No position remained untested, no part of either of their bodies remained unexplored, no thoughts about sex were left unspoken, as the two melded together as closely as Siamese twins.

Onward and upward to ever greater peaks of pleasure as the night wore on. Finally, they lay exhausted in each other's arms, tenderly stroking delicate spots discovered during the hours they had just spent 'getting acquainted.'

Victor thought this had possibly been one of the most erotic experience of his life, as he prepared to leave her flat, the sun just beginning to peek over the horizon. Opening the bedroom door to leave, Victor saw Alex rouse from her slumber.

She came to the door and draped her arms about him. She ran her tongue around his ear and whispered, "I'm having a small dinner party here tonight for a few of my friends. I'd like to introduce you to them. So please tell me you'll be able to come."

The look in her eye told him that this was also an invitation to an encore performance after the guests had departed. How could he resist?

"With pleasure. What time? And what should I bring?"

"Just bring yourself! The party begins around 8 o'clock. Why don't you come half an hour earlier, so we can get reacquainted first?" she urged with a small stroke to his lower regions.

"Done," Victor said. He was already looking forward to the evening.

*

The guests at the dinner party were an eclectic selection of Alex's London friends. They ranged from some loud-mouth, fellow New Zealanders she knew from somewhere, a couple she worked with at Merit, the male half of which was actually a pretty interesting currency analyst, but whose wife was a shrill, anemic French woman who immediately grated on Victor's nerves.

Finally, there was Alex's friend and neighbor from down the hall—the onerous Maerta (Hart, Heath, Harmon . . . , Victor could never quite remember her last name). She impressed him as a dim-witted, blonde, South African artist, dragging behind her one of the blue-collar phone repairmen or steam-roller drivers she seemed to favor.

Maybe she likes these types for the sex, Victor speculated idly, although he immediately revised this hypothesis when he took a longer look at her.

All the guests were at least twenty years younger than Victor, a generation gap that didn't really bother him much. Before he left Alex's flat that morning he'd asked Alex if it bothered her:

"Don't you think you're a little too young for me?"

"I've always had relationships with older men," she replied. "So if you think I'm too young for you, that's your problem, not mine."

He certainly didn't see it as a problem—at least not then. He most definitely wasn't about to let something as trivial as the 24-year age difference between them get in the way of the kind of sex he'd had the night before.

Even so he couldn't help but notice how Alex introduced him to her friends.

"This is my new friend, Victor," she said. "Don't mistake him for my father now just because his hair is a bit grayer than yours. Snow on the chimney doesn't necessarily mean the fire is out down below."

Perhaps she was saying this to let her friends know that the age difference between them really *did* matter to her.

As the evening wore on, her possessive manner showed itself when Victor happened to find himself in the kitchen talking with the artist. Alex abruptly burst into their chit-chat, and she grabbed him by the arm.

"Come with me, Daddy," she said. "I need your wisdom in the living room right now." With that, she dragged him off to meet a late-arriving guest.

Later, Alex managed to irritate Victor yet again when she went out of her way to make a variety of gratuitous, anti-American remarks based on what he knew to be a superficial understanding of American life and values.

It seemed clear to Victor that Alex was not-so-subtly trying to show to her friends that he was her new 'toy,' and that she could play with him in whatever way pleased her at the moment.

By the end of the evening Victor was not feeling too positive toward Alex and was even strategizing how he could get out of there, among the first guests to leave.

In fact, he did attempt to join the artist and her friend as they headed for the door, but Alex loudly stopped him by saying, "Don't leave yet Victor. I need you to stay and help me clear up a few things around here." The look in her eye as she said this broadcast the signal that what needed clearing up would be matters in the bedroom once all the guests were gone.

Strangely to Victor, the sex with her later that night was, if anything, even more electrifying than the night before, as Alex insisted that they do and say things to each other that were beyond even his considerable experience.

Yanking him back to reality, Victor found the pillow talk rather disconcerting as Alex offhandedly mentioned a number of experiences she'd had with other lovers.

She began by asking, "Did I ever tell about the time I had a threesome in this bed with two other guys?" she asked. "Wow, we were all so drunk that night. It was very different than with a normal twosome, like us."

"What was so different?" asked Victor.

"For me it was very exciting being double penetrated at the same time. A totally unique feeling, one that I guess only a woman can have."

That led her to describe the time she picked up a guy at a bar and brought him home, only to discover that the 'he' was a 'she.' What a shock! But they managed to sort out the gender problem without too much difficulty, although Alex confessed that she didn't really enjoy that kind of lesbian sex as much as she'd imagined she would.

"Very interesting, Alex. Maybe we should redo some of your experiences one of these evenings."

"Oh, what a good idea, Victor. Let's do that when you return here to London to start our project."

To be honest, though, Victor was puzzled as to why she thought he needed to know about her sexual antics with other women, groups, and transvestites. Next thing you know, she'll be telling me about encounters with lawyers!

Not very good 'saleswomanship' in his opinion.

At that juncture his reptilian brain was not being too discriminating about salesmanship or anything else above the waist. Perhaps he should be thankful for small favors—and big sexual appetites.

"I'm really hoping we can get our project going very soon," Alex said the next morning as they were parting. "I'm going to miss you, Victor."

"Me, too," he agreed, as they promised to stay in contact electronically and to meet again as soon as circumstances allowed.

Hopefully, the consultancy with Merit would be settled in the coming days, because Victor was already counting the minutes until he could get back to the sexual playpen defined by the cozy sheets of Alex's bed.

With some reluctance he left for Heathrow airport and the long flight back to Santa Fe. Happily, when he got to the gate and was waiting to board his flight, his cell phone pinged with a rather plaintive email from Alex:

Dear Victor,

Oh, I already miss you so much, and I'm seriously unhappy without you here next to me. I really don't know what I want from life, other than to be happy and have a family with at least two children. Please come back to me very, very soon. I know we can have a lovely life together.

With all my love,
Alex

Victor thought that was an odd, almost childish message. After all, who doesn't want to be happy?

In his view, this message was distinguished by its strange combination of vagueness and precision—vague on the big issues of life, the universe, and everything else, and super precise on the rather trivial matter of *exactly* how many children she wanted to have.

Why was she telling him all this? Had he become her father confessor? Or a candidate for the altar? He hadn't staked out either of those roles for himself in this game—and, with annoyance, he would ponder this for much of the long flight across the Atlantic.

Episode V

The Holiday

Vienna

The taxi brought Victor from Vienna International Airport into the city center along the Danube Canal, a tributary of the Danube River created by far-sighted engineers and city planners in the late 19th-century to protect the inner city from high-water flooding. Victor saw that the *Donaukanal* was a recreational area with bicycle and walking paths along both sides, together with numerous small cafés and restaurants to serve walkers and cyclists taking a breath of fresh air.

As the taxi made its way into the city center, he remembered that at one point he was seeing ads and displays in stores in Santa Fe, encouraging would-be Lotharios to step-up their game by offering a lovely present to the lady (or ladies) of their affection.

At that moment, Victor really missed Alex and wanted to do something to reposition himself by remote control onto her radar. He again sent her a huge bouquet of roses as he had in London, along with a cheery card recalling their time together in her flat.

But as time came and went for Victor in Santa Fe with no thank-you message from Alex, his paranoia began stirring. Just before it reached the boiling point, however, a lovely email arrived from Alex in which she told him she wished he were there in London to hand the flowers to her in person. She also said seeing him again could not come soon enough to suit her.

While he was both pleased and gratified with Alex's response to the flowers, Victor wondered about her rather sharp swing in mood from the aloof, 'ice queen' of their London dinner at her flat to the warm, endearing, school-girlish tone she displayed in this email. This was not to mention her voracious sexual appetite for him after their earlier dinner together in London.

Despite the way she generally treated him in London, in his mind she was still a problem to be solved. And once he'd identified a problem to be solved, either in mathematics or in life, he would start working on it until he figured it out. Victor always figured things out.

Reflecting on these rapid swings in Alex's behavior, Victor recalled a former lady friend who used the term 'narcissist' to describe what she saw as his erratic behavior at the time. He then looked up what it meant to be a narcissist, and now wondered if it might enter into some of Alex's own behavior.

Victor really could not say he thought of her as being a narcissist. She didn't really fit into that pattern. *While Alex is almost certainly not a narcissist,* he thought, *she definitely is a problem*—currently Victor's biggest problem—and he had try to to solve this problem.

To do this, Victor believed he had to get to the heart of who Alex was and why she acted the way she did. And psychological labels like 'personality disorder' or 'narcissist' didn't really help much. They were simply labels, much like the labels on the jars and cans at the supermarket. In the end, what counts is the contents, not the label.

Victor felt that to solve the 'Alex Problem' he just needed to get the right point of view. As with every problem he'd ever encountered, once he had all the pieces constituting that 'right' point of view, the pieces would come together and the solution then almost magically appeared.

When he left Santa Fe, Victor knew he would be going first to Vienna in order to deliver a lecture at the Austrian Academy of Sciences. In a momentary fit of enthusiasm, he sent an email to Alex from Santa Fe, half-jokingly suggesting the 'wild idea' that she join him in Vienna for a day or two before he came to London to meet her colleagues at Merit and sign the consulting contract they'd just finished negotiating.

Her reply startled him: She asked why his invitation termed this visit 'wild.' She then accepted his invitation with great enthusiasm.

Again Victor was puzzled by her yin-yang behavior. First, a seeming failure to react more positively to the idea of getting a bit closer during the early part of his last visit to London. Then bringing out her scorpion's tail to sting him with the almost childish query as to why he might think that spending a bit of time together in Vienna would now be a wild idea. Doesn't she recognize any of the usual signs of males sniffing around her turf, he wondered? Could she really be so naïve?

Victor recalled his time in Vienna when he was first a Visiting Professor *(Honorarprofessor)* at the Technical University of Vienna (TUW), then a Research Scholar at the International Institute for Applied Systems Analysis (IIASA) in Laxenburg, a small village located about 12 miles south of Vienna. When Victor joined IIASA in the early 1970s, he was barely out of short-pants, coming to Vienna as more of a life experience than for real intellectual work. IIASA at that time was brand new itself, a joint venture of the USSR and USA Academies of Science with ten junior partners, the host country Austria, Japan, Canada and many of the countries of Eastern and Western Europe.

In those days, Vienna looked a lot like it did in Carol Reed's famous 1949 film *The Third Man:* dark, gloomy and a nest of spies. Years later, when Victor returned to the city for his next stint at the TUW, he could hardly believe his eyes. Vienna had somehow blossomed into the highest quality-of-life major city in the world. What a shock!

The taxi dropped Victor at the *Hotel König von Ungarn* (King of Hungary) located in the very center of the center of the city, just behind St. Stephan's Cathedral. Victor always loved this classic old hotel and was pleased that his hosts at the Academy of Science had been able to book him there. *Much better,* he thought, *than the fancy-shmancy modern, international chain hotels that now dotted the central areas of almost every major city in the world.*

At least the *König von Ungarn* still retained more than a touch of the nineteenth-century, which after all was one of the principal reasons tourists came to Vienna. A visit to this city is like going into a time machine back to a more leisurely, bygone era when emperors ruled the world, people waltzed in the street, and problems were 'Desperate, but not serious.' The *König von Ungarn* fit perfectly into that type of ambience.

Tonight Victor planned to have dinner at the *Zum Schwarzen Kameel* (To the Black Camel), an ancient bar-restaurant established in 1618. It was located at one end of the Graben, the main tourist street in central Vienna, with St. Stephan's Cathedral at the other end.

It was only a five-minute walk from Victor's hotel to the restaurant, so he thought he'd spend a few minutes beforehand just strolling around the central city, reacquainting himself with some of those many sweet memories from his youthful past in this fantastic place.

Victor began by walking down the second main tourist street in the central city, Kärntner Strasse, which ran from the cathedral down to the famed opera house, the Vienna *Staatsoper.* He reached the Vienna Casino, across the street from the Hotel Sacher's cake store, famed for its nearly infinite supply of Sachertorte in wooden boxes, ready for immediate shipment anywhere in the world, giving the street a bit of cachet.

Victor then turned on to the Ringstrasse, where instead of wall-to-wall tourist shops and the babble of a dozen languages each shouting for its own slice of attention, not to mention thousands of people aimlessly wandering about with no seeming purpose, he could enjoy the charms of 19th-century Vienna instead of the hustle and bustle of the early 21st.

Glancing at his watch, Victor saw that time was fleeting and he'd have to move along if he was not to be late for his reservation at the restaurant. But he thought there would be just enough time for a quick *Wiener Melange,* a Viennese coffee with foamed, not whipped, cream. As a bonus, he would also get a glimpse of the famed Café Landtmann before heading back to the center of town to the restaurant.

Landtmann occupies the ground floor of a classic Viennese palais, directly across the street from the Vienna City Hall, the Rathaus. It now had the most extravagant and lavish interior of any *Kaffeehaus* in the city. Viennese habit is for writers, philosophers and other struggling intellectuals to sit for hours in a café working on their respective *magnum opuses.*

Every Viennese person has their regular coffee house. Unfortunately, Victor had time only to drop into a seat in the main hall of the café, drink his *Melange* and then head out to the restaurant for dinner.

As he sipped his coffee, Victor came to the conclusion that for him Alex is just another problem. In the end, either the problem would get solved or he would discover that it was logically unsolvable. There is no in-between. Sometimes, though, he wondered whether the game was really worth the candle. Was the solution really *that* important? This was the question Victor was pondering as he settled his bill and left Landtmann.

While it was at most a ten-minute walk over to the restaurant, Victor had the bad luck to have a spring shower start up just as he left the café. The absence of an umbrella didn't help his humor much either, as the rain served to support his long-held belief that the weather was one of the few truly negative aspects of this city.

As one of his friends put it, "No one ever came to Vienna for the weather." So true. Luckily, the shower turned into nothing more than a passing patch of clouds without too much rain, and Victor got to the restaurant before it developed into the thunderstorm that came pouring down shortly after his arrival.

Victor then spent the better part of the next couple of hours reminiscing over past Viennese experiences, thinking about his new life developments and, in general, renewing his acquaintance with Vienna and his future over a delicious Viennese meal.

Setting down his empty glass, Victor finally decided that he had to get a bit of shut-eye tonight and get ready for his presentation at the Academy tomorrow. He paid his bill and started heading back to his hotel.

Following a totally uneventful lecture at the Academy of Science the next morning and a so-so lunch afterwards, Victor called Alex and arranged to meet her at their hotel following her arrival the next day in the afternoon.

*

As Alex came from the Vienna airport into the city, she thought about a conversation she'd had with her friend and neighbor Maerta about her experiences with and feelings for Victor. Maerta had asked her, "How do you feel about Victor?"

Alex looked closely at her and then said, "I find Victor very, very appealing in many ways: good-looking, very smart, sophisticated and, in general, a high mate-value companion/partner. But there are also negatives: he's at least twenty-five years older than me, which doesn't really bother me all that much, since for me age is just a number."

"So what is it that does bother you, baby?" enquired Maerta.

"Much more troublesome is the distinct feeling I have that Victor is not serious about me. And I don't want just a good-time companion, or a player. That's simply not my game."

Or is it? she wondered.

When Maerta asked why Victor might not be a serious suitor, Alex recalled catching Victor in the kitchen at her dinner a few nights earlier when he was getting just a bit too friendly with the French artist married to Alex's colleague from Merit. Alex said the way Victor was looking at this singularly unappealing woman really irked her, and she almost had to grab Victor and drag him back into the living room to get him away from her.

Maerta didn't think that this little episode made Victor 'unserious.' But she let it go, and the conversation moved off in another direction.

When Alex reflected back on that conversation, she thought that she had been rather ingenuous with Maerta. While she wasn't looking for just a one-nighter with Victor—especially if he was nothing more than a player—she was equally uncertain whether she was really looking at him as a long-term companion or not. Her objective at the moment was to capture his attention and not to make it too easy for him to capture hers. She hoped this trip to Vienna would contribute to that goal.

As Alex's taxi made its way into the city, Victor was waiting in their hotel room for the front desk to call and tell him she had arrived. Around three o'clock the receptionist finally rang and said that Frau Lynne was at the front desk, and could he come down and check her in. Victor thanked her and said he'd be down immediately.

Leaving the elevator in the lobby, Victor saw Alex and his emotional energy went up a couple of levels. *Strange,* he thought, *that while his mind was vacillating between Alex, the tempting schoolgirl and Alex, the temptress, his body made no distinction.* Regardless of her persona, his heart always stepped-up its pace when she was around.

At the desk, Victor and Alex shared the customary European hug and air kisses on both cheeks, although the hug was a bit longer and the kisses a bit sweeter than would ordinarily have been the case.

"Lovely to see you again Alex," he said. "I hope you had an uneventful trip over from London."

"Yes," she replied with a charming smile. "The trip was perfect. Totally uneventful—but too long. I was so eager to meet you that I could barely sit still in my seat."

Alex had a modestly-sized carry-on bag that Victor immediately took. He then ushered her to the elevator.

"Let's get upstairs to the room. You can freshen-up a bit and unpack your things. Then we can discuss what to do between now and dinner."

"That sounds fine, Victor. I just love this old-style hotel. The nineteenth-century is already coming alive for me here. Thanks so much for inviting me to join you. I know I'm going to enjoy this visit very much, short as it may be."

Victor accepted the compliment about the hotel and suggested that perhaps they could take a short stroll around the central city on their way to dinner.

She agreed that it would be good to stretch her legs a bit after the flight. Once they entered the room and closed the door, they each looked at the other for a moment, then literally fell into each other's arms in as loving an embrace as Victor had ever experienced.

Their hands and lips were already exploring each other like two blind people trying to feel, smell and touch each other in places that could not be accessed by sight alone. What is it about this lady, he wondered, that made him feel like a lovesick teenager again? Amazing, the power of testosterone and pheromones!

"You know," Victor said, " this room has a lovely old bathtub, easily big enough for two. Why don't we take a bath together? We have several hours until dinner, and that would be a good way to get rid of the tensions and stress of your travel and my public presentation earlier today. What do you think?"

Slightly taken aback at this suggestion, Alex was silent for a moment or two. Then her face broke into a big smile and she nodded her head in agreement saying, "I want to unpack my bag first and sort out my clothes and cosmetics. Why don't you draw the water and get into the tub? I'll come join you in a few minutes."

"Great! But don't dawdle," said Victor as he took off his shoes and socks and began unbuttoning his shirt on his way to the bathroom.

The tub was filled with hot, but not too hot, water as Victor eased into it and lay back to relax. For a moment, his eyes closed and he imagined Alex scrubbing his back, or maybe it was his front, he couldn't really be sure.

When he came back to reality from this erotic interlude and looked at the bathroom clock, he was surprised to see that fifteen minutes or more had passed since he entered the tub.

What happened to Alex? How long does it take to hang up a dress and set out a few makeup items?

Victor called out through the bathroom door, asking when she would be joining him.

The bathroom door opened and Alex entered. Stopping for a moment, she gazed down at Victor lying in the tub. The look in her eye was as impersonal and pitiless as the noonday desert sun. She said nothing at all but only gave Victor a 'What are you doing here?' type of look, as if she was more annoyed than happy to see him.

All of a sudden a sense of danger was palpable, as real as the faint scent of her perfume drifting into the room.

The reptilian part of Victor's brain, programmed to make instinctive life-or-death decisions, was working overtime, screaming silently that something had happened while Alex was in the bedroom and that she had now slipped into a totally different personality than when she arrived.

Victor forced a smile and shivered involuntarily as he leaned back in the womb-like warmth of the bath water. Glancing up at Alex, he raised his eyebrows by way of invitation to take off her robe and join him.

Instead, she strode resolutely across the room to the counter next to the tub and opened a drawer by the sink. With her back to Victor, she reached inside and took out a hair dryer and plugged it into a socket next to the mirror.

With his eyes again closed, Victor asked her, "What's taking so long? Come into the tub with me."

Turning quickly to face him, Alex held the dryer out over the water, letting it hover out of his reach somewhere just above his thighs.

"Come into the tub with you?" Alex said in a flat tone of voice, frigid as a blast of arctic air. I don't think so. But this hair dryer might join you. How would you like that?"

As she spoke, Victor opened his eyes and saw the hair dryer. A flurry of thoughts raced through his mind, a kaleidoscope of images each vying momentarily for his attention.

Scheisse! What the hell's going on here? I never thought she would be physically abusive or homicidal. I don't recall ever seeing her this cold and remote. Will she really do it? Just stay calm and try to get out of the tub.

Struggling to fight down these images and impulses, he put on his most engaging face and looked up at her.

"Okay. Let's go to bed and talk. Whatever's troubling you, I'm sure we can work it out," he said soothingly, hoping his voice didn't betray the deep fear and tension he was feeling.

"No one would think it was anything other than an accident if I dropped this dryer into the tub right now. One of those thousands of accidental deaths that happen every year in the home," she said in a soft, almost conversational tone, oblivious to his invitation. "I'd tearfully tell the police, 'The dryer just rolled off the edge of the sink and fell in.' They'd try to console me, and I doubt they'd suspect a thing."

Staring her directly in the eye, he tried once again. "I'm falling in love with you. I don't want you to be upset. Let's talk." He started to rise from the water. "And please put down that hair dryer."

Her hand remained rock-steady and unwavering. He stopped lifting his body, fearing that trying to escape the tub might provoke her to drop the hairdryer. He settled back down, taking his weight off his hands, hoping to knock the dryer away if she dropped it.

"Oh, you don't want me to be upset, do you? Just think over why I might be upset," she cried, as she switched on the dryer. "And be damned quick about it, too. My arm is already getting tired. I just might 'accidentally' drop this dryer."

Christ, he thought. *What's put her into this hysterical state? Can she hate me enough to kill me? What* am *I involved in here?*

At that moment, a wide, welcoming smile emerged on Alex's face.

"Hah! Did you really think I was going to drop this dryer into the tub? It's just a little joke to liven things up a bit," Alex said with a touch of maniacal laughter. "Don't get your knickers in a twist."

"Very funny," said Victor. "Maybe I just don't have a macabre enough sense of humor to start laughing when someone holds a loaded gun to my head. Or in this case a plugged-in hair dryer over my balls."

Victor then started getting out of the tub.

Alex looked at him in mild astonishment asking, "What are you doing? I thought we were going to have a nice bath together."

Victor looked over at her rather coldly, asking if she'd be kind enough to hand him a bath towel.

Alex replied, "Maybe the hair dryer could do the job instead. What do you think?"

At that point, Victor reached out, grabbed the towel himself, and went to dry off in the bedroom, leaving Alex alone with the hair dryer still in her hand.

After finishing drying with the towel, Victor got dressed and told her, "Okay, Alex, I'm going downstairs right now and will wait for you. Come down when you're ready. We can then set out on your micro-tour of Vienna."

"Fine," she replied in an even tone of voice, as Victor left the room.

*

As he sat in the lobby, Victor couldn't stop running and re-running the hairdryer scenario through his mind, looking for what could possibly have triggered such behavior by Alex. Hard as he tried, he simply could not understand whatever possessed her to flip into such a potentially murderous mode. There was no way he could accept her remark about her behavior as being simply a 'joke.'

Nobody would take it that way. For her to imagine he would just laugh it off as an idiosyncrasy on her part was asking him to believe in fairy tales. But this was no fairy tale. And it would be a long time, if ever, before he'd believe that.

At that moment, his view of Alex shifted like the movement of two tectonic plates. This woman is dangerous and he knew he would have to keep a close eye on her from now on.

Finally, Alex joined him in the lobby, seemingly back to the same spirit she showed when she had arrived earlier. From her behavior, one would have found it difficult to imagine that the hairdryer scene had ever taken place.

Victor, too, decided to set it aside for now and went back to his original plan for a small tour, followed by a dinner. He would still like to believe that the dryer scene was just her way of making a black-humor-style joke.

Leaving the hotel, he suggested they walk a block from the hotel to Stephansplatz so Alex could see St. Stephan's Cathedral, the very heart of the center of Vienna. From there they began to stroll up the big tourist street Graben, which would lead almost directly to *Ofenloch* (The Oven Hole), the ancient restaurant where Victor had booked dinner.

The window-shopping on the Graben was equal to any that Alex had experienced in London, and she remarked to Victor that the town was so clean. Not a bit of trash on the street or any vagrants passed out in doorways. Victor told her that this was one of the charms of living in Vienna, as the city fathers and mothers paid special attention to the town's physical and aesthetic appearance.

He added that for this reason, along with many more, Vienna had been named the best city in the world for quality of life—for the past ten years! Alex nodded her head in appreciation, as her gaze focused on the offerings of Chanel, Louis Vuitton, Prada and all the other chi-chi boutiques at the end of Graben.

Walking past these shops, Victor motioned Alex down a small street to the right, which was directly across from the *Zum Schwarzen Kameel,* the restaurant he'd eaten at the night before. This street was Kurrentgasse, a narrow, winding, ancient cobblestone passage where the restaurant *Ofenloch* was located.

Here you drink beer since 1704! said the menu at the restaurant. "Not many restaurants can say that," Victor pointed out to Alex.

"No, they certainly can't," Alex nodded in agreement.

"At the beginning, *Ofenloch* was a tavern with a rather disreputable image, actually," Victor explained. "But through the centuries it developed into an upmarket restaurant, now one of Vienna's finest."

The table Victor booked was right in the corner of the main dining room, which consisted of half a dozen wooden tables and chairs of ancient style, sitting on a wooden floor that may well have been in place from the very beginning of the old tavern. In the corner of the room was a counter with several spigots for different beers, along with a collection of waitresses in the country-style Austrian dresses called *dirndls,* fluffy blouses and wide skirts covered with an apron.

"How utterly charming this all is, Victor. I'm so glad we came here. It's like going back a few centuries to a totally different era," Alex gushed.

"Indeed. I think a yearning for a type of time travel is one of the principal reasons tourists come to this town," said Victor. "But now I'm getting hungry. Let's order some drinks, look through the menu, and experience Austrian food, old-style."

Alex asked Victor what he would recommend. When she responded positively to his question about whether she liked fried chicken, he suggested she have Old Viennese fried chicken. He said that to make the fried chicken particularly juicy, Viennese chefs developed a special trick. Before coating the chicken with a mixture of eggs and breadcrumbs, it was soaked in a special marinade of sour cream and herbs.

Alex agreed that it sounded delicious and told the waitress to bring a portion for her, while Victor ordered *Tafelspitz,* boiled beef in broth, with applesauce mixed with horseradish and sour cream dressing. This was the same dish he'd had the night before. He mentioned this to Alex, explaining that he always liked to compare restaurants with their competition by ordering the same dish, especially if it can be done on back-to-back evenings. During the course of their meal, the two discussed not only the food and the style of Vienna, but also their upcoming meeting at Merit, where Victor would give a much more detailed presentation of his simulator to his new work colleagues than he had during his previous visit.

Even more importantly, he would sign his consulting contract as well. They also spoke briefly about Alex's role in the project. They each expressed how happy they were that they'd be able to work together and see each other more often in the coming months.

After dinner they were both tired, too tired even to stop off for an after-dinner drink at one of the many bars and cafés between the restaurant and the hotel. Besides, although neither of them explicitly stated it, they both were ready for a bit of privacy and some intimate reacquaintance. So they walked slowly, but with purpose, back to their hotel along the same path they'd followed earlier.

When they entered their room, Victor went over to the mini bar and asked Alex if she'd like a glass of wine or something perhaps a bit stronger to relax before they went to bed. She said a glass of red wine would be very welcome.

She then asked if Victor would excuse her for a few minutes while she went into the bathroom. He continued rummaging through the mini bar, saying through the bathroom door that her red wine would be on the table when she came back. Taking a small bottle of fairly decent single malt whisky for himself, he took off his shoes, coat and tie, and sat down on the sofa to await Alex's return.

Sipping his whisky, he thought that it was so nice seeing Alex and that they had had such a lovely stroll and dinner tonight that he wondered why he had harbored those dark thoughts about her during his recent time in Santa Fe.

Perhaps the hairdryer episode this afternoon was reviving those thoughts. He hoped that that aberration was just a one-off and that these thoughts would start to drift out of his short-term memory.

Just then Alex returned from the bathroom. But instead of the dress she'd worn to dinner, she was now wearing an off-white, see-through shortie-type negligee that left absolutely nothing to Victor's imagination.

"Oh my!" exclaimed Victor. "You look fantastic. Come a bit closer so I can get a better look."

As Alex walked across the room to join him, Victor handed her the glass of red wine and held her other hand directing her to the place on the sofa next to him. She took a sip of wine, then set the glass on the table and leaned-in to embrace Victor and give him a loving, tender kiss that took in not only his lips, but his tongue as well. Finally, he managed to come up for air and returned her greeting.

"Now that's my kind of kiss. I guess the old-world charm of Vienna is working its magic on you. It's certainly doing something for me, as I sense that I'm already turning to stone like a statue in one of the museums."

"I think we're going to have to do something about that, aren't we?" Alex replied, a very coquettish look on her face. "Why don't you get into something a bit more comfortable yourself while I enjoy this excellent wine?"

"You're reading my mind," he said. "I'll be back momentarily," as he went into the bedroom.

As Alex was laughing to herself about the incident earlier in the bathtub, Victor reappeared in one of the high-class robes supplied by the hotel and rejoined her on the sofa.

"It seems that we're not as tired as we thought," he said, taking Alex's glass and setting it gently down on the table. He then moved close and put one arm around her, leaning-in to give her another steamy kiss.

At the same time, his free hand was busy unbuttoning the front of her negligee and fondling her perfectly-sized breast and teasing its nipple with his fingertip. Alex leaned back, closed her eyes and sighed contentedly as Victor continued stroking her breast, applying just the right pressure to the nipple to speed up the pace of her sighs.

At that point Victor thought it wasn't fair that he'd taken off Alex's robe and not his own, so he evened things up by slipping out of the hotel robe. Alex reached out for his lovely erection, stroking it to generate considerable heavy breathing and gasps on his part to match her own.

"The sofa is nice," Victor whispered quickly. "But I'm an old-fashioned-type of guy. Let's move to the bed."

"Yes," Alex managed to choke out before Victor picked her up and carried her to the bedroom, laying her onto the bed.

In contrast to the frantic, almost animalistic, devouring of each other that they'd experienced in London, here they were very gentle, edging on delicacy.

Victor tenderly stroked Alex's sensitive regions with his hands, fingers and tongue, while she did much the same to him. This foreplay went on to such an extent that Alex finally whispered in Victor's ear that she wanted him inside her—and not just with his fingers and tongue.

He responded by saying that he could hardly wait to feel her wrapped around him again. This time he'd like it if she would take the dominant role and get on top of him.

Jokingly, he said, "Now it's my turn to relax and enjoy it." And that was exactly what happened: they relaxed and enjoyed each other for the next half an hour, changing positions, varying the tempo and, in general, doing what they had both wanted to do since the first time they'd met in Tortola.

After expending all their vital bodily fluids, liquid and vapor, Alex and Victor were exhausted and dehydrated. The latter problem was easily cured with a bottle of mineral water sitting conveniently on the nightstand.

As for the former problem, they lay down on their pillows spooning and wishing each other happy dreams, each promising to wake up in the morning and do it all over again.

*

Perhaps not surprisingly, Victor and Alex both overslept and so had no time the next morning for an encore performance in the sheets. They promised each other to make up for that when they got to London that evening.

At the moment, though, they barely had time to get downstairs to the breakfast room before the dining hours ended. As they munched on their toast and eggs, Victor asked Alex what she'd like to do between now and mid-afternoon when they'd have to head for the airport to catch their five o'clock flight to London.

Alex reminded him that she'd never been to Vienna before, but what she'd seen yesterday had fascinated her. She explained to Victor that she'd like to spend her remaining time having another Victor Safir-guided tour of the inner city. She thought they could stop somewhere for a nice lunch too, and then come back to the hotel and collect their bags before going to the airport.

"Perfect plan, Alex. I'll be more than happy to act as tour guide again today," he said. "Let's get going. Go get your coat and I'll meet you in the lobby."

As Victor took his by now accustomed seat in the hotel lobby, his thoughts seemed to go with the chair as they turned again to Alex's strange, threatening behavior yesterday with the hair dryer. He even wondered if perhaps he should turn down the contract at

Merit, especially if Alex was going to be his main contact on the project. On the other hand, why do that? He really wanted to develop his simulator for real-life work. And Merit was definitely a good place for that.

Besides, maybe he'd be able to figure out what kinds of things set Alex off into her 'second personality' and try to avoid those triggers in the future. In any case, she certainly seemed back to the old Alex in bed last night. So maybe the relationship will work, after all. *Only time will tell,* he thought, as she joined him in the lobby.

They left the hotel going in the same direction as the previous evening, across the square in front of the cathedral, then up the Graben. But when they came to the end of the Graben, instead of turning to the right past the *Zum Schwarzen Kameel,* they turned left up Kohlmarkt and walked one block to Michaelerplatz and the entrance arch leading to Heldenplatz and the Hofburg Palace. The square had the Austrian National Library on one side, the Volksgarten on another, and the entrance to the Hofburg Palace on a third side.

Looking up at the gigantic portico at the entrance to the National Library, Victor told Alex about Hitler's famous speech given from that portico on March 15, 1938, the so-called *Anschluss* speech, that united Germany and Austria just prior to the Second World War. *What a day that must have been,* he thought, trying to imagine this huge square filled with people displaying the Nazi salute and shouting their allegiance to Hitler. How satisfying that must have been for Hitler, returning to this city as leader of the entire nation after having been refused entry to the art school here many years earlier.

Turning away from the National Library, their gaze fell upon the winter residence of the Austrian emperors, the Hofburg Palace.

Just one more astounding monument built to represent what many at the time must have believed would be a monarchy that would last forever. In this case, though, 'forever' was less than two hundred years.

While the monarchy was now long gone, the fantastic buildings that housed it lived on. So, too, did the bureaucracy, Victor wryly told Alex, recalling his own experiences with it during his stay here at the university. Not coincidentally, in today's world the offices of the President of Austria are now in the Hofburg, with those of the political leader, the Chancellor, in the building right next door.

They then walked through the Volksgarten, which bordered Heldenplatz, and exited in front of the Burgtheater, another empire-style building arguably the principal theater for live stage productions in the entire German-speaking world.

Directly across the Ringstrasse sat the Vienna City Hall, the Rathaus, with its imposing gothic towers and huge square in front, where films of opera and classical music are shown every evening in the summer, while it turns into an outdoor ice-skating rink in the winter. The Rathaus itself was flanked on one side by the Austrian National Parliament, a building whose architecture is meant to evoke thoughts of the buildings on the Acropolis in Athens. On the other side of the Rathaus is the main building of the University of Vienna, where the Renaissance meets the 19th century, architecturally speaking.

Victor then asked Alex if she was ready to have a bite to eat. She responded with an affirmative nod of her head and a tighter grip on his arm.

"There's quite a good restaurant right here in the Burgtheater, a place called *Vestibül.* Let's go there for a bite."

Entering the restaurant, they were fortunate to be coming early, said the maître d', who was able to show them to a nice, secluded table for two in the main dining room.

Like *Ofenloch,* where they had dinner the previous evening, *Vestibül* had beautiful traditional decor, although from the 18th century, not the 17th, as with *Ofenloch.* Victor mentioned that the restaurant's signature dish was very special, lobster and cabbage, a must-have for visitors and Viennese alike. They both ordered it, together with some very fine Austrian white wine to complement.

During the meal, their conversation turned again to Victor's visit to Merit the next day.

Victor told Alex, "I want to give a short demo of some of my financial models to your colleagues as background for moving forward on the collaborative project we will finalize with your bosses."

She agreed wholeheartedly with this plan, and thought this would serve her interest well too, given that the project will now involve her as the principal point person from Merit's side. They both ended up believing that the simulator project would be a win-win proposition for everyone.

The waitress who came for their dessert order turned out to be a lovely lady named Dagmar. Quite coincidentally, she was one of Victor's former students from his TUW days.

"How have you been, Dagmar?" Victor enquired. "Why are you waiting tables here instead of doing experiments in the lab?"

"Oh, a very long story, Victor. Maybe you can come back for dinner one day and I'll tell it to you," replied Dagmar.

Victor then introduced her to Alex and the two women measured each other silently as they shook hands. Alex could not escape the feeling that Dagmar had had many experiences with

Victor that she would like to relive the next time Victor came in flying solo.

After declining desserts, Victor excused himself to go to the men's room. To his shock, a minute or two later Alex joined him there and took him into one of the stalls, unzipped his pants and gave him a quick blow job. Afterwards, she asked, "Is that what it was like with Dagmar?"

Victor was now seriously wondering about Alex's mental stability and quickly hurried them back upstairs. He then settled the bill, luckily with the original waiter and not with Dagmar, and they left the restaurant to return to the hotel and get their luggage for the trip to the airport and their flight to London.

Victor hoped that this visit to Vienna and the next couple of days in London would be both professional and personal watershed moments in his life trajectory.

Episode VI

The Collaboration

London

After gathering their bags, Victor and Alex quickly grabbed a taxi at Heathrow Airport to take them into town. On the plane, they had agreed that they would not stay together tonight as they both needed a good night's sleep in preparation for the 10 o'clock meeting the next day at Merit. During the drive, they recapped how the meeting would be structured.

"I'll look for you at our offices around half past nine tomorrow morning," Alex said. "We can then go to the conference room I've booked for our meeting with the two programmers and Jerome."

"Sounds just fine, Alex. Maybe you can have a screen and projector set up. I want to show a couple of overheads at the meeting."

"No problem at all."

They agreed Alex would open the meeting with the re-introduction of Victor to her boss Jerome, as well as an introduction to Bob, an experienced trader who would handle the trading aspects of the simulator upgrade, and to Bill, a programming *Wunderkind,* who would implement the changes.

Victor would bridge the gap between their areas of expertise, as well as contribute higher-level ideas regarding the structure of the simulator. Finally, Alex would take care of day-to-day management of the project, as well as interface with the upper management at Merit, meaning Jerome and his boss, Michael Zilk.

The taxi stopped in front of Victor's hotel. Before opening the door, he leaned over and gave Alex what was a far from *pro forma* goodbye kiss, saying again how much he enjoyed their time together in Vienna.

He added, "I am so glad we are going to be combining work and play while I am here in London. You are really something special, Alex."

"Victor, I feel exactly the same about you," she replied. "Tomorrow cannot come soon enough. I'll see you at Merit, and we'll take things from there. Meanwhile, have a few happy dreams about the future, and don't dwell on the past."

He gave the taxi a long farewell look as it pulled away from the hotel to take Alex to her flat. He made his way into the hotel and checked-in, thinking about how quickly his relationship with her was developing.

That evening Victor had an early dinner at a fish-and-chips place near his hotel, then returned to his room for a last review of the meeting structure and his plan for presenting the simulator to Alex and her colleagues.

Before going up to his room, he dropped into the hotel bar for a shot of Glendronach single malt. No place like the UK for getting his favorite whiskies, he thought as he sat with his drink at the bar. The bar was neither busy nor empty, which suited him perfectly for thinking about not only his talk in the morning, but also his experiences with Alex in Vienna.

He was still troubled by the incident with the hairdryer. If that's her idea of something funny—as she claimed it was—he had better keep a careful eye on her during their upcoming encounters, both personally and professionally.

She obviously had the capacity to go very cold, very quickly, without any particular actions on his part to provoke her. And if this same behavior intruded into the professional landscape, it could make working with her on this simulator project very problematic.

Anyway, nothing he could do about that now other than wait and watch. Finishing off his drink, Victor went up to his room and was asleep almost as soon as his head hit the pillow.

*

He arrived at Merit the next morning about twenty minutes before the meeting was scheduled to begin. Alex met him at the reception area, greeting him in the friendly, but not effusive, way she would greet any colleague and then took him to the meeting room.

The others came into the room as Alex and Victor were sorting out the technicalities of getting the computer, projector and screen in harmony with one another for the overheads Victor wanted to use to illustrate his presentation.

By the time that was done everyone was present, so Alex called the meeting to order and re-introduced Victor to Bob, Bill and Jerome. Victor then took the floor and began his presentation by saying that he was looking forward to working with everyone here at Merit during the coming months to sharpen the simulator into a tool that would ultimately make a lot of money for all of them.

He then went into some detail about the many pieces that composed this 'market in a box,' displaying all the components of the simulator for their examination.

The major items were the traders, the set of trading strategies they each had at their disposal and the market rules specifying what actions the traders can and cannot take at any given moment. The simulator also took into account information from the outside world, such as geopolitical, economic and governmental news, as well as from the inside world such as regulations impacting trading.

Perhaps most importantly, the system also has publicly-available information on the market itself, such as the current market price of each security, the volume of shares being traded in each stock and so on.

After giving a short demo of the simulator in action, Victor asked if they had any questions.

Alex had been listening intently to what Victor was saying, particularly that the simulator was a kind of computer game, with the traders as the players competing against each other in a continually changing environment.

"Victor," she said, "every computer game I've ever seen—-a football game, a war game, a real-estate game or whatever—has been a slimmed-down version of reality."

Victor nodded in agreement and the men from Merit leaned forward a bit to see where Alex was going with this.

"The game *always* leaves out aspects of its real-world counterpart that we know are there," she continued, "aspects that the game designer felt were unimportant, or even irrelevant, to the purposes of the game. I'm sure your simulator is no exception. It's a 'toy version' of the real stock market and will always be that. So how can we take seriously the idea that this stockmarket game can—or even should—be used as the basis for decisions about the *real* stock market, decisions that will make—or lose—money for all of us?"

Wow! thought Victor. *Alex has cut right to the heart of the matter with this question. This lady is not just a heavenly beauty. She's a supremely* intelligent *heavenly beauty!* He paused for a moment before replying.

"Alex, you're one-hundred percent correct. My simulator is indeed just a *model* of a real stock market. And it will never be more than a model, in the sense that there will always be things about the real system that are left out of the model. That's the very essence of a model. Whether the model is useful or not depends on the type of question(s) it's designed to answer, whether what you've left out of the model seriously impacts the answers, and most importantly, are the answers *useful.*"

At this point, Jerome stepped into the discussion:

"This is all fascinating, Victor. But you know Merit is not an academic research institution. We don't have a big budget for speculative projects like scaling up this simulator to real-world size. In fact, we don't have a budget for this at all. Tell me how close to reality you think you could get with the people in this room? And how long do you think it would take to get there?"

Victor was not surprised by this question, and had been considering the answer ever since meeting with Alex in Tortola. Now he was ready to put it on the table.

"You are quite right to raise this issue, Jerome. This *is* a research project, not simply a case of development, or as you say, 'scaling up.' Nevertheless, I believe a six-month effort will go very far toward addressing the questions you pose."

Jerome persisted, "Do you mean in six months we'd have a simulator ready to jump-in to real-world trading?"

"No, I mean in six months we will be able to estimate with some confidence how much longer it would take and what resources would be needed in order to 'get real.'"

Jerome replied, "Okay, thanks for your answer and your frankness," and sat back down.

"In fact," added Victor, "that's what we're here for. We want to shape and polish the model so as to eliminate as many of those answer-changing factors as we can before we start putting real-world money on the table. When you boil it down to its essence, that's what our simulator project is all about. Making sure the model and the real world are sufficiently aligned for the model to mirror prices changes accurately enough to make money on those computer-generated price changes."

"Yes, thanks very much, Victor," Alex said. "Now I understand where we're going with the project."

Bob then stepped into the discussion with a somewhat more operational question:

"Tell us, Victor, what do the trading strategies look like that are used by the traders in your market?"

"First of all," Victor said, "I wouldn't really call them 'strategies.' They're more like tactical rules for deciding at any given moment whether to buy, sell or hold. And remember, in my toy world as it currently stands there is just a single stock being traded, not the three thousand or more that are traded every day on the New York Stock Exchange."

"So what form does a trading rule take in your simulator?" Bob persisted.

Victor thought for a moment before replying.

"Each rule consists of a collection of Yes or No questions. For instance, has the stock gone up during the last period? Has the volume of trade increased or decreased during the last period? Have there be any political developments in the last period affecting the stock? And so forth."

Jerome interrupted with the remark, "These rules all seem to be 'technically-based,' in the sense that they rely mostly on information from within the market itself. Price changes, volume of stock traded and so forth."

Victor replied, "Yes, at least to some extent that's true. At the moment the rules incorporate very little 'fundamentalist' information from outside the market, such as corporate profit-loss statements or geopolitical considerations. That's all part of what we hope to do here at Merit by way of beefing-up the simulator."

Victor then continued his description of the trading rules:

"Altogether there are sixty such questions. What distinguishes one trading rule from another is that each rule is composed of only a *subset* of those sixty questions. In numerical terms, there are 2^{60}, or about one billion billion, possible rules, which is a number that commands some respect. At any moment, each trader is using one of those rules to decide what to do."

Then Bob asked whether a trader can change their rule from time to time if they see the current rule is not working so well? That is, it's not making any money. Or at least it's not making enough money.

"Absolutely, yes," Victor said. "The simulator contains a 'rule for changing rules,' which in effect makes it an adaptive system.

"I'll be very eager to dig into this, Victor, and see how we can 'soup-up' what you've done to bring it up to everyday trading standards."

"Well, that's what our project is all about," Alex chimed in.

Jerome then stood up, and the others looked to see what he was going to do.

He said, "I have another meeting to attend, so I'll have to leave."

Alex told him, "We really appreciate you coming here this morning, Jerome. It's important for you to see what we're planning for this activity."

"Let me thank Victor for this very illuminating picture of how the stockmarket simulator works." Jerome said. "We will certainly have plenty of time over the coming months to address all these matters that you have raised, along with quite a few others that I'm sure you are all keen on hearing about and digging into."

As Jerome left the room, Alex stood up. "This is a good time to end the discussion for today," she announced. She then echoed Jerome's comments, saying "Victor's 'fixes' to the simulator have now made it ready, if not for prime time, at least for a thorough off-Wall Street vetting, over the next few months. Thank you, Victor, for an edifying presentation to get us started on this project."'

Bob and Bill both thanked Victor as well as they filed out of the room, leaving behind just Victor and Alex.

Alex reiterated what Jerome had told Victor earlier in an email, namely that Merit would be pleased to offer him a six-month consultancy contract. It would involve a consultancy fee that made his mouth water, not to mention a generous allowance for travel and living expenses if he would temporarily relocate to London and lead the charge on developing the simulator for real-life trading.

Victor quickly agreed, saying, "To finalize the contract, I will have to formally clear the situation with the management of my Institute in Santa Fe. But I've already discussed the matter with the Institute's president, who told me a temporary leave-of-absence should be no problem."

All Victor needed to do now was return to Santa Fe and get himself organized to move to London for a few months. He told Alex, "This arrangement with Merit will probably call for me to make the odd trip back to New Mexico, just to keep the pot boiling there. But since the pot in London and the pot in Santa Fe are essentially the same pot, it should be easy enough for me to attend to both."

He continued, "Why don't we celebrate my soon-to-become new status as a 'Meriter' with a nice dinner together tonight?"

"A terrific idea, Victor. I'll even volunteer Merit to pick up the tab as the first 'business expense' of your new consultancy."

For the dinner, Alex suggested Maggie Jones, one of her favorite restaurants in London. "It fits the situation perfectly; it's a quirkish, down-home-type of bistro tucked away on a side street in Kensington, oozing with charm and a very particular 'Olde English'-style menu."

According to Alex, the secret to Maggie's success was a warm, friendly atmosphere and a generous menu full of beautifully cooked, classic English dishes. She also said that if the restaurant were personified, it would be an eccentric Englishman of the old school.

"Don't expect any dainty salads or 'free-from' dishes," she said, with a laugh. "Hearty stews, classic pies, steaks, and yummy things for dessert like bread-and-butter pudding are what you'll see on the menu tonight."

By the time she finished her 'advertisement' for Maggie's, Victor's mouth was already watering. If he was going to be a temporary Londoner, it sounded to him to be the perfect place to start.

Just before he left her to go to the taxi stand and return to his hotel, he said, "Let's get my London life started right. I can hardly wait to see you at Maggie's tonight. I suggest we meet there at seven o'clock."

She replied that she would make the reservation and see him then.

*

Victor was surprised by how quickly Alex began baring her soul during their pre-dinner drinks.

She immediately launched into her concerns about her future, problems she'd been having at work with her colleagues and her boss Jerome, who was being just a bit too bossy for her tastes, especially in the touchy-feely department.

"How long has this been going on, Alex?" Victor enquired.

"Well, for most of the past year, at least," she responded.

Alex was really concerned with what she should do with her life. This existential issue was compounded by the fear of losing her position in an upcoming merger Merit was currently negotiating with a much larger financial house in New York.

During the course of this litany of uncertainties and complaints, it finally dawned on Victor that the difficulties he'd been having in relating to her were part of a much broader pattern that had been scratching at the back of his brain almost from their very first encounter in Tortola.

For the first time, he now saw how deeply worried Alex was about how others perceived her as a professional and as an intellect.

Victor suddenly realized he was going to have to tread very carefully in his future dealings with Alex, especially as matters moved from the personal domain into the professional realm during the coming months. Once again he found himself returning to the thought that this woman, with her sweet little-girl looks and charming naïveté, was going to be an extremely tricky and potentially even dangerous liaison.

Victor set these concerns aside as the waitress arrived to take their order. They each opted for the set dinner. Alex selected a prawn cocktail appetizer, grilled salmon with Hollandaise sauce and a lemon sorbet for dessert. Victor's choice was an appetizer of duck liver paté, followed by Maggie's creamed fish pie and then a plate of Stilton and celery to finish things off.

During dinner, they engaged in banal small talk about British life, the weather, comments on the food, and office gossip at Merit.

Over coffee Alex told him, "I booked a two-week holiday next month to Thailand. But now I'm wondering whether I should go or cancel. My friend Maerta was going to go with me. But she has backed out at the last minute, so the trip now seems somewhat problematic."

Victor half-jokingly said, "Nothing would please me more than to take Maerta's place and cruise down the Chao Phraya River with you Alex, exploring the sights and smells of Bangkok together."

Glancing up at him with a long, searching look, Alex breathlessly replied, "What a lovely picture that would be."

Oh, oh! Could this be another twist of the scorpion's tail, thought Victor, as alarm bells started ringing.

While the idea of such a trip held great attraction for him, he could not escape the subconscious feeling that it could well turn into another case of the huntress on the prowl. Perhaps he should find out right now, but in a more restricted, controllable context. He leaned toward her across the table and said softly, "You know, I'm not leaving London until the end of the day on Sunday. So all of tomorrow and half of Sunday is free time for me," he said. "I was thinking of using it to go to a restaurant-hotel up near Oxford that I just love. It's called *Le Manoir aux Quat'Saisons.* Perhaps you've heard of it?"

"No, I haven't," Alex replied.

"So much the better. Maybe we could go up there together tomorrow? I'll rent a car in the morning and we could then drive to the restaurant. It's only about an hour's drive from London, so we'd have time to explore the lovely Oxfordshire countryside, have some fantastic food and even stay over in one of their luxurious rooms for the night. There would still be plenty of time for me to get back here in time for my flight to the US on Sunday evening. How does that sound to you?"

The idea seemed a no-brainer to Alex, who immediately agreed with Victor's suggestion. She then upped the ante:

"That excursion sounds lovely. As a preview of coming attractions, why don't we leave here right now and go back to my flat and finish what we didn't have time to complete yesterday morning in Vienna?"

"You're reading my mind," said Victor with enthusiasm. "I'll settle the bill and we can get out of here."

As he signaled the waiter for the bill, Alex reminded him that this dinner was on Merit.

*

Victor and Alex returned to her flat to celebrate their new business partnership with what Alex hinted, with her eyes and body language, would be a night of sexual games, leaving Victor flush with anticipation.

He was thinking how happy he was that they did *not* have time for a morning eye-opener in Vienna the day before, as his pent up energies were definitely ready for something more than a simple encore.

Quickly, the activities even took a somewhat frightening turn for Victor, when Alex asked him to undress and lay down on her bed, as she disappeared into her walk-in closet. Moments later, dressed in form-fitting black leather-and-lace, she brought out a handful of black silken cords and asked if she could tie him up. Bondage had never been much of a sexual turn-on for him, especially when he was the one being bound. But the ecstatic, almost dream-like look in Alex's eye was so seductive he told her to go ahead and tie him to the bedposts.

Quietly humming the childhood song *Four and Twenty Blackbirds* that her mother had often sung to her as a child, Alex finished the binding. She was a bit surprised when she looked down at him.

"Don't be scared, Victor. This will all be in the spirit of good fun and play between us. Not to worry."

"Yes, Alex, I understand those words. But I'm pretty unfamiliar with these bondage games, and I know they can sometimes get out of control. Please go easy on this neophyte, okay?"

"We're partners now, Victor. In business and now in life. My role is to help you feel better with both, not to threaten you. I'm going to treat you like my most valuable friend in the world, which you are."

Well, Victor thought, *here's one more chance to get inside Alex's psyche.* And that was what Victor needed more than anything else at this time, even if it entailed a potentially fatal, or at least dangerous, risk. Nothing ventured, nothing gained—especially if you are hot on the trail of the solution to a major unsolved problem.

To his great surprise, when she finished securing his arms and legs, she brought out a golden cord that she used to wrap his neck. Then she looped the cord over the top rail of the bed in a way that by pulling on it she could tighten or loosen the noose around his neck as she wished.

"What's with this cord around my neck, Alex? I thought you were simply going to tie my hands and feet to the bedposts."

"Oh, Victor, this is a variation on the bondage game. It's well-known that when the oxygen flow to the brain is reduced during sex, the orgasms are indescribably spectacular. Wouldn't you like to experience an 'indescribable orgasm?' "

At that point, Victor was really starting to take seriously his inner warnings about how potentially dangerous this woman might be. Alex then walked over to the stereo and put on a Bach CD, telling Victor playfully that a little 'fugue music' is just the thing for the 'fugue state' she wanted to put him into.

She then proceeded to stimulate him orally and by hand, while she gradually pulled on the golden cord to tighten the noose. The cord finally reached a point where Victor was just one tug away from total asphyxiation.

Eventually, Alex took the cord from around his neck and, in a cheery voice said, "Wasn't that fun?"

His arms and legs bound, Victor could only nod in agreement, remembering how he'd felt just two days ago in the bathtub in Vienna. *Just like the tub, I'll be lucky to get out of this bed with my sanity intact, not mention my life. The hairdryer incident was* not *a one-off. This is an integral part of Alex's psychological makeup.*

Eventually, as Victor continued to 'cooperate', Alex came down from her state of sexual ecstasy— or was it a different kind of ecstacy?—and untied him. Without showing it, he considered leaving. But he couldn't help himself, and now there was a lot of money involved, too. It was dangerous. And delicious. *And dangerous.*

But as their play continued, he wondered if he should reconsider ... *Just say No,* he told himself when his thoughts started wandering down such byways like rekindling the idea of a truly meaningful relationship with her. *This is one mixed-up lady,* he reminded himself, *and definitely not the kind of woman to settle-in with for the duration. Maybe not for* any *duration.*

They finally left the bedroom and retreated to the sofa, where Alex poured Victor a double shot of pretty decent Scotch, while she picked up the glass of red wine she'd set on the table for herself earlier.

She took up the conversation they'd begun before, with no indication that what they'd just experienced in the bedroom was anything out of the ordinary.

Alex was staring at Victor now in a way that was beginning to make him feel uncomfortable.

"Would you like to hear a recording of the bondage game we just played?" she asked him abruptly.

"What do you mean?" he asked.

"I mean that there was an audio recorder underneath the bed, and it got a pretty good record of what we were both saying back there. I thought maybe it could be interesting for you to hear yourself when you're in a state of sexual stress."

This was a first for Victor. He'd had many sexual experiences. But he'd never been with anyone who recorded their sexual adventures.

"Do you record all your sexual encounters?" he asked. "Kind of like photos in a scrapbook or something?"

"No, nothing like that," she said. "Just the S&M encounters. Mostly because there's a lot more potential danger and stress then, and I like to hear how people sound and react when their very life might be being threatened."

"Well," replied Victor, "I can't say I really want to hear that tape. Keep it in a safe place for future reference, though. I could change my mind later."

"Oh, don't worry about that," Alex said. "I keep the tapes in a special place for extraordinary encounters."

Then, without missing a beat, Alex shifted the topic again, "I'm really looking forward to that trip tomorrow up to Oxfordshire," she said. "Thanks so much for inviting me. We're going to have a wonderful time. I just know it."

Victor was having so much trouble making up his mind about Alex that he didn't know what to say. On the one hand, his fears about her unstable nature were just now confirmed in a quite dramatic and definitive fashion. On the other, he had after all invited her for a short holiday tomorrow, including another evening together in a luxury room at the restaurant-hotel.

He was also embarking on a professional relationship with Alex and her firm that had just been cemented earlier that day. He could hardly walk away from it now before it had even begun. So he decided he'd just have to keep his wits about him and his eyes and ears open, while at least going through the motions of satisfying his obligations to Alex and to himself.

Suddenly, he felt a bit like a caged bird. Or a bear with his paw caught in a trap. Except it wasn't his paw!

"Yes," Victor said, "I'm sure we'll have a wonderful day and night together tomorrow. Now I think I should be getting back to my hotel. Since I'm not totally familiar with London road-traffic patterns, my suggestion is that I have the rental car delivered to my hotel, and we meet there at ten o'clock tomorrow morning. Is that all right with you?"

Alex agreed and the deal was done. Victor quickly dressed and they shared a loving embrace at the door as he left.

*

The next day Victor and Alex overslept and got a bit of a late start from London on their fifty-mile drive up to Great Milton in Oxfordshire, where the restaurant-hotel was located.

Le Manoir aux Quat'Saisons was in a 15th-century manor house surrounded by countryside. It was notable for its two-acre garden that supplied 70 types of herbs and 90 types of vegetables used in their world-famous kitchen. The hotel also had its own cooking school, where students got plenty of hands-on experience in developing their own culinary skills.

Unfortunately, Victor and Alex got to the hotel after the luncheon hour had ended, so weren't able to enjoy any of the renowned cuisine immediately after checking in. In any case, they'd both had decent-sized breakfasts and were not suffering hunger pangs for dinner quite yet.

The room was a one-bedroom garden suite, with both courtyard and garden views. The suite had its own terrace and private garden, along with a large sitting area and sofa in the living room, a huge king-sized bed, and was themed in a way to capture the French heritage of its owner and chef.

"Wow," said Alex when they walked into the room. "This place must cost a fortune."

"Better not to know," replied Victor. "Just enjoy. But so you won't feel too badly about the price, the Michelin-starred meals are included in the price of the room."

After leaving their bags in the room, they decided to drive into Oxford and have a look around the fabled place.

It was only about a fifteen-minute drive, and on the way Alex asked Victor, "Have you ever been to this town before?"

He replied, "I've never lived in Oxford. But I have visited several times for conferences and to make presentations at one or another of the colleges." He added, "I actually prefer Cambridge to Oxford, but please don't mention that to anyone, especially if they are an old Oxonian."

"Why?" Alex asked.

Victor replied, "Oxford is a town with a university, albeit one of the world's great universities. But Cambridge is a place where the university *is* the town! So somehow in Cambridge I always felt as if I was wrapped up in a kind of intellectual cocoon. But I've never felt that way in Oxford."

They spent a couple of hours poking around Magdalen and St. John's Colleges, admiring the fantastic architecture of these medieval structures. Alex noted that Balliol College was founded in the 13th century.

Alex joked, "That makes this place even older than you, Victor." She also noted that, "Some of these colleges bear a striking resemblance architecturally to our hotel. Or maybe it's the other way around. I'm not sure. In any case, the feeling I get is a lot like what I had in Vienna as we were walking around the historic area in the central city there."

From Balliol College, they walked a block or so down to the famous Bodleian Library and the Ashmolean Museum, two fixtures of the Oxford landscape. After a stroll down High Street for a look into the shops and other commercial establishments, Victor suggested they get back to their car and return to the hotel.

He told Alex that he'd like to take a pre-dinner walk through some of the lovely gardens surrounding the hotel before it got too dark. She said she'd like that too, so they started moving back to the parking garage where they'd left the car.

Once they had taken their walk in the countryside and returned to the hotel, it was almost time for dinner. The ambience in the restaurant was regal enough that they thought they'd change into something a bit more formal for the meal. They went to their room, where Alex put on a very stylish, elegant black dress, while Victor donned a dark suit and tie.

In the dining room, they perused a menu that would tempt anyone. Even someone indifferent to fine food would be moved to revisit their prejudices upon seeing this menu. The items on offer had a distinctly French leaning, with appetizers such as wild risotto and mushrooms, seared duck liver, and Cornish crab with lime, coconut and passion fruit as sauces. For the main courses that day, the chef tempted their palettes with filet of Angus beef, Anjou pigeon, roast grouse or pan-seared Dover sole. Finally, the desserts included a pear almondine, raspberry soufflé and a 64% dark chocolate coffee cup filled with various textures of cappuccino. And, of course, in characteristic French style, there was a final course consisting of a variety of exquisite French and British cheeses.

"I think we could simply close our eyes and make a random pick for each course and not go wrong," said Victor. "What do you think?" Alex agreed that to make a logical choice was a fool's errand and that she might do just as Victor suggested. She'd just close her eyes and simply point three times. Following dinner, they stopped in the hotel bar for a glass of Hennessy XO cognac to settle their stomachs before proceeding upstairs to enjoy their lovely suite.

Snuggling on the plush sofa in their living room, Alex thanked Victor for the invitation to spend this day with him. She said it was one of the finest experiences she'd had since moving to England and really wanted to express her gratitude. "But not with sex."

Victor was nearly shocked into a state of speechlessness, but managed to croak out a query, asking what she had in mind.

With that, she took his hand and led him to the bedroom where she said the gratitude would still be expressed physically, as well as emotionally, but not the way he expected.

Alex asked Victor to take off all his clothes and lay down on the bed. She then went to her travel bag and took out a tube of gel for massaging, not for penetration, and put a big squeeze of it onto both her hands.

Naked herself by then, she climbed onto the bed and began to give Victor one of the most relaxing, soothing and stimulating body massages he'd ever experienced.

What followed was a very loving, tender and totally non-sexual experience that Victor would never forget. Alex was still applying her massage magic when she asked Victor to turn over.

But by then Victor had fallen totally asleep. As he slipped into his slumber, he reminded himself of those previous experiences with Alex that he would also never forget. His task was to discover how to make the 'nice' Alex with her tube of massage gel appear and remain, leaving the 'naughty' Alex with her silken cords and hairdryers buried somewhere in her psyche, hopefully forever.

Following a sumptuous English breakfast the next morning, the couple set off back to London with their stomachs stretched and all their appetites sated.

Once they were in the car and headed back to London, Alex grew very quiet for the first fifteen minutes or so, before reaching over to stroke Victor's arm. Then she leaned a bit closer to him and said, "Do you recall my litany of concerns at dinner the other night at Maggie's?"

Victor nodded his head, as she continued, "I want to tell you how much this trip has helped me see a better path in life."

"Really?" replied Victor. "Tell me about it."

"I feel so comfortable with you, safe and secure from all those things I spoke of at the restaurant. I'm really going to miss you for the next days while you're in Santa Fe. I'm feeling so close to you now, Victor, that I just want to put my arms around you and keep you here in London with me."

"That's very sweet, Alex. I will be thinking of you every day and counting the hours until I can get back here to you."

Alex looked at him very seriously, hesitating for a moment, before saying, "We're now partners in both business and love, Victor. When you come back from the USA, I'd like us to discuss getting married."

Victor was stunned. His first thought was that she must be joking—again! But it didn't really sound like a joke, and as he absorbed that fact, he actually almost lost control of the car. Luckily, there was another car about to cut into their lane at that moment, so Victor had a good excuse for a rapid turn of the steering wheel and a blow on the horn before he had to respond to Alex's request.

"Oh, Alex. I want us to be happy and successful together, too. Yes, let's talk about our personal arrangement when I return. We'll both have a couple of weeks or so now to reflect on what we want from each other and see how that fits into our individual life patterns. In this sense, it's lucky I have this trip coming up."

Alex nodded in agreement and they each sat back contemplating what being 'together' would mean to each of them.

Victor drove back to the hotel to collect his luggage and return the rental car, while Alex asked the doorman to call a cab. As they were waiting for the taxi to arrive, she hugged Victor once again, gave him a loving kiss and said she was already missing him. He reciprocated her feelings and said he would try to clean up the dangling loose ends in Santa Fe and get back to London and to her *post haste.*

Later that evening, Victor was sitting in a business-class seat on his flight from Heathrow to Atlanta, thinking ruefully that he was becoming a regular commuter on this flight back. That would soon end, thank God.

He would be happy to get settled in London for his consultancy and at least get rid of this boring aspect of his life. Something to celebrate, he thought, as he asked the hostess for another gin and tonic to relax his mind on the long flight back to New Mexico.

There were two Alexes. He asked himself whether the 'bad' Alex with the hair dryer and ropes was bad enough to actually follow the implications of that paraphernalia through to their deadly end? Or would she always pull up just short, saying, 'Wasn't that fun?'

As a scientist, Victor knew that he now had an hypothesis, namely, that Alex would play at dangerous sexual situations like asphyxiation or electrocution. But she would always back away when she got close to the point of no return. Unfortunately, he also knew that to test the hypothesis he must do a real-life experiment.

Otherwise, it remained simply armchair philosophy supported by few facts and a lot of guesses and intuition. But that was just one possibility among many—including the possibility that some day she wouldn't back off. The only way to pick one hypothesis from the many alternative contenders would be to construct an experiment that would eliminate the pretenders. His task, then, over the coming weeks and months, would be to create and carry out just such an experiment.

He now had the additional burden of trying to figure out how to defuse Alex's marriage request without torpedoing their project at Merit and destroying his relationship with her.

For starters, at the moment he wasn't even formally divorced from Karin. Furthermore, marriage to anyone right now was not part of his game plan. And even if it was, Alex would be far away from his vision of the ideal partner. *What a mess!*

To a large degree it was a mess of his own making, of course. While in Santa Fe he would have this huge new problem to face, and hopefully solve. Fortunately, he was good at solving problems. He hoped this gift would not desert him at this moment when he needed it most.

Episode VII

The Competition

Santa Fe

Shortly after his return to Santa Fe, Victor checked his calendar and was reminded that almost a month ago, he had accepted a dinner-party invitation for the next evening. This was the very day before he was leaving on a short trip to San Francisco to meet with Martin Manry, a Silicon Valley zillionaire interested in forming a new institute for research on extreme events, or X-events, as Victor termed them.

This was an area close to his current interests on stock market prices movements because a financial X-event is basically a crash, a boom or, in other ways, an extreme market movement. Victor was understandably eager to talk with Manry about serving on the organizing committee for the new center.

Having just flown in from Europe and with this trip to California the next day, Victor was tempted to beg off on the dinner. But the hostess of the party was Stephanie Fitzgerald, a very old friend he hadn't seen for ages, and he really wanted to attend. Besides, there was always a likelihood he would meet some genuinely new and interesting people at her parties.

This factor was yet another of the many attractions of living in Santa Fe. Almost the entire Anglo community consisted of middle- and post-middle-aged, native-born American intellectuals—artists, writers, sculptors, photographers, scientists, potters, clothes designers, et al.

Yet the town had very little night life of the commercial variety, so the vast majority of social encounters took place in private homes at parties just like this one. Victor seldom knew who would be present at one of these parties. But he did know that whoever was there would be interesting.

And right now he needed a bit of intellectual variety in his life. So an evening with Stephanie and her friends held some definite appeal.

When he arrived at the party, a bottle of nice Merlot in hand for the hostess, Victor was met at the door by an especially attractive woman of indefinite middle age whom he'd never seen before. She introduced herself as Natalie, and said right away that she was a newcomer to Santa Fe, from Texas of all places.

"You must be Victor," she said with a radiant smile as she invited him in. "Stephanie told me a lot about you. She said you knew everyone worth knowing in this small town, and I should get to know you tonight and you might show me around."

"I'm very pleased to meet you, Natalie. I'll do my best to obey Stephanie's command."

"Maybe you'd like a drink to get things going?"

"Thanks for those very welcome words. A gin and tonic with a twist of lime would really hit the spot right now," replied Victor, taking a long look as Natalie turned and went into the kitchen to fetch his drink. A lovely lady with a charming personality, Victor thought.

Just then Stephanie showed up, gave him an air kiss and accepted the bottle of wine with pleasure.

"Caught you, didn't I?" she said.

"What do you mean?" Victor replied, a sly smile on his face.

"You know damned well what I meant. You were checking out Natalie as your next conquest," she smiled back, with a look that said she knew Victor—and he knew her.

"You know I always admire your friends, Stephanie. And I'm certainly pleased to see you're maintaining standards for this party tonight. I hope you'll sit me down next to Natalie at dinner so I can welcome her to town, hear her story and not just tell her a few of my own."

"Since you know just about everybody here Victor, why don't you and Natalie start circulating," Stephanie told him, as Natalie reappeared with his drink.

"Victor will introduce you to some of the other guests, while I have another look at what's happening backstage."

Offering his arm to Natalie, Victor guided her out onto the patio and joined the party. Not more than a few seconds after reaching the patio, Victor heard a hearty greeting behind him. He didn't even need to turn around to know that the Institute's President, John Casey, was on his way over to greet him.

"What a pleasant surprise to see you here, John," Victor said, shaking his hand. "Let me introduce my new friend, Natalie. Sorry, but I haven't known her long enough yet to know her last name."

"Nice to meet you, John," Natalie said charmingly, shaking his hand.

"Say John, while you're here," Victor said, "I was in touch with Jenny in your office the other day, asking her to set up a time for us to meet before I have to go back to England. She told me your calendar was full, but she thought maybe we could squeeze-in a phone call or go over some things via email," said Victor.

"Well," John replied, "if it's something short and simple maybe we can settle it right now. What's on your mind?"

"My apologies, Natalie. I just have to say a few words in private with John. Then I'll be right back to you."

"No problem, Victor. That's what parties like this are for," said Natalie with a smile.

Victor nodded and gestured for John to move over to the corner of the patio where they could talk a bit more privately.

"What I wanted to ask is whether there would be any problem if I took a leave-of-absence from the Institute for a few months to complete some business that's come up in London?"

"Is this to do with your stockmarket simulator?" John asked.

"Exactly. A financial firm there, Merit, wants to acquire rights to the simulator and move it forward into the realm of real-world trading. They've asked if I could come over to London for a few months to spearhead this transition. I told them I didn't think there would be any problem, but I had to talk with you about it first."

"I don't see anything standing in the way of such a leave. Of course, it would have to be without pay. But I suppose the Merit folks will take care of that. And you know the Institute's policy on intellectual property rights for things like your simulator."

"My understanding is that the Institute faculty owns all property rights on their work, even if it is carried out with Institute funding. Is that correct?"

"That is indeed the policy, Victor. All we ask is that if you walk away with a few zillion in your hand, you remember us fondly when it comes time to make those juicy, tax-deductible, charitable contributions."

"You can count on that, John. I'll talk with the people at Merit and see if we can nail down the dates for my stay in London."

"Sounds good. Now let's get back to the party."

Whew! Victor had been lucky that John was at Stephanie's party. Now he could really fix the details of the Merit project and make definite plans to go back to London. It would be very nice to be there for a long enough period of time to really get 'acquainted' with Alex.

He rejoined Natalie just as Stephanie began tapping a glass to call the guests to the dinner table.

The evening passed in the usual fashion with lots of chit-chat about local issues in Santa Fe—an upcoming mayoral election, whether the summer thunderstorms would be sufficient to recharge the water reservoirs, the dropoff in the art market, and other such matters, not to mention recurring themes about literature, music, science or whatever took the fancy of the person introducing the topic.

Victor's flight the next day was early, and he had to get up around four o'clock to get to the Albuquerque airport in time. So right after the dessert, he paid his compliments to Stephanie for a lovely dinner and made his apologies for an early exit from the party. But before leaving, he spoke privately to Natalie saying, "I'd really like to meet you when I return to Santa Fe a few days from now."

"That would be very nice," Natalie replied, and scribbled her phone number on a napkin and gave it to him before he left. Good way to end a nice get-together thought Victor, as he headed back up the hill to his house to finish his packing and get at least a few hours sleep.

On his way up the hill, Victor thought about his upcoming meeting in Silicon Valley with Martin Manry. He really didn't know much about Manry at all. He'd made early investments in several tech companies that quickly became worldwide household names, and had an academic background in law, but a life-long interest in science.

In particular, that scientific interest was now focused on developing ideas and tools for anticipating and managing human-caused extreme events, such as financial collapses, political revolutions, power-network failures, Internet crashes and the like.

Since complexity ideas are crucial in understanding the likelihood of the appearance of such an X-event, Manry had read a few of Victor's articles and books on these themes. Out of the blue, he had sent Victor an invitation to join together with half a dozen other name-brand thinkers for a couple of days in a discussion on how to move forward in creating a think tank-style institute for applied research on X-events.

Victor's feelings about this meeting were much the same as he'd felt about Stephanie's dinner party. He didn't really know who would be at Manry's meeting or what would happen, but he knew it would be interesting. So he had agreed to participate.

*

When Victor returned to Santa Fe from California late in the evening two days later, he was exhausted. The Manry meeting turned out to be a lot more interesting than he'd anticipated, and he was left with a lot of thoughts about X-events floating around in his mind.

He would definitely have to sort out how to integrate these new ideas into his current work on the stock market simulator, as well as consider Manry's offer to join in the planning of his new research center. He was sure this offer would be an entrée to people who would be able to help him develop the stock-market simulator in its second phase.

While he was in San Francisco, Victor received two emails from Alex. But the all-day meetings were a cell-free zone, where no recordings or photos were allowed by the organizer. And the evenings were filled with cocktails and late-night dinners. Between this schedule and his travel to and from Santa Fe, Victor hadn't had any realistic possibility to call and speak with her directly.

The best Victor could do by way of immediate response was to reply to Alex with a quick email, explaining his situation and telling her he would get in touch with her as soon as he got back to Santa Fe. He told her he was missing her very much, and was looking forward to being together with her again 'shortly.'

Awakening from a long sleep the next morning, Victor saw his house was a mess. Not only did he need to call the cleaning lady and ask her to make an emergency visit, he had to wash clothes, tidy-up the kitchen, and take out some pretty foul-smelling rubbish. In general, he needed to return the house to some semblance of livability.

While gathering up his pants, shirts and coats to take to the cleaners, a piece of paper floated out from the pocket of one of his jackets. Reaching down to pick it up, he saw it was the napkin Natalie had used to jot down her phone number during his farewell to her on the night of Stephanie's party.

He had been thinking of her on the flight back from San Francisco, as well as his promise to Alex to call her as soon as he returned home. Those two calls were both action items for this afternoon.

Just as these thoughts were passing through Victor's mind, he heard his phone ringing in the kitchen and went to answer it. On the other end of the line he heard an immediate gasping kind of sob, followed by Alex's voice:

"Victor! I'm so happy to hear you again. I've been thinking about you every moment since you left and I started to become very concerned about your silence. Last night, I even had to take a heavy dose of sleeping capsules to get some rest. Thank god you're safe."

Oh, oh, thought Victor. *Alex sounds like she's on the edge of hysteria. It's going to be tricky getting her calmed down.*

"Alex, how nice to hear your voice again. I just got home late last night and was planning to call you this afternoon."

"I can't stop thinking about you, Victor. I need you so much. Come back to me *right now!*"

"I've got business here in Santa Fe, Alex. I'll be there as soon as I can. But first I have to put things in order at both my house and at the Institute. I'll let you know by email as soon as I've gotten everything sorted here."

Alex was silent for a moment, before saying, "I'm holding you to that promise, Victor. I'll be counting the days and don't want my count to have to go beyond six or seven. Hurry and travel safely. I need you. I want you in my arms and in my bed again—ASAP!"

"I understand," he told her, saying once again they would be together again soon.

With that the called ended.

Oh God, thought Victor. *Deeper and deeper with no end in sight.* He was going to earn that juicy consulting fee with this job! That's for sure.

By late afternoon Victor could turn his attentions to Natalie. With a much-needed cool beer in his hand, he sat down and dialed her number. A couple of rings later he heard her slight Texan drawl:

"Hi, this is Natalie." her recorded message said. "I'm not available to take your call right now. Please call me later or leave a message at the beep."

Victor decided to leave a short message:

"Hi Natalie. This is Victor, your escort at Stephanie's party a few nights ago. I'm back in Santa Fe and would love to get together with you again. If you have the time, please give me a call. My number is 986-2017. I look forward to hearing from you."

As Victor put down the phone, he suddenly asked himself,

What the hell do you think you're doing? What about Alex? What about the relationship with her that you were so upbeat about on the plane coming back to Santa Fe and on the phone earlier today? All it takes for those thoughts to vanish into the mist is meeting a lady that you were attracted to at a dinner party?

These were very good questions. And he did have to wonder what *was* going on with him? Then in his usual manner, Victor quickly banished these thoughts back to where they came, finished his beer and headed into the kitchen to start putting together his dinner.

Victor was a moderately advanced amateur cook. While he frequented many of the greatest restaurants in the world while traveling, he seldom went out to eat when he could prepare meals for himself.

Tonight he was making one of this favorite dishes—a Moroccan tagine of duck breast with dates, honey and orange flower water served on a mound of couscous sprinkled with roasted, chopped almonds. Luckily, except for the fresh duck breasts, Victor's shelves contained all the ingredients he needed, and his trip to the food market would be a short one. He thought he might also purchase a couple of oranges and prepare a fluffy soufflé to eat for dessert while he watched the ball game tonight on TV.

Soon after he returned from the store, and while he was getting all of the ingredients together, his phone rang.

"Hello, Victor here," he said.

"Hi Victor. This is Natalie. I got your message and called as soon as I could. How are you? Back in Santa Fe, it seems."

Victor was very pleased with how promptly she was returning his call, and he loved hearing the tone of her voice.

"Indeed, I'm back and eager to see you again. What about lunch one day this week?"

"Sounds lovely," she said without hesitation. "How about day after tomorrow, Saturday?"

Victor already had the right place in mind, a pretty upmarket restaurant just a short walk down the hill from his place.

"Great! Let's meet at *The Compound* on Canyon Road at half past twelve. Would that suit you?"

Natalie agreed and said she she was really looking forward to seeing him again.

The deal was done. Victor returned to the kitchen to begin cooking his tagine and soufflé.

*

On Saturday, Victor was already sitting at a corner table at *The Compound* when Natalie arrived, looking a bit flustered because she thought she was late.

"I have a habit of being early and you're right on the dot. So not to worry," Victor told her.

While he was reciting these reassurances, Victor observed how really lovely Natalie looked in her flowery summer dress and flat-heeled shoes, not to mention her fashionable, but unobtrusive, hair-style, a kind of mid-level bob that set her dark hair in nice contrast to the light tones in the dress.

And, of course, Victor noticed her long, tanned legs, curvy waist and the rest of her figure.

As she took her seat, the waitress arrived with the menus and took their drinks order. The usual G&T for Victor, a margarita for the lady. They clinked glasses and began the pretty meaningless idle chatter that almost every couple engages in when they meet for the first time at lunch. But this chit-chat was somewhat less meaningless than most, at least for Victor, as he found himself really wanting to know more about Natalie.

"When we met at Stephanie's party, we hardly had a chance to talk about your situation here in Santa Fe," he said. "If you'll pardon me sounding like a journalist, tell me how, when, and why you came to be here? Maybe also a bit of where, at least where you're from in Texas?"

"I'll give you the condensed version, Victor. Then you can decide how many details I've left out that you simply *must* know," she said with an enigmatic smile.

"Fire away. And be sure to include all the juicy parts. Otherwise, I'll have to try to squeeze them out of you," he said, only half-jokingly.

"Okay. Here's my story, abridged version. I was raised just outside Dallas and got married when I was twenty. Two children appeared by the time I was twenty-three. I then spent about eighteen years as a housewife, married to a successful businessman whose mind and body were always in some distant time zone. Finally, about a year ago my children grew up and left for university, my husband ran off with his assistant, I got divorced and found myself with no family and no husband but a tidy sum of hard cash in my bank account."

"You were then facing the existential questions: 'What should I do'? 'Where should I do it'? 'Who should I do it with'?" said Victor.

"Precisely. But I had to do it somewhere fairly close to Dallas, as I wanted to be able to see my children frequently. I then recalled several trips I'd made here to Santa Fe when my husband and I were still a couple. I met Stephanie at a gallery showing a few years back and we hit it off. I called her and inquired about possibly moving to Santa Fe. She said she'd kill me if I didn't! And since I'm not ready to check out quite yet, here I am."

"Where is 'here'?" Victor asked.

That's when the waiter appeared, as waiters have a nasty habit of doing just when a conversation is at a critical point. He asked if they were ready to order. That put Natalie's answer on hold while they told the waiter what they wanted. A foie gras and a jumbo crab and lobster salad for Natalie, a bowl of summer corn soup and seared rare tuna niçoise for Victor, along with a bottle of light white wine for them to share.

"Okay, Natalie, let's get back to 'Where is here'?" Victor prompted after the waiter finally departed.

"Geographically, 'here' is just a few blocks down the street. While I'm getting myself settled in Santa Fe, I've rented a cozy little house over on Cerro Gordo for a year. So far I like it very much. The location is convenient, my friends all live nearby, and I can walk to a lot of places worth going to. This restaurant, for example."

"Just to add another item to that list, you could also walk to my house from yours," said Victor. "I live just up the hillside on San Acacio, off Camino Cabra."

"Oh, I know that street. It's that old Santa Fe-style street with no paving, just a dirt road. Very charming."

“Indeed, I like that old style too. A few years ago the city of Santa Fe actually wanted to pave our street, saying it would be a lot cheaper to maintain than sending around a road grader to skim it off twice a year. We all complained bitterly, saying we didn’t come to Santa Fe to live on a street with a paved road. The city finally relented. But as our penalty for complaining, they now come around with the grader only once a year! The price of a dirt road is that we have more potholes and washboard sections than ever before, although it’s a small price to pay for being able to believe you’re living here in an earlier century.”

As the afternoon progressed, Victor discovered more and more about Natalie and she about him. He decided she was probably in her early forties, loved to eat but didn’t like cooking all that much, and was a devoted patron of the arts, which accounted for her residence just a few hundred yards from the wall-to-wall galleries up and down Canyon Road.

Over coffee and eclairs, Victor asked Natalie what she’d like to see in Santa Fe. She said she wanted to visit galleries and museums, go skiing in the winter, hiking in the summer, visit Taos, go up to Los Alamos and see the Atomic Museum, and so on and so forth.

“Sounds like you have a pretty big program in front of you,” he said, “at least for the coming year. Hey! I have an idea. One of the items on your hit list is a visit to Taos. Why don’t we drive up there together tomorrow? The weather will be perfect, and we can go up for lunch and look around that charming town. What do you think?”

“Oh, Victor, that sounds divine. All the items on my list will be so much more fun if I do them with friends. I accept your invitation. Where and when should we meet?”

“Jot down your address on Cerro Gordo, and I’ll be at your place at half past ten tomorrow morning. Is it a date?

They jokingly shook hands and walked out of *The Compound,* through the parking lot and up the slight hill back to Canyon Road, hand-in-hand like two very old and close friends.

They then gave each other warm hugs and parted company at East Palace Avenue, where Natalie turned left to go to her place, while Victor continued on up Canyon Road a bit farther before taking a right at Camino Cerrito to hike up the hillside to his own *casita* on San Acacio.

*

As they drove on Highway 68 to Taos the next morning in Victor's Jeep Cherokee SUV, they reveled in the beautiful scenery on the Low Road to Taos. It's a winding road through the valley along the Rio Grande River, twisting through high desert mountains, the forest and little farms.

Along the way, they passed small art galleries and studios of traditional artisans and artists. No wonder, thought Victor, that the state of New Mexico has declared this stretch of road an official Scenic Byway.

Natalie was fascinated by the diverse scenery, and she remained pretty much silent during the drive, other than to express a few oohs and ahhs at particularly lovely spots. Shortly before they reached Taos, there was a turn off from the road at a very scenic elevated location.

It was an especially good spot for visitors to take panoramic photos of desert and mountains. Victor pulled over for just that purpose, as well as to nuzzle a bit closer to Natalie.

By this time they were getting hungry, so as they returned to the SUV, Victor suggested they continue on along Paseo Del Pueblo Sur, the main street running through Taos, and visit the Historic Taos Inn for something to eat and for a peek at local history. "The Inn is made up of several adobe houses," Victor explained, "which date from the 1800s, and it is surrounded by a small plaza—now the Inn's magnificent lobby.

In the 1890s, Dr. Thomas Paul ('Doc') Martin came to Taos as the county's first, and only, physician. He bought the largest of the houses—now Doc Martin's Restaurant, which is incorporated into the Inn. Doc was a rugged individualist, but dearly beloved for his deep concern for his fellow men and women. Covering the county to treat his patients meant hitching up a team of horses and later firing up his tin lizzie to travel for miles through mud and snow to set broken bones, break fevers and deliver babies."

As they arrived in the town, Natalie was clearly amazed. "This is still a living memorial to the time when New Mexico was a hotbed of cowboys, Indians, gunfights and all the rest," she declared. "Just like jumping into a time machine and going back fifty years to star in one of those famous mid-twentieth-century western movies."

"Here you get the cowboys," Victor said in agreement. "After lunch we'll see the Indians. The only difference is that the Indians are still here."

"I can hardly wait," gushed Natalie. "Let's have a quick lunch and get back to the tour."

Doc Martin's restaurant offered a simple combination of breakfast and brunch items, mostly northern New Mexican food interspersed with sandwiches and salads. That suited both Victor and Natalie just fine. He ordered a Huevos Rancheros, eggs on a blue corn tortilla, black beans, grated cheese and chili.

Natalie opted for a Mediterranean spinach salad, with roasted red peppers, feta cheese, toasted pine nuts, red onion and Kalamata olives. For drinks, they split a big bottle of sparkling water.

As they were eating, Natalie commented that it was simple but just the thing they needed to ease the pains of no breakfast and get back onto the road. Victor nodded his agreement as he ate, and they soon paid the bill and left.

"First stop, the oldest inhabited building in the entire state of New Mexico," Victor declared.

"What is it?" she asked.

"It's the Taos Pueblo," Victor replied." It was built sometime between the years 1000 to 1450, so it might even be a thousand years old. Now about 150 people from the Taos Indian tribe live in it. It's only about a mile up the road. So we'll be there in no time."

As they walked into the pueblo site from the parking lot, the first thing that grabbed their attention was the magnificent Taos Pueblo itself, a multi-storied residential complex of reddish-brown adobe constructed on either side of the Rio Pueblo, a small stream that flows through the middle of the pueblo compound.

Surrounding this residential building were several other smaller pueblo-style buildings, much like you'd see small shops and stores surrounding a large apartment complex in a major city. These buildings were occupied by small homes and one or two shops for tourists. One of these buildings was the Pueblo de Taos, a quite lovely church dating from around 1620.

"This is just unbelievable, Victor," Natalie said. "I'm so glad you suggested we come up here. I'd heard earlier about how special Taos was. But you hear those kinds of remarks about many places. Now I'm a believer. To be in a compound hundreds of years old where everyday life is still going on is really mind-blowing."

"Yes, it's definitely something special," Victor agreed. "Luckily, it's just an hour or so from Santa Fe. You'll have many more opportunities to come here again once you're settled. But now we have other sights to see, and not so much time or light to see them. If you don't mind, let's go back to the car and head a few more miles up the road to the next amazing sight."

Natalie took his arm and gave him a very special smile. Victor did not fail to notice the look in her eye as she glanced over at him on their way to the parking lot.

Leaving the Taos Pueblo, Victor's phone began ringing. He saw on the screen that it was Alex calling, and excused himself from Natalie for a moment to take the call, walking quickly away and speaking in a low, somewhat hushed voice.

"Hello, Alex. It must be middle of the night for you. What's wrong?"

All Victor heard at first was crying and sniffling, before Alex finally said, "Oh, Victor, I miss you so much. When are you coming back to me?"

"I promise I'll be there when I can. Right now I'm closing down my life here in Santa Fe. At the moment, I'm out on the highway driving over to the house of our institute's president for an early dinner. I can't talk long. Just hold on and I'll be there with you very soon. I think of you every moment," he lied like a thief.

"Okay, I'm feeling a bit better now that I hear your voice again. I love you, Victor. I need you here with me in London, not out in the middle of nowhere in New Mexico."

"As soon as possible, honey. I promise. Now I have to run. Big hugs and kisses."

When Victor got back to the car, Natalie glanced over at him with a quizzical look in her eye.

"There's no problem is there, Victor? I hope not."

"Just some confusion with one of the programmer's on our project who mixed up two very different—but very important—sides of the project. But I got him straightened out—I hope. Nice to see he's working late to get everything done right. This is just one example why there's no substitute for me being there in person for a few weeks. These sorts of things have a nasty way of coming up at just the wrong moment."

They drove a couple of miles in the direction away from the Taos city center before encountering a traffic light. Turning left at the light, there appeared to be nothing but flat desert landscape and a two-lane road bisecting it.

Setting off on that road, they passed the Taos airport, little more than a paved strip for prop planes to land. Ahead they saw several cars parked on both sides of the road, just before the beginning of a nondescript bridge that presumably would take them over a little stream or tributary of the Rio Grande. Victor pulled over to park with the other cars, and invited Natalie to join him in a short walk to the bridge itself.

When they got there, Victor told her to look over the railing. What a sight! The small stream was indeed there—but more than 500 feet below the bridge—so it was no 'small stream' at all but the Rio Grande River itself!

Natalie exclaimed, "This looks like a miniature Grand Canyon! I can't believe it. Out here in the middle of nowhere."

"Yes, it's called the Rio Grande Gorge Bridge," said Victor. "It's the seventh highest bridge in the USA and the 82nd highest in the whole world. Who would have imagined such a sight out here in Nowheresville?" he laughed. "So now you've seen the most surprising sight in Taos. But not much more we can see today, really. Didn't you mention you wanted to stop in the souvenir shop we passed on the way out here? This would be a good time for that, as it's nearly five o'clock and we should start heading back to Santa Fe pretty soon."

On the drive back to Santa Fe, they started a deeper conversation about their respective past lives—especially Victor's—since Natalie had given her abridged version at lunch the previous day at *The Compound.*

"You know, Victor," Natalie began. "Yesterday at lunch you asked me quite a bit about my past life. Why I'm here in Santa Fe, as well as one or two other things of a semi-personal nature. In the spirit of fair play, now it's your turn. Of course, you're a well-known scientist and there's plenty about your professional life on the Internet, so you don't need to tell me about that. I want to know the same things you wanted to know about me yesterday, the juicy personal stuff. Okay?"

"Fair enough, Natalie. Let me start with the essentials. I came to the Institute about ten years ago from Zürich, where I was a professor at the ETH, the main technical university in Switzerland. My family background is Italian, Sicilian-style. I studied in Milano and then got a graduate fellowship in computer science at the ETH, which eventually morphed into a faculty position."

Natalie interrupted him, "Yes, I know all that stuff from the Internet. I said I want to know about your *personal* life."

"Sorry. While I was in Zürich I married Karin, a student from Sweden, who was studying psychology. That was only a year or so before I was offered the opportunity to come to New Mexico."

"Do you have any children?" Natalie enquired.

"No, and I'm quite sorry about that. I'm embarrassed to say that my career always seemed to get in the way. Karin had the 'strange' idea that raising a family was a two-person job. It never happened. She and I split up less than a year ago, and that was one of the principal reasons. She's now in her early forties and needed to find a real partner instead of being what she described as a 'junior partner' in Victor L. Safir, Inc."

"How old are you, Victor, if you don't mind my asking?"

"Not at all. Besides, I suspect you already looked it up on the Internet anyway. I'm now fifty-two years-old—going on a thousand. Past due for a mid-life crisis, wouldn't you say?"

"What are your plans, personally, professionally, or otherwise? Do you intend to stay in Santa Fe indefinitely?"

"I'm not big on long-term planning, I'm afraid. I pursue my work and my life on the basis of what looks right at the time, keep my eyes open for opportunities as they arise, and am ready to take a risk if something very attractive presents itself. If an irresistible opportunity popped up in my professional, personal or any other part of my life, I would be ready to jump on it. Basically, I try to maintain lots of degrees of freedom in my life, keep my nose down and do my work. That way I'm ready when Dame Fortune comes knocking on my door."

"Or any other 'dame,' as local gossip tells it," remarked Natalie drily, with an ironic smile.

"Sometimes that too, I guess," replied Victor, taking the turn-off from Highway 285 into Santa Fe. "I admit that I simply 'like' women."

They pulled up in front of Natalie's house and as she was getting her handbag and preparing to leave, Victor leaned over, put his arm around her shoulder and drew her near. She fell into his arms and he gave her a rather passionate farewell kiss, one reciprocated in kind by a big hug and kiss from her as well.

"I'll have to leave Santa Fe tomorrow for some lecturing obligations in South America. But I'd love to have you come by my place for dinner when I return in a few days."

She looked him in the eye for a moment, and then said, "Well, I guess I'm as big a girl now as I'll ever be, so why not? I enjoyed today very much Victor, and look forward to seeing you again soon. Give me a call when you get back and we'll fix the timing."

He nodded saying, "I'll stay in touch while I'm away."

As she left the car, she looked back and blew him an air kiss to seal the deal.

And so it was as he drove off in a state of euphoria up the hill to his own place, thinking about what the menu should be for that dinner together—and not just for the dinner.

He also felt a twinge of conscience about how these developments with Natalie were going to affect his future interactions with Alex. It was going to be tricky to deliver on his promise to be back in London within 'a week or so.' He thought he could just about make it.

He could already sense that his emotions were in a tug-o'-war between the two women, and he was relieved that he would have a couple of days in Brazil and Chile to decompress.

Episode VIII

The Dinner

Santa Fe

Victor's return flight from South America to Santa Fe was a long, convoluted one, totaling the better part of twenty hours of travel before he finally reached home. Such a trip from hell gave him plenty of time to ponder where he should be focusing his attention, on Alex or Natalie?

The more he thought about it, the more it was beginning to look like an undecidable Gödelian proposition. Hopefully, his upcoming dinner with Natalie would help him see the answer more clearly. First, though, he needed sleep—and lots of it.

Ten hours and a good night's rest later, he was attending to bits and pieces of administrivia at his office late in the morning, along with a short meeting with John Casey's assistant to confirm his upcoming leave of absence in London. Business taken care of, Victor headed back home to start preparing the dinner with Natalie.

They had agreed to meet that evening at 6 o'clock at his house. So he had the better part of a day to plan the meal and get himself physically and psychologically ready for her appearance at his front door on Camino San Acacio.

Victor thought about the emotionally-laden phone calls Alex had made to him in Santa Fe, as well as the one on the day he and Natalie went to Taos. He really didn't know how to interpret her behavior.

On the one hand, they gave every appearance of being calls from the heart. On the other hand, he had seen enough of Alex to know that calls from the heart can quickly turn into life-threatening, heart-piercing situations.

Recalling Alex's topsy-turvy shifts in behavior and comparing them with Natalie's seemingly quite stable and mature actions, Victor began to wonder again why he hadn't broken off the personal relationship with Alex by now. He thought it was his instinctive need to solve any problem that came his way. Or maybe it was his need to gain control over Alex in a battle of wills. Or maybe it was his desire for the opportunity to move his simulator into the real world. Or maybe it was his *need* for the consulting fee from Merit to satisfy the continuing demands from Karin's lawyer. Or maybe it was all of these—or none of them. He couldn't really tell.

What he could say for sure was that his dilemma with Alex was a quagmire of his own making. He should certainly have been experienced enough to know that when you mix personal and professional lives, it almost never comes out well.

Getting back to realities, he concluded these sad reflections thinking that perhaps he should call Alex tomorrow, or at least send her an email, to reassure her that he really is on his way. Given that she will formally be in charge of the project at Merit, he couldn't afford to alienate her now. Maybe later he could find a good way to escape from her and defuse her outrageous idea about getting married. But now was definitely not that time.

Today, though, Natalie was his focus and he had a bit of shopping, a little chopping and a lot of cooking to do before she arrived at his place that evening.

Victor chose a pretty easy menu for the dinner. A Caesar salad to start, followed by a big dish of lobster seafood pie. The pièce de résistance would be a blueberry cream cheese pie, one of his favorite desserts. If that didn't turn Natalie's heart in his direction, Victor smiled to himself, nothing would.

Luckily, the upscale foodstores in Santa Fe were the equal of those one would find in any major metropolitan area. Victor's shopping expedition was again a short and successful one, leaving a few minutes to drop by the wine shop for a couple of bottles of the red-and-white and one bubbly to get things started when Natalie arrived. Then back to the kitchen.

Victor had made all these dishes many times before. Soon the seafood pie was ready to start baking, the blueberry cream cheese pie was cooling in the fridge and the salad was ready for final preparation more-or-less in real-time.

With everything moving according to plan, Victor had a moment to put some comforting background jazz on the stereo, pour himself a decent shot of Bunnahabhain, one of his favorite single-malt Islay whiskies, relax in his reading chair and await Natalie's knock on the door.

That knock came right on the dot at six o'clock. She was wearing a bright smile, another lovely spring dress of many colors and was carrying a bottle of fine Pinot Grigio that she thought might go well with Victor's promised lobster seafood pie.

She looked around as she entered, complimenting Victor on the old Spanish style of both the house itself and the furnishings. She remarked that the combination of a classic stressed-wood dining table, coupled with a lovely overstuffed dark brown leather sofa in the sitting room, was just the thing. She mentioned that she had been keeping her eyes open for Santa Fe-style furnishings for her own house. Perhaps Victor could give her some tips on where to look.

The exploration of the house continued on into the kitchen, where Natalie's eyes really popped out. The counters showed just about every upmarket type of table-top oven, food processor, mixer and other kitchenware imaginable. There was even a special Japanese-made oven for preparing toast 'just right.'

As the kitchen ceiling was a series of *vigas,* wooden logs supporting the house's flat roof, Victor took advantage of these to hang many pots, pans, and other cooking instruments so they'd be immediately at hand when needed. In addition, there was even a sous-vide cooking pot, next to a combi-oven that could do steaming, convective heating—or both together.

After catching her breath, Natalie proclaimed that this kitchen would put many a restaurant kitchen to shame.

"I remember that you said you liked to cook," she said to Victor. "But I had no idea you were so serious about it."

Victor just smiled and shifted the topic by asking her if she'd like an apertif to get the evening off to a good start. She agreed with his suggestion of a glass of champagne for each of them, at which point they retired to the sitting room.

"This is a truly magnificent house, Victor. How many years have you been polishing it to such a luxurious finish?"

"So far, you've only seen the visitor's half. I'll show you the working half, along with the garden and other outdoor charms, later. But to answer your question, I've been living here for over eleven years now. Most of that time was with my former wife, Karin. What you see before you now is the joint effort of her and myself. Believe me when I say that that's plenty of time—and money—to devote to putting things into a form that one can feel comfortable with. The only pity is that as you know I travel way too much. As a result, I don't really get as much enjoyment from the house and the town of Santa Fe as I'd like. Maybe in my next life," he joked, asking if she'd like a refill of her champagne.

"Not quite yet, Victor. But I really would like to have a look at your garden while we still have a bit of light."

Once out the door, they walked alongside the house where there was a fence sheltering many lovely bushes and southwestern, desert-style plants and flowers. The main garden was actually behind the house, adjacent to the outdoor patio with a grill and a redwood picnic table, bordered by a path that continued up the hillside of the narrow, but very lovely, garden.

Natalie looked up the path and saw a structure that she didn't immediately recognize.

"What's that building up there at the end of the path, Victor? It looks like it could be a sauna. But in Santa Fe?"

"Indeed in Santa Fe—by way of Finland. I saw this sauna on a visit to Finland and fell in love with the big tempered glass panels on the door and sides. I thought how great it would be laying in the sauna and watching the sun coming up or the snowflakes coming down. I foolishly ordered it at a price I won't even mention and got it installed here a couple of years ago. I'm glad you like it."

"I don't just 'like' it, I love it. If I get the chance, I usually take my sauna at the end of the day, not the beginning. Somehow it seems to serve as a relaxant helping me get a good night's sleep."

"Well," Victor said with a smile, "maybe you'll have to show me the virtues of an evening sauna one of these nights soon."

"With pleasure," Natalie replied, giving him a look suggesting that she was fully aware of the implications of Victor's suggestion. "Now what about that fabulous dinner you promised as we left the house?"

*

Leaving the sauna on the agenda for later consideration, they made their way back to the dining room where Victor had already laid out the plates, glasses and silverware for the meal.

First up was the Caesar salad, looking delicious in a wooden salad bowl brimming over with Romaine lettuce, olive oil, a coddled egg, grated parmesano, chopped anchovies, toasted garlic bread cubes and smelling of all sorts of nice spices.

"I hope you're one of those people who like anchovies in their Caesar salad. But if not, or they're too salty, then just set them aside when you run into them and I'll help you out," Victor said as he generously filled two salad bowls, pouring two glasses of dry white wine to accompany the salad.

"Victor, this is absolutely delicious. You should be a chef, not a complexity scientist, whatever that is," she declared.

"I'm really only interested in cooking for myself and a few good friends. I can't imagine anything that would kill my interest in cooking faster than trying to run a restaurant. Then it becomes a job, not an avocation. If you don't mind, I'll stay a complexity scientist who cooks, not the other way around."

Next up was the main course, lobster seafood pie. This is a dish consisting of five types of chopped fish and seafood—lobster, crab, bay scallops, shrimp and a white fish like sea bass. It's all put together with onions, celery, garlic and special seafood spices and then mixed with *lots* of melted butter combined with breadcrumbs. Then everything is put into a big glass dish and baked for half an hour or so in the oven.

Victor had put the lobster seafood pie in the oven just as they sat down to eat the salad. This gave him the opportunity to ask Natalie a bit more about herself and her life in Santa Fe.

"I recall you telling me earlier, Natalie, that you are a recent divorcee, who came to Santa Fe because you wanted to be out of Dallas but near enough to still see your college-aged children. Otherwise, I don't know too much about you and what you're planning to do in Santa Fe once you finish off your sightseeing punch list."

Natalie replied, "I don't really know myself what I'll be doing. In order to meet people, I'm thinking of taking a part-time job at a gallery owned by a friend of Stephanie's. Luckily, my divorce settlement was generous enough to keep me off the breadline. But not quite so generous that I can live a life of luxury, Santa Fe-style."

"Well, I think you made a good choice to come to Santa Fe," Victor told her. "And not just to meet me," he added with a grin.

Just then the kitchen timer went off, and Victor left to take the lobster seafood pie out of the oven. Generously filling two plates with the seafood combo, he brought them to the table and refilled their wine glasses and sat down.

"Oh, Victor, this smells heavenly. But you've put enough on my plate to keep me filled up for the next three days!"

"Don't worry. This is a dish that can be easily reheated and eaten as leftovers. In fact, since I'll be leaving town day after tomorrow, which I'll tell you about later, I'm counting on you to take a goodly-sized portion home with you for just that reason. Think of it as a 'Welcome to Santa Fe' offering."

Natalie looked at him with a tender smile and a gleam in her eye as she ate, thinking to herself what good luck it had been for her to meet Victor at Stephanie's party a couple of weeks back.

How could you not like a man who was smart, handsome and knew how to cook? Indeed, Victor seemed to be the kind of trifecta every woman was looking for.

As they finished all the lobster seafood pie they could handle, Victor had a suggestion:

"I'm too full right now for dessert. How about if I take you up on your preference for an evening sauna and invite you to join me there to rest up a bit before we come back to the table? I see that in the time it will take to heat up the sauna, the sun will be just right for us to watch it set. What about it?"

This really put Natalie into a quandary. On the one hand, she had just met Victor, having spent maybe a dozen or so hours with him. Her 'good girl' sense of propriety was shouting, *No Way!* On the other hand, why was she in Santa Fe at all if not to change her life? What better way to start than by doing something daring with Victor? After all, he wasn't inviting her to a sleep-in, at least not yet. And even if he was, so what? She wasn't exactly a totally inexperienced *ingénue,* was she?

"That's a great idea, Victor. I'd love to experience the sauna with you as the host."

This was just what he wanted to hear and hoped the joint sauna might move things to another level with Natalie before he had to leave town again.

He told her there was a clean robe, towel and sauna shoes in the bathroom downstairs. While she changed, he'd start up the sauna and then go upstairs and get changed himself. They agreed to meet back downstairs in ten minutes.

*

Dressed for the sauna, they walked out the door and strolled into the garden. "It will take the sauna another fifteen minutes or so to become really hot," Victor said. "While we wait, let me show you around the garden a bit."

Natalie thought that was perfect. She needed a breath of fresh air anyway to settle both her body and her mind. She sneaked a peek at Victor in his robe and thought he looked even more dashing than when dressed in his party clothes.

He snuck his own look at her in her robe, envisioning how delightful she would almost surely look without it. And that hypothesis would be tested soon enough, in about fifteen minutes to be precise. Meanwhile, they sat in one of the garden chairs and enjoyed the spectacular view of the Jemez Mountains as the sun began to set.

Finally, the sauna was ready and they walked inside and took off their shoes and hung up their robes. They were both pretty nervous, but they covered it up very well by acting as if it were almost a family get-together that just happened to be in the sauna, and that they had seen each other stark naked many times before.

How they were acting and what they were really thinking and feeling were, of course, two very different matters!

Victor's thoughts could best be described as 'astonished.' Natalie had a narrow waist, long, slender legs and a beautiful, heart-shaped butt. Smooth skin, too, certainly not what one would expect from the mother of two college-age children. And when it came to the upper half of her body, his astonishment doubled. Natalie had full breasts, not like melons but more like over-sized oranges, with firm support and large aureolas. Of course, her face was already familiar to him, and when he placed it in the context of the rest of her lovely body, she became red-hot, photo-model material. And definitely not a forty-something photo model, but one who looked at least seven or eight years younger than her true age, maybe even more.

Natalie was also pleasantly surprised, although perhaps not as surprised as Victor. What she saw was a very well-preserved older, but definitely not old, man who looked to be in his late-forties, not more. It was a relief for her to notice that he didn't have the kind of paunch so many men of that age usually acquired through a lot of serious beer drinking and a lack of physical exercise. His proportions were good, his chest and biceps showing the effect of a lot of exercise and general physical activity.

She didn't doubt for a moment where much of that physical activity had taken place. But strangely, at least for her middle-class American values, she wasn't disturbed by that thought at all, but rather excited by it. All in all, coupled with his obvious intelligence, social position and general style, she was actually quite eager to test out the last qualification, if the next hour or two went well.

The sauna had the customary upper and lower benches for sitting. They chose to sit on their folded towels, side-by-side, on the upper bench to get warmed up a bit. Victor splashed a couple of ladles of water onto the heating element, creating a good burst of steam to aid the warming process.

Initially, they sat in silence, looking out through the heavy glass panes in the walls of the sauna at the slowly-setting sun as it dipped down below the mountains in a pinkish glow characteristic of Santa Fe sunsets at that time of the year.

Finally, Natalie uttered the single word, "magnificent," which described perfectly the views they were experiencing.

Victor agreed that this view was surpassed only by watching the snowfall coming down in the winter. Luckily, they could do both. Look at the sky when there were no snow clouds and/or look at the snow coming down when the clouds were there. He then ladled on more water, after which he couldn't see Natalie in the mist of the steam coming from the heater.

After another fifteen minutes or so, Victor saw the solar-powered lights alongside the path back to the house start blinking as they came on. He suggested to Natalie that perhaps they could start making their way back and get cleaned up for dessert.

Initially, she seemed a bit reluctant to leave the warm cocoon of the sauna. But when Victor got up and grabbed his robe, she joined him and they put on their shoes, shut off the sauna and started back to the house.

When they reached the living room, Victor told Natalie she should go into the shower and get rid of the steam and sweat from the sauna. He would then follow when she'd finished.

"You know, Victor, Santa Feans are always worried about water" she said, looking directly into his eyes. "Why don't we do a good turn for the city and have our shower together?"

She never imagined saying such a thing! "I saw earlier that you have a very nice walk-in shower, certainly big enough for two," she remarked.

Victor couldn't think of a reason to disagree. After all, it wasn't as if they weren't already familiar with each other's naked bodies. So why not?

As they walked to the shower, they took off their robes and shoes and hung up their towels. Victor turned the shower on to a medium-hot level temperature and they stepped in to rinse away the residue of the sauna. Fortunately, that didn't take long.

The next step was to break out the shower gel and start washing each other from top to bottom. Victor began this long-awaited moment by starting with Natalie's neck and working down to her calves—very slowly.

She reciprocated and soon they were facing each other. The process of washing and rubbing continued now, face-to-face. Then Victor began soaping her when she asked if he would be kind enough to soap down her lower back. This was music to Victor's ears, and Natalie's last word was hardly out of her mouth before

Victor's hands were on her shoulders moving down her back to her exquisite butt.

At that point, Natalie leaned back into Victor, turned her head, and breathlessly suggested she do the same for him.

*

And so it went until each of them had explored every square inch of territory on each other's skin. They then quickly dried off and fell into a deep embrace, using kisses instead of hands to explore each other again as they wordlessly headed for the stairway leading up to the bedroom.

Falling into bed, Victor proposed that they alternate in choosing which position to explore next. And as she was a lady and his guest, he suggested she begin.

Natalie's body displayed her choice when she climbed on top of Victor. Instead of simply inserting himself between her sweet lips, he brought her up a bit higher so he could reach those lips with his tongue. He then slowly put the tip into every part of the space between her lips, essentially marking out the letters of the Greek alphabet (since he was a mathematician!) as he moved his tongue up, down, this way and that as Natalie panted and squealed in delight.

After fifteen minutes or so of this 'linguistic' foreplay, Natalie barely managed to choke out her wish that Victor fill her completely, a request he was more than ready to grant. But what he was not ready to do yet was complete their sexual interaction. *There's much more to come,* he thought, smiling to himself a bit at this unspoken double entendre.

Following Natalie's first orgasm, she lay down on top of Victor breathing heavily, whispering, "Now it's your turn." He answered by rolling her off him and assuming the conventional missionary position. Entering her again, Victor began the age-old rhythms that have ensured the human race's regeneration for countless millenia.

Finally, as they lay side-by-side in a state of mutual exhaustion, Victor remarked, "This was definitely the best dessert I've had in years. There will certainly not be a recipe for it in any cookbook I might write. It's more like the chef's secret blend of herbs and spices than a simple formula for satisfying even the most jaded foodie."

A few minutes after calming down from their workout, Natalie said she had to use the toilet. Since Victor did too, they crawled out of the bed, put on their robes and slippers and stumbled toward the bathroom, as always, ladies first.

Afterwards, they went downstairs and sat in the kitchen, thinking about the blueberry cream cheese pie, which was their supposed dessert for tonight.

Both of them were still digesting the dessert upstairs, so the pie in the fridge would have to await its moment another day.

"Perhaps you'd like to take two pies with you when you go," Victor said, "the rest of the lobster seafood pie and the dessert pie. I'm sure you can put them to better use than I can, as I must leave soon and certainly cannot eat this amount of food beforehand, especially the cream cheese pie."

Natalie agreed she would do that. Then she suggested, "Perhaps you'd like to come by for a little snack sometime tomorrow afternoon?"

He told her, "There's nothing I'd like more than a little snack at your house. Unfortunately, though, I have way too many things to do tomorrow to get ready for my trip. Besides, when I have my next 'snack' with you, I don't want to be distracted or rushed.'

Instead, I suggest we meet immediately upon my return. But before you leave, I have something to tell you."

"I'm listening," Natalie replied, moving to the chair next to him.

*

"I recently accepted an invitation for a six-month consulting job with a financial firm in London. They want to have me help them develop the stock market simulator I've been working on into an operational, practical tool for trading on real exchanges," said Victor.

"I see. So you're going to be away quite a bit over the coming months. Is that right?"

"Yes, I will be away for awhile. Of course, I could hardly refuse such an opportunity to get my work into mainstream life and out of the cloisters of academe. This means that when I leave here in a couple of days, I will actually be moving my life to London temporarily."

"Well, six months is not forever, Victor. I will surely miss you during that time."

"I had no idea when I accepted this offer that I would meet you here in Santa Fe. But now it's all set. During my stay in London, I will very likely come back here a time or two to keep an eye on what's happening at the Institute. Basically though, I'll be living in London."

Victor then took her hand and leaned closer saying, "I'd like to ask if you would consider coming to visit me in Europe a time or two or three during the next few months? Think about it and let me know if you're as interested in seeing me as I am in seeing you. Then we can make a plan that works for both of us. Okay?"

Natalie nodded her head and said, "I intuitively felt you were on the brink of saying that you would be away for an extended period. I hope it works out well for you."

She then told him that she would give very serious thought to what he'd just said. Her initial feeling was *Why not?* After all, look what he did by way of guiding her around in Taos!

"I've never been to Europe, and couldn't imagine a better guide than you."

Strangely, she once again thought back to the fact that even though her former husband traveled extensively, the combination of mothering two children and her husband's intoxication with his assistant ensured that he never asked her to join him on even one of his many 'business' trips to Europe.

Returning to Victor, she told him, "I'll think over the situation, yours and mine, and let you know in a few days how I feel about the whole matter."

At this point, Natalie understood it was time for her to start making her way back to her own house. She left the kitchen to find her clothes and get dressed. Victor remained in the kitchen, reflecting on what had happened over the past few hours.

He also flashed on Alex and wondered how this evening was going to affect his future with her. *Well,* he thought, *nothing I can do about that right now.* At least he could be thankful for the separation of half a continent and an ocean between Alex and Natalie.

As that thought faded, Natalie came downstairs fully dressed, ready to say her farewell. By then Victor had also dressed, packaged up the food for her and placed it in a carrying bag. They walked out the door together and Victor followed her to her car.

A kiss carrying both the excitement of potential and the satisfaction of immediate pleasures ended this very special encounter.

As she pulled out into the street, Natalie gave Victor a sad, fleeting wave and drove off into the distance. Victor slowly walked back to the house, his mind confused and overwhelmed with a sense that he was entering an entirely new phase of his existence.

Episode IX

The Dreams

London

Alex sat up abruptly from a deep slumber on the sofa, shaking herself awake after a nightmarish vision she'd had involving people from her past and present. It had jarred her because these were people who in one way or another were opposing her actions and wishes.

Entering principally into her now-awake thoughts—and causing her great agitation—was her current boss, Jerome. Alex saw him as a continuation of so many of her earlier antagonists. Jerome was obsessed with demonstrating and exercising his power over her, and occasionally employing that power in the form of sexual innuendos.

That didn't mean he wasn't capable of shifting to a demon without disguise whenever she rejected his sexual advances or remarks. Sometimes she thought it would have been a lot easier if she simply found another job and been done with it.

Enough, she thought. *I can't lay here on the sofa all night going over these greatest 'hits-on-me' of my past. I've got enough to worry about in my current life, especially how to interface Victor with Jerome.*

She had been hoping that having Victor working at Merit on the simulator project on a semi-regular basis might provide a buffer between her and Jerome. But it was now clear it would be a delicate back-and-forth act she'd have to script very carefully so as not to antagonize either of them by paying too much attention to one or the other at the office.

In any case, she was pleased that Victor would be in London within a few days and ready to rock-and-roll. The 'new regime' could then begin in earnest—she hoped. But right now she had to get to bed and prepare herself for another day at Merit, hoping against hope that Jerome would keep his job pressures, sexual 'hits', hands and other instruments of influence off of her.

*

Alex woke up in the morning determined to make it a good day. But before she'd even reached her desk, bad luck seemed to be shadowing her. Walking into Merit's offices, the first person she encountered in the elevator was Jerome.

Fortunately, there were others in the elevator as well, so Jerome limited his attentions to a neutral, "Good morning, Alex," and let it go at that.

When the elevator reached their floor, Jerome didn't get off, which meant he must have an appointment elsewhere with even more senior management of the company. *Thank God for small favors,* thought Alex, as she headed for her office and settled in to begin making preparations for Victor's arrival.

Her first task was to confirm with Merit HR that they had sorted out an office for Victor, one big enough to accommodate the entire simulator team for group discussions, along with an apartment for the duration of his stay in London.

After getting confirmation of those logistical items and attending as well to a few other administrative matters, Alex leaned back, breathed a sigh of relief, and began to think about lunch.

At that very moment, Jerome stuck his head into her office doorway.

"How about joining me for lunch?" he asked, suggesting they go down to the cafeteria and grab a quick bite together. "I'd like to hear more about your plans for Victor and the project."

While a 'bite' with Jerome was one of the last things she had in mind, Alex had very little choice but to agree, since unfortunately, Jerome was the formal head of the project.

"I'll meet you downstairs in about five minutes," she replied, sparing herself the irritation of having to share the elevator with him going down to the lunchroom.

For her lunch, Alex chose a simple tomato and avocado salad with mineral water, hoping that she could finish eating quickly and say an equally fast farewell to Jerome. He sat down with a chicken sandwich and a soda and asked, "Did you set up the logistics yet for Victor's stay with us?"

"Yes, I confirmed everything this morning," she said. "He has a lovely office with plenty of room for small meetings. The personnel department also kindly volunteered to let Victor stay in one of those nice apartments that we keep in Mayfair for high net-worth clients who come to visit their money. Things seem pretty well set for his arrival."

"You know, Alex," Jerome said, looking her directly in the eye, "you do a good job here for Merit. As your boss, I appreciate that. But what I'd appreciate even more would be one of these days soon we could get outside the office and socialize together in a more personal way, a bit of business mixed with a lot of pleasure you might say. I like you and would appreciate the chance to get to know you better. How would you feel about doing that?"

Alex *knew* this was coming. And as they say, forewarned is forearmed.

"First, thanks for your kind words," she replied.

"Well, they are given sincerely, Alex," he said. "Of course, it is the second part of what I said that I hope you will consider now."

"Yes," Alex replied. "I noted that. I feel compelled to say that I think the kind of socializing you're talking about is a very big 'no-no' in our situation."

"A 'no-no'?" he snapped back at her. "Be careful what you say next."

Alex paused and took a breath. Jerome was staring at her intently, yet with a forced smile meant to convey that for as light-hearted as he was about the socializing, he was also completely serious.

Even so, Alex felt she had no choice other than to continue with what she wanted to say. "The separation of business and pleasure, professional and personal, is one of the first principles of harmony in both of these dimensions of one's life," she began. "And that's especially true when the pleasure is between an employee and her immediate supervisor. So while I appreciate the thought, I cannot take you up on your invitation. Please don't offer it again."

"Oh, come on, Alex," Jerome spat back at her, a bit indignant now. "Get real. There are plenty of office romances going on here right now. And you know it. Don't start getting prudish on me. Life has a way of being very strange sometimes. Don't forget this conversation. I definitely won't."

Alex put on her sternest look and asked cooly, "Are you threatening me, Jerome?"

"I don't think 'threat' is quite the right word. I'm just pointing out the realities of life, both inside and outside of Merit."

"Well, one definite reality—and it is also not a threat—is that you and I are not going to become an 'item.' "

"Please keep this conversation in mind when Victor shows up," Jerome shot back. " At that point, he's inside Merit too, not outside. Just in case it might slip your mind."

With that, Jerome quickly got up from the table, took his tray to the collection window and left the room.

Well, there it is, thought Alex. *I see the coming weeks are going to be rather tricky. How to balance work and play, not to mention the play with Victor and the work but no-play with Jerome. How in the hell did I get myself into such a situation? A boss that's an asshole, one that cannot even do his own job very well, but who doesn't hesitate to take credit when the credit is due entirely to others, myself included, and worse, who feels his position over me should grant him privileged—no, extorted—access to my body and affections.. But this is not the time to start going through all that again.*

She left the lunchroom, telling herself to get back to work and be cool.

*

Alex then went back to her office. As much as she wanted to shake it off, Jerome's behavior in the lunchroom was still nagging at her as the afternoon continued. She also couldn't keep from connecting today's happenings with Jerome's abysmal attempts at seducing her at last year's British Financial Analysts Convention in Bristol.

Following the conference dinner, Alex and Jerome left the dining area to go back to their rooms at the same time. As bad luck would have it, both of them were staying on the same floor, so they left the elevator together. When Alex turned to walk down the hallway to her room, Jerome grabbed her arm and mumbled, "C'mon Alex, let's go in my direction instead. We can have a goodnight drink together."

Shaking off Jerome's grip on her arm, Alex said, "Get away from me, Jerome. Just back off and I'll write-off your outrageous behavior to it being a bit too much alcohol at the party getting the better of you."

Jerome came for her again, at which point Alex gave him a strong push and maneuvered around him to go back toward her own room. As she left, he shouted, "You're going to pay for that, Alex. I guarantee you won't forget it."

And, in fact, Jerome delivered on this threat when it came time to distribute the year-end bonuses. Alex found that her bonus was at least 25 percent lower than the previous year, even though Merit's overall profits had increased considerably.

When she complained to Jerome about this, he looked her straight in the eye, saying her performance had been unsatisfactory and she should consider herself lucky to have received any bonus at all.

Alex was shocked by this statement and asked him, "What do you mean my performance was 'unsatisfactory?'"

"More than once I gave you a set of figures to analyze and you came back with what later turned out to be erroneous results," he said.

"Well," answered Alex, "if the results were wrong it was because you gave me the wrong numbers."

"Sorry, Alex. The numbers were correct. It was your analysis that was faulty. And this caused me a lot of trouble with the big brass here."

At this point, Alex realized she was in a no-win situation. If she made a formal complaint, it would be just her word against Jerome's. No way she could win that contest. She simply turned and stomped out of his office.

Her recollection of this disgraceful episode only further stoked her resentment against Jerome, making her angry that fate had saddled her with such a incompetent and boorish boss.

That shit, she thought. *He's the one who ought to be paying, not me.*

Before she left work that afternoon, Jerome called to remind her that he would be going to Paris the next day to meet with one of Merit's best customers, Henri Lions, a major player in the Parisian business world. Jerome knew that Alex had been watching Lions' account carefully. He told her that he might have to contact her about details of the account during his meetings in Paris, and said she should be able to readily access Lions' files throughout the weekend.

Just great, she thought, as she left the office to head back to her flat. *Now I can't escape this incompetent fool even during my so-called 'days off.'*

*

Walking up the steps to the entrance door of her apartment building, Alex ran into her neighbor, Maerta. After their usual friendly greeting, Maerta said, "Hey, I never see you anymore, stranger. What about having a few drinks and a bite to eat tonight at the bistro down the road?"

"That's just the kind of evening I need," replied Alex. "I'll meet you on the porch in about fifteen minutes."

Maerta gave her a hug and they went to their respective flats to change clothes and freshen up a bit before leaving for the restaurant.

"You know, baby," Maerta said after they'd settled into their preferred corner in the bistro, "I think the last time we met privately was when you were fretting over your feelings about Victor.

That must have been at least a month ago, if not longer. How are things going with him?"

"To be truthful, I haven't seen much of Victor since that conversation. He's been in the United States preparing to come to London for several months on a consulting job with my firm. It turns out that I'm going to be administratively in charge of that project."

"Sounds tricky to me, having to boss around your lover during the day and soothe his ego at night. How do you think you'll manage that juggling act, honey?"

"I don't know. We'll just have to see how it goes when he's actually here and we do the experiment. Right now, I have a much bigger problem I'm grappling with."

"Oh, I love bigger problems," Maerta said gleefully. "I hope this one's got some hot-and-heavy parts. But before you tell me the gory details, let me get a refill of my margarita. Would you like one, too?"

"Why not?" Alex replied. "It may stiffen my resolve not to omit those 'hot' parts you're so eager to hear," she joked, as Maerta headed for the bar to get their drinks.

With a fresh drink in hand, Alex began the sad story about her interactions with Jerome and how they were starting to reach the breaking point, at least as far as she was concerned. Maerta listened attentively, and then offered the suggestion that Alex simply try to avoid Jerome as much as possible.

"Pretty hard to avoid your boss," said Alex. "About the best I can do is try to hand-pick the situations when I see him and make them ones where there are other people around. Or at least situations in which I have limited time before a meeting or some other bona fide excuse arises to make a quick disappearance."

"That sounds like a tricky juggling act, but at least you have a plan, baby."

"But there's something else going on with me now that transcends this disgusting business with Jerome. It involves my emotional fantasies."

"What do you mean your 'fantasies'? What kind of fantasies?" asked Maerta.

Alex told her, "I've been seeing visions where people from my past who have caused me stress and pain continue to appear. Not only have I been losing a lot of sleep because of these unpleasant fantasies, I'm starting to wonder what the actual *meaning* of these visions is."

"I wouldn't worry too much about these emotional upheavals," Maerta advised with an air of authority. "There are so many competing theories of what these things mean, why we even have them and so on, that you can take your pick as to what your fantasies might really mean, if they mean anything at all."

Alex was a bit taken aback by Maerta's seeming knowledge of the research literature.

"Well, what do you *think* these visions I'm having might mean?"

"I think there is no meaning at all in emotional fantasies. So forget about yours and enjoy a good night's sleep for a change."

"Okay," Alex said, with a smirk on her face that said she knew that Maerta's advice about her dreams was not going to be as easy to follow as it sounded. "Let's get back to my problem with Jerome. Trying to avoid him, as you suggested earlier, is not really doable under my circumstances."

"Okay," Maerta said, holding-on to the last syllable in order to emphasize that she still didn't understand.

"I have to interact with him on a lot of matters at work. Do you have any constructive ideas about how I might handle that?"

Maerta gave Alex a long look asking, "Would you ever consider sleeping with him? That might be the lesser of two evils."

"I'm not sure," replied Alex. "I could imagine a situation when it might be possible—but only if it would lead to me getting some leverage to use against him if he ever tried to harass me again."

"Like what?" asked Maerta.

"Well, maybe if I had some photos or a recording of his pressuring me to have sex. With something like that I could blackmail him into leaving me alone."

As they got ready to leave the bistro without ever actually having had a meal, Maerta stated, "We seem to have agreed that Jerome is a problem to think about over the coming days."

"Yes," replied Alex. "We can discuss it again the next time we meet."

On that note they settled their bar bill, and left.

Episode X

The Confrontation

Paris

Alex decided to do a bit of shopping at Harrods on Saturday morning to cheer herself up. On her way there and back, she planned to stop in some of the chi-chi boutiques in her neighborhood. After all, what's the point of having a decent salary—not to mention, putting up with a jerk like Jerome as a boss—if she didn't spoil herself every now and then?

As she was putting on her makeup, the phone rang.

Oh, oh, she thought.

Something told her this was going to be Jerome calling from Paris, and she warned herself not to answer. *Just let it ring.* But her sense of responsibility, not so much to Jerome, but to Merit, forced her to pick up the phone and see if she had figured correctly. Sad to say, she had.

"Good morning, Alex," Jerome mumbled, sounding as if he had just gotten up from a Friday night bender in some Parisian bar.

"I have a huge favor to ask. Last night I met with Lions, who had some rather pointed questions about his account. To be frank, I didn't really know the answers since they are sitting in your files, not in my head. I am meeting him again on Monday. Could you go to the office, get those papers and bring them to me here in Paris tomorrow?"

Alex should have been surprised by Jerome's request, but she wasn't. It was typical of him to think that she or anyone should ever have a day off, particularly on a weekend. She was seriously annoyed about this, but considering how things had been with him lately, the last thing she needed was trouble because she said no to a request from him concerning the needs of a major client. She made an effort to keep a strident tone out of her voice, as she replied,

"Is it really necessary for me to come to Paris just for this, Jerome? Can't I simply give you the information over the phone?"

"You could do that if I knew exactly what information I need," he said. "Besides, what I really need is your expertise to walk me through some of the details in Lions' account."

"Okay, but you know this account, too," Alex said. "I've regularly been keeping you up-to-date on what's been happening with it."

"No Alex, you're the office expert on that account. I need to tap into that expertise *now.* When I meet Lions again on Monday, I really want to have the entire file in my hand, as well as in my head, just to make sure there are no more mistakes like I made last night."

Alex made a notable sigh into the phone, which she knew even Jerome would understand, considering that his request was at the last minute and also on a weekend.

"So please be a dear and hop on the Eurostar and come over," he said. "At most it will only take a few hours, and you'll get a nice lunch and a free trip to Paris out of the deal. Okay?"

Alex silently stomped her foot, but she really had little choice but to agree. And he was right. It was only a couple of hours on the train from St. Pancras Station in central London to the Gare du Nord in Paris. She could easily go over in the morning and be back in London by dinnertime, if not earlier.

"Okay, Jerome. I'll do as you wish. I'll call you when I'm on the train tomorrow and tell you my time of arrival. You can then let me know where we should meet."

"Great, Alex," Jerome said, his tone now soothing. "I'll look forward to seeing you in Paris."

That last phrase had a suggestive tone Alex couldn't miss. "Uh-huh," she replied, tempted to call it off. "Gotta get to work now." She hung up without waiting for a reply.

Shit, thought Alex. *Now half of today will be lost digging up all those files instead of digging-in to the clothing racks at the boutiques. Shit, shit, shit!* she said to herself again, as she finished her makeup and headed out the door—but to the office, not to the boutiques.

Gathering the papers from the files, Alex wondered once again whether it was really necessary for her to go to Paris to meet Jerome. Phone and email can work, of course, but she realized there's no substitute for going over the files in person. First-hand contact is still the best way to sort out confusions. It's also true that Paris is easier to reach from London than most of the cities in the north of England. Jerome did have a point in asking her to come in person. It's not really much of a trip. But his motives were clearly mixed, as always.

On her way to the Eurostar terminal the next morning, Alex called Jerome and left a message telling him she would arrive at the Gard du Nord in Paris just after 11:30 that morning. "If you could call me back and tell me where we should meet, I'd appreciate it," she said in the nicest tone of voice she could muster.

To his credit, Jerome returned her call just as she reached St. Pancras and told her to take a taxi from Gare du Nord to the *bistro Au Bougnat* at 26, rue Chanionesse, where they would have lunch.

She jotted down the address of the restaurant and hung up. *Sounds promising,* she thought. At least he didn't tell her to meet him in his hotel room!

As the train started into the dark of the Eurotunnel, Alex once again thought about the strategy she had worked out as to how to handle Jerome if circumstances took a negative turn and he became touchy-feely to an unacceptable extent.

She felt that could happen only if he forced her into a situation in which they were together in his hotel room. And even then, she wondered whether she'd be able to go through with actually sleeping with him for the sake of getting some kind of evidence she hoped would shut him down forever. A short-term loss for a long-term gain, she concluded, a tried and true principle in investment circles for ages.

If only human life were as simple as investment strategies, we'd all be prospering she thought.

She spent the remainder of the trip reviewing the notes she'd made about the Lions account, so she'd be ready to coach Jerome and provide the information he needed to pacify Monsieur Lions when the two of them met tomorrow. Just one more example of Jerome's incompetence. They should and could have gone through all this earlier in the week when he was still in the office and she wouldn't have to give over her Sunday on this damned train. But that's Jerome. And as long as he's the boss, she'd just have to swallow her feelings and deal with it.

Maybe she'd get lucky and his incompetence would get him promoted—she'd seen that happen to many other men she'd encountered. Then she'd be out of his direct line of fire.

*

The train was a few minutes late arriving at the station in Paris. But as the bistro where she was meeting Jerome was only a short taxi ride from the station, Alex wasn't worried about being late.

She gathered her briefcase, along with her handbag, and headed for the taxi stand. The driver happened to be one of that small number of friendly faces in Paris, maybe because he was a foreigner, who spoke excellent English.

He said he had 'migrated' to Paris when he met a lovely *mademoiselle* and came to France to be with her. When he heard the address of the bistro, he told Alex that the street she wanted, rue Chanionesse, was probably the oldest street in the entire city, right next to the Cathedral Notre Dame. It was the heart of the high-rent district.

En route, she began to wonder about the bistro, especially as she never regarded Jerome as a high-rent-district type of guy. He could very easily be an expense-account-type of guy though, trying to impress her with a bit of pseudo-sophistication. Anyway, she was hungry and looking forward to lunch. A good, expense-account meal at a chi-chi Parisian bistro would be just the thing. And Merit could afford it.

The restaurant itself looked rather charming from the outside, if a bit nondescript, with a well-maintained wooden façade and a stylish green awning. Its interior had the traditional bistro look, with wooden chairs and tables, all slightly worn but cozy.

The only thing not cozy was Jerome, who was sitting at a table by the window already looking a bit cross. At the moment, he was the only customer in the place, as Sunday lunch at a Parisian bistro generally doesn't get going until at least 1pm, if not later. For now they had the entire place to themselves.

Jerome waved and motioned for her to join him. He got up and pulled out a chair for her to sit down.

"Hello, Alex. I'm glad to see you got here almost on schedule. Nice to see you in this 'distant' land."

Alex shook his hand, but said nothing by way of reciprocating his less-than-warm greeting other than to give him a short hello as she sat down.

At that moment, the waiter arrived with menus and asked what they'd like to drink. Jerome voted for an apertif, while Alex told the waiter she'd just have a small bottle of Perrier water, at least for now. Following the waiter's departure, Jerome looked at Alex's 'luggage':

"Does that briefcase contain the Lions material?"

"Indeed it does," she responded. She thought she should try to be friendlier to Jerome, since if things went her way she might find a way to get him under her control before the day was out. "But if you don't mind, I'd prefer to wait until after we eat before entering into discussion about it. Right now I'm too hungry to be able to focus on the details of Mssr. Lions' finances, interesting as they may be."

"Of course," said Jerome. "First, sustenance for the body, then for the mind—and for the pocketbook."

They spent a couple of minutes perusing the menu before the waiter returned for their orders. The offerings were appealing French favorites like foie gras terrine, entrecôte of beef and crème brûlée with vanilla bourbon sauce. They gave their choices to the waiter and Jerome asked for a bottle of the house red wine along with another sparkling water for the lady.

Following the main course, Alex offered to give Jerome a quick overview of the Lions account, even though she was much hungrier for her dessert order from the kitchen than for questions on finance from him. He stopped her, saying he'd prefer they enjoy the rest of their meal without business talk getting in the way.

"Plenty of time for that afterwards," Jerome told her just as the waiter arrived with their desserts.

When the plates had been cleared away and the cheese was almost finished, Alex asked when he'd like to have his 'lesson.' He appeared to think about this for a moment.

"Let's go to my place for that," he said. "It's just up the street. We can talk privately there and afterwards you can go sightseeing or just grab a taxi to the station for your train back to London."

"Where is 'your place?'" she asked. "I didn't notice any hotels around here when I arrived."

"Ah, it's not a hotel. I'm staying in a private apartment here that belongs to my friend, Alain. He's on a business trip of his own right now and was kind enough to let me use his place for a few days."

Oh, oh, thought Alex. A hotel room would have been tricky enough. But a private apartment is an entirely different level of privacy and seclusion. *Nothing I can do about that now, it seems. I guess I could insist that we go to a bar or cafe, maybe even just sit in the lobby of some hotel where nobody will pay any attention to us. But if I ever want to get the goods on Jerome, this private apartment could well be more of a blessing than a curse. I want to get this business with Jerome over and done with, once and for all.*

"Oh, that sounds convenient. Shall we settle up here and go to your friend's place and take care of this things? I'd really like to finish our business so I can get back to London."

"Perfect," Jerome replied, signaling the waiter for the bill.

*

Jerome and Alex left the restaurant and walked up to the corner, then and turned away from the River Seine. Jerome stopped at the second building on the right announcing, "Here we are, Alex.

Home, sweet home. I'm staying in this lovely nineteenth-century house right here."

He opened the door and led Alex to the typically micro-sized Parisian elevator. They squeezed-in with almost no room to spare between them, a situation Alex was painfully aware of as Jerome was basically pressing her against the elevator door by the time they arrived at his floor. He led her out of the elevator to the first door on the left and ushered her inside.

The apartment was a lot more spacious than the elevator, having a large entry hallway leading to a quite decent-sized living room with a classical-style sofa, armchairs, fairly well-stocked bookshelves and bar, along with a coffee table. A doorway from the living room led to a small room that Jerome's friend had converted into a cozy home office, having a desk and chair, together with a side table with two chairs of its own. Jerome suggested they sit there and discuss the Lions material.

On the way into the office, Alex had noted another open door off the living room that was clearly the bedroom. It contained a large four-poster double bed, two clothes cupboards next to a chest of drawers, a standing mirror and a chair. She also noticed an open suitcase in the room that she supposed contained Jerome's traveling clothes and other personal items.

Once they were settled in the office, Alex put her briefcase on the table and took out the folder of papers that Jerome needed for his meeting the next day. She placed them on the table.

"What can I tell you about the Lions account that you don't already know, Jerome?"

"Oh, pardon my manners, Alex. I forgot to offer you something to drink before we start. You probably noticed that Alain has a pretty well-stocked bar in the living room. Speaking for myself, I could use a small digestif to settle my stomach from lunch before we get into these papers. What about you?"

"I'm okay, Jerome. But if you're getting something for yourself, a glass of sparkling water would be lovely if there's any in the fridge."

Jerome went to get their drinks. Alex used his absence to quickly reach down into her handbag and switch on the small recorder she'd bought before leaving London. Hopefully, she could maneuver Jerome into a compromising situation and get a record of everything said between them from here on. She just managed to finish adjusting the recorder when Jerome came back and handed her a glass.

They toasted each other, after which Jerome edged his chair next to hers so that they could both look at the documents. She noticed his re-positioning but made no statement about it preferring to wait and see what might happen next.

The two of them then spent a few minutes going over the fundamentals of the account. Alex answered a couple of pretty basic questions as to how Lions' money was allocated, then asked Jerome if he had any more detailed questions. She was a bit surprised when he said he didn't, since what he'd asked about so far was absolutely plain vanilla stuff that she could have easily answered over the phone from London.

What was all this about him needing her expertise and coaching him for the meeting the next day? Now she knew he'd maneuvered to get her here for something very different than the Lions briefing. Before she could even ask him about this, she felt a hand under the table beginning to stroke her thigh. When she looked over at Jerome his face was now just a few inches from her own. He looked her in the eye.

"You, uh, must know by now Alex that I'm crazy about you." he said. "Could we, you know, take this opportunity to get a bit closer?"

Alex wanted to be sure the recorder heard what she was about to say so she raised her voice.

"Stop it, Jerome!" she said, rather forcefully. "We've been through this before with your disgraceful behavior in the hotel at the Financial Analysts Convention in Bristol. I do *not* want to mix my business activity and my personal life. So take your hand off my thigh and back off."

"I'm sorry Alex, but I can't do that," he said, coming even closer to her and moving his other hand up to put it behind her head for a kiss.

At that point, Alex was trying very hard to balance her revulsion for Jerome's behavior with how to get some some permanent leverage against him.

In a split-second, she decided, choked back the protest in her throat, and let Jerome's hands remain where they were.

As Jerome leaned in to kiss her, Alex opened her arms and began to pull him even closer.

This got an immediate reaction from Jerome, who wasn't expecting her resistance to have given away so easily. He was surprised she had changed so quickly, but sure of himself now, and was instantly receptive.

They kissed rather clumsily at first, then with something approaching passion. Alex began making sounds—grunts and moans, even muffled cries—that could be interpreted as either passion or distress.

At that point, Jerome began to rise from his chair and pulled Alex up too, suggesting they retire to the sofa in the living room to continue their activity.

Before Alex joined him, she grabbed her handbag to make sure the recorder came to the sofa as well, and they then more-or-less fell onto the sofa together rather than sitting down upon it.

This made Jerome laugh. "What? You need your bag for what's about to happen now, Alex?" he asked. "Do you have a present in there for me? Were you counting on this?"

"Sorry, Jerome," Alex replied in her best little-girl-scared voice, designed for the recording, but which seemed to turn Jerome on even more.

She grabbed her bag again as they left the sofa and only dropped it once they were near the bed. But from the way it landed in the fall, she wasn't sure if her recorder would still be picking up the sounds and voices in the room.

Jerome was now all over Alex, kissing her, continuing to stroke her upper leg and now reaching up to caress her breasts.

Despite her instinct to fend off these comical efforts, Alex pretended she was an actress playing a role and reciprocated his passions as best she could, with her by now routine pained moans, each of which seemed to drive Jerome wilder, encouraging him to start unbuttoning her blouse and move his mouth down to her breasts.

As he was grappling with the fastener on her bra, Alex was looking over his shoulder, trying to see if her recorder had spilled out of her purse onto the floor, all the while trying to avoid letting loose with the scream of disgust and or laughter forming in her throat, whichever it was.

Once he finally managed to sort out the intricacies of her bra, Jerome began licking her. After a minute, he came up for air.

"I want to fuck you, Alex. Do you want to fuck me?"

She bit her lower lip and made another one of her pained moans. She began removing her clothing for him, somewhat seductively, letting that form her answer.

She said nothing in reply and that seemed to irritate him. "What do you say, Alex? Do you want to fuck me?"

He removed his shirt and pants and was soon wearing only his underwear. At the same time, Alex noticed there were a bunch of black cords and other items stacked up in the corner of the room next to the bed.

"What's all that stuff over there, Jerome? It looks like bondage equipment."

"That's exactly what it is, Alex. My friend Alain has a fondness for erotic asphyxiation. He likes to have his girlfriend tie him up and choke him nearly to the point of unconsciousness. He says it's like getting a snort of cocaine and the orgasms are literally out of this world. Did you ever try it?"

"No," Alex said, breathlessly, trying to sound scared. "I've never tried asphyxiation ... ."

At that moment she had an inspiration.

"What about you, Jerome? Did Alain's story tempt you to try S&M-style sex?"

"I have to admit that I found his stories not only exciting, but intriguing. I've never actually done it, though. It's not how I imagined our first time, Alex."

She gave him a wry look and an almost girlish smile that asked, 'Why not?

"Would you like to be my dominatrix?" Jerome asked shyly.

At that Alex laughed along with Jerome, but broke off their momentary bit of nervous laughter.

"Let's do it!" Alex said, losing all signs of the little-girl-scared. "What a novel way to start our new relationship. Don't you agree?"

Hoping that Jerome would be so thrilled by her sudden enthusiasm for him that he would agree immediately to almost anything, Alex went over and picked up some of the cords and other apparatus and dropped them on the bed.

She was betting Jerome would regard her actions as a welcome challenge and not want to put her off at this critical juncture in what he surely now saw as their emerging new intimate friendship.

"Yes, Alex, let's do that. You can tie me up to these bedposts and take the woman-on-top position and we'll see how it goes."

They were now completely naked. Jerome gave Alex a very big kiss and stroked her top, bottom and in-between before laying down on the bed, arms and legs stretched out to the four corners.

"A bit on the puny side, Jerome, for a big boss man," she said. "But I'll soon get you in shape."

"Oh, I love that kind of talk, Alex," he responded. "I want to get much bigger and stronger under your tutelage."

"Not to worry, Jerome. I've got a plan for you."

Alex then quickly tied him up, hoping again that he wouldn't change his mind before she finished the job. Fortunately, he didn't. She then reached down to the floor and brought up one more item, a rubber ball with four elastic bands fastened to it in an X-pattern.

"What's that?" Jerome inquired.

"I'll show you right now," Alex said, coming up to the top of the bed and gently pushing Jerome's head back to give him an extremely sexy kiss, sticking her tongue deep into his mouth.

As she withdrew from the kiss, she quickly pushed the ball into Jerome's open mouth before he knew what was happening. Taking the elastic bands running through the ball, Alex stretched them around to the back of Jerome's head and secured the ball firmly in place.

"Now you see what this gadget is for," she told him. "It's to make sure you don't do any yelling or make too much noise while I'm cutting off the air supply to your brain as I literally fuck your brains out."

Jerome immediately started squirming, trying to get the cords off the bedposts. But Alex had knowledge and experience in fastening these kinds of items securely. The cords remained in place.

She then sat firmly on Jerome's chest and stomach, further pushing him into the mattress, while she wrapped a fifth cord around his neck.

"Isn't this fun, Jerome? Aren't you feeling excited? Somehow I don't see the kind of excitement in your lower regions that either you or I were hoping for. Perhaps another twist of the cord around your neck will get you going."

With that, she took the ball out so her recorder would capture Jerome's voice and shouts, wrapped the cord tighter around his neck, giving it a strong tug.

Jerome gasped and squealed more than shouted at this and began having trouble breathing. His bulging eyes focused on Alex and silently cried out for her to ease up on the cord.

Sing a song of sixpence
A pocket full of rye

When he saw the look in Alex's eyes, he became even more frantic. She wasn't looking at him at all, but seemed to have flipped into a fugue state, staring off into some other realm of space and time, where there was no Paris, no bedroom and, most importantly, no Jerome.

Just a cord that her mind was telling her to pull tighter and tighter around the man's neck, which she did.

*

At some point, Alex's mind stopped telling her to tighten the rope and she opened her eyes—and her mind—to her surroundings. She was shocked. A dozen questions presented themselves: Where am I? Why am I in this bed? Where are my clothes? Who is this person I'm laying on top of? What am I doing here? ...

As her consciousness snapped back into contact with reality, answers came to these questions like bullets from a machine gun.

I'm in Paris. This man is my boss, Jerome. I'm in bed with him because I wanted to use his sexual hunger to gain some leverage over him so he'd stop hitting on me.

Shocked by these realizations, Alex looked down at Jerome and realized he was totally silent and seemed to have stopped breathing. She feared he might be injured or even unconscious.

Rolling herself off of Jerome and on to the bed, she looked back and called out to him, asking if he was okay. He remained silent.

She called out again. When he again failed to reply, she felt his wrist, looking for some sign of life. His pulse was as silent as his voice. She felt again for a pulse, this time on the side of his neck. Again, no reaction. Starting to panic, Alex again called out to him: "Jerome, wake up!"

To no avail.

At this point, Alex became very frightened, believing that somehow the sex game had gotten totally out of hand and she had inadvertently choked Jerome to death.

How exhilarating it was, though she thought, seeing her nemesis Jerome stretched out on the bed, dead and never to trouble her again. *Finally, one less oppressor to get in the way of me simply carrying on my life.*

Why are all these men continually trying to prevent me from just doing my job?

I'm beginning to think that Victor is going to be another one on the list.

Unlike the others, I actually have some strong personal feelings for Victor. I'm going to have to be careful dealing with him in the coming days.

Regaining her equanimity, Alex realized that if Jerome really was dead, it need not be a disaster for her. It could be a boon.

She was aware that the death of a foreigner, an Englishman no less, by strangulation in some kind of S&M sex play was bound to arouse suspicion of foul play. It might be a blessing in disguise, though, since no one knew she was here in Paris.

She took a moment and searched her mind to be sure that was true. She had no way of knowing if Jerome had told anyone she was coming to see him, but she couldn't imagine why he would have, considering his intentions.

Only the messages on Jerome's phone and her own would tell any such tale.

She quickly grabbed her phone and erased the records of all the messages they had sent back and forth since he'd called her yesterday in London. Then she found his phone in his jacket pocket hanging in the entry way.

Luckily, he had not turned it off so she could easily find his messages to and from her since yesterday and erase them, too. Of course, the cell phone companies might keep a record of these messages for a week or two. Unless some suspicion was cast in her direction by the Paris police, though, the likelihood of anyone asking the phone companies for this information was tiny, especially if she simply took Jerome's phone with her and trashed it after she left the flat.

Now she had to carefully examine the apartment for even the smallest trace of her having been here. A hair, a fingerprint, some forgotten item could be catastrophic for the 'accidental death' theory she was already constructing in her mind.

A fingerprint would be by far the worst, since she knew there exist international databases for them, unlike other body traces like hair, toenails, nail polish or whatever, for which there are no such archives. Those kind of objects would be fatal *only* if she were to become a suspect.

Alex dressed quickly, brushed her hair and put on a dab of makeup. She then went to the kitchen and, looking under the sink, immediately set eyes on what she was hoping to find: a pair of latex dishwashing gloves. She immediately put them on and, no longer concerned about leaving fingerprints, proceeded to inspect the apartment for any of her belongings, finding only her briefcase and the papers on the table in the next room, along with her handbag, as well as her coat hanging in the hallway. She consolidated all these items and then went into the kitchen.

As she suspected, there were a collection of bottles under the sink for various types for cleaning, pots, pans, windows and most importantly, furniture and glass. She grabbed one of these bottles, put some solvent onto a cleaning rag and went to work on the tables in the living room and office, the frame of the bed, the door handle in the office, bedroom and so on.

While she was doing this, she kept a careful eye out for items such as hairs from her head or pubic area or anything else that may have come from her body.

She realized, of course, that *if* the police searched hard enough they'd surely find some hairs. But why should anyone think they are hers? No one knew about her being in Paris or about her and Jerome having lunch at the bistro. It's very unlikely the police were going to start interviewing everyone and anyone who might just have happened to see her walking on the street with Jerome from the restaurant to his flat.

Finishing her inspection of the apartment, Alex returned to the kitchen and grabbed a small hand vacuum she'd seen hanging there on the wall. She used it to very carefully vacuum the floors, tabletops, chairs and other areas and items in the house that she'd touched. Finishing this task, she opened the vacuum, took out the cleaning bag and sealed it in a plastic sack from the kitchen, putting in a new cleaning bag. She then put the sack into her handbag, telling herself to remember to dump it into a trash bin somewhere on her way back to the train station.

She then thought of the cassette in the voice recorder. She would have to erase that and throw it into the trash too, along with everything else.

When she found the recorder, the thought momentarily passed through her mind that perhaps she should *keep* that tape! It would be a souvenir of this strange visit and her final victory over Jerome. It might even be fun listening to it again some day. But then practicality stepped in to tell her it would be crazy to keep the one piece of evidence that would surely convict her of murdering Jerome.

Don't be an idiot, Alex, her sense of self-preservation said. *Erase that tape and get rid of it.*

But in the end she listened to the voice that said, *'Keep it. It might be amusing to play it back one of these days.'* She left the tape in the recorder and packed it away to take back to London with her.

In order to sow as much confusion as possible, Alex took all of Jerome's travel and personal documents, as well as his phone with her. She also rummaged around in his suitcase and clothing to see if there were any other items that might help identify him, such as luggage tags, airline boarding passes and the like.

By the time she finished, Alex felt pretty confident that Jerome would not be identified until his fingerprints were taken and/or Alain returned and found him in the bed.

With all these cleanup items taken care of, Alex returned to the bedroom and once again inspected Jerome. His body was still laying silently on the bed, in exactly the same position and state as before. She concluded that he had definitely died of asphyxiation and would now be out of her life forever, both in body and in spirit.

As one last clean-up item, she went back to the kitchen and got a rag with cleaning fluid and brought it to the bedroom. There, she carefully wiped down the knots on the ropes that held Jerome's body, along with the rope around his neck. She didn't really think ropes could retain fingerprints. But she didn't know for sure.

Better to be safe than sorry, she told herself.

Alex returned the rag to its place beneath the kitchen sink and then made a very careful circuit of the entire apartment, looking for anything that might indicate she had been here. She also opened the windows in the flat in order to allow the smell of the cleaning fluids to dissipate.

Finding no more potentially incriminating signs, she took her coat from the rack in the hallway, and still wearing the latex gloves, picked up her bag and briefcase, and then realized: *I'd better not be recognizable when I go out.* She headed back to the bedroom and into the walk-in closet, hardly noticing Jeromes cooling corpse. She found an assortment of fashionable Parisian men's clothes, including just the thing: a rack of several scarves. She grabbed one of the more muted ones and held it to her face, looking in the full-length mirror at the end of the closet. Perfect.

She carefully wrapped it around the top of her head, being sure to hide every trace of her brunette locks, then tied it tight with a nice knot. She dug into her purse and put on her dark glasses, took another step back from the mirror and looked. *No one knows me in Paris, and no one ever will,* she nodded to herself, picking up her bag and briefcase once again and heading back to the entryway. There, she paused and listened for any sounds from outside the door. Hearing nothing on this quiet Sunday afternoon, she noticed that Alain's front door had a spring lock. *Thank God for that,* she thought, as she wouldn't have to lock the door from the outside and then have to worry about how to get rid of the keys.

She took the latex gloves off and stuffed them into her purse, then slid her hand inside her coat sleeve and used the covered hand to push down on the door handle to open the door. Stepping cautiously out into the hallway and seeing or hearing no signs of neighbors, she carefully and quietly closed the door behind here and went to the stairway, not wanting to chance using the elevator and possibly leave a fingerprint or have to share a cramped ride with one of the residents.

Once on the street, Alex walked in the direction of Cathedral Notre Dame and the Metro station Saint Michel. She knew it was only one subway stop from there to the Eurostar station at Gare du Nord, a five-minute ride at most.

She preferred the Metro over a taxi, as the anonymity of the subway would further lower the chances that she'd be remembered by anyone in Paris. On her walk to St. Michel, Alex passed a couple of trash bins; she threw the vacuum cleaner bag into one, Jerome's phone and papers into the other.

She then entered the station, where luck was with her at the Eurostar terminal when she saw that the next train to London would be leaving in just ten minutes. That allowed her to get on and find a seat before departure, thereby eliminating any sitting around waiting in the terminal.

On the train, Alex could finally relax a bit and review her situation. Though she certainly hadn't had any premeditated intentions of murdering Jerome, she could not honestly say she regretted what had happened. She was confident that his absence would improve her life in several dimensions, personally and professionally.

It wasn't even totally clear to her that tidying up the scene and vanishing had been absolutely necessary. Even though she felt justified in removing Jerome from her life, others might disagree. Besides, accidents do happen, even in the bedroom. She could have simply told the police the true story. But that would have caused her to lose her job, at the bare minium. And it may well have turned against her if the French authorities took a hard line on the event. An unnecessary risk.

All things taken together, she believed that killing Jerome had solved one of the world's major problems, and she had done other women like herself a big favor. Now she just had to scrupulously avoid any statements or actions, especially with her work colleagues, that might throw a shadow in her direction regarding Jerome's death.

Alex realized that in her heart of hearts, she was very happy that Jerome was dead!

He deserved it, after all the trouble he'd caused her. Yes, indeed, this trip to Paris was providential in many ways.

Savoring her peace of mind, Alex leaned back, closed her eyes and slept the entire way back to London.

Episode XI

The Return

London

Alex returned from Paris to her Knightsbridge flat at around 6 o'clock Sunday evening. As she made her way home from St. Pancras Station, all the events of the past few hours came rushing through her mind like a hurricane, giving rise to jumbled thoughts and ideas of every sort involving how Jerome's death will impact her job at Merit, how Victor will act toward her when he returns from Santa Fe, how she can avoid giving any signs that she had a hand in Jerome's death.

Oh, why does life have to be so complicated, she complained to herself.

Once inside her flat, she made herself a bowl of chicken soup and a sandwich, then sat down on the sofa and opened a bottle of wine. As she neared the bottom of the bottle, she began focusing on that single, overriding question in life: *What should I do now?*

She decided there were really only three possible courses of action she could take. The first was simply to pretend she was never in Paris and that Jerome's death had nothing to do with her. In short, denial.

The second involved physical, as well as mental, escapism. She would put as much distance between herself and London as she could—and she would do this as soon as possible. She could easily manufacture some sort of family emergency, maybe an accident or sudden illness to her mother, forcing her to return to New Zealand immediately.

The third possibility was acceptance, which meant going to the London police and confessing everything.

Even in her half-inebriated state, she didn't have to spend much time before rejecting the last option.

Some argue that confession is good for the soul—but in Alex's experience, it was usually pretty lousy for life. She suspected that this option carried with it the very high likelihood of her spending a lot of time in a very unpleasant prison, where she would accumulate years of reflection on what the other two options might have offered.

Even at their worst, the first and second options could lead her to that very same prison. So why volunteer for it? Bad enough if it comes via just plain bad luck. She concluded there was no reason to deliberately inflict that bad luck upon herself.

Escaping to New Zealand had some immediate emotional appeal. But she also knew that if there were any investigation of Jerome's colleagues, she would jump right to the top of the suspect list if she just 'happened' to have left the country the day after his death. Alex didn't think anyone other than Maerta knew about Jerome's unwelcome advances or how she really felt about him. But she couldn't really be certain about that. Perhaps someone in her department at Merit had accidentally overheard a remark or caught a glance she didn't know about. So, no, a disappearance to New Zealand would also be asking for trouble.

By a process of elimination, Alex decided that her best strategy to deal with the events in Paris was simply to tough it out.

She'd go to the office the next morning as if nothing had happened and act accordingly. Considering how Jerome had summoned her to Paris on a Saturday, she couldn't imagine how anyone knew she had gone there, anyway.

She was also pretty confident that her clean-up of Alain's flat had left no obvious tell-tale evidence she had been there. She might be wrong, of course, and overlooked something in the flat that pointed directly at her. All things taken together, though, she felt that even that kind of bad luck was much less likely than with either of the other two options.

After drinking the last bit of wine, Alex made her way to the bedroom and settled in for what she hoped would be a decent night's sleep before putting on her best face before going to the office the next day.

In the morning, Alex came through Merit's front door with a smile on her face and greeted her colleagues and asked about their weekend in much the same way she always did on Mondays. On the way to her own office, she passed Jerome's and looked in the window, irrationally wondering if perhaps he would be there.

Get a grip, she told herself. *I killed Jerome. I strangled him. He will never be here. He was a bad boss. Maybe that office will be filled by someone nice. Maybe it will even be filled by me.*

No one in the office expected to see Jerome today anyway, because they knew he was on business in Paris and not due back until tomorrow. That gave her at least a day to get herself adjusted to office life without Jerome before everyone else began wondering where he was.

One bright spot for Alex when she sat down at her desk was finding an email from Victor.

"I'll be arriving in London on Thursday," his message said. "Should I go to a hotel or come directly to Merit in order to get the information and keys for the apartment they've arranged for me?"

She replied, "Just call me from Heathrow when you arrive. I will then meet you at your new flat, give you the keys and welcome you to London."

In her reply she told him the address of the flat in Mayfair, explaining that it was only a few blocks from there to her own place near Harrods. She closed by saying, "I'm very pleased you'll finally be in London to begin our project, and very much look forward to seeing you again."

Alex then contacted the other simulator team members, Bill and Bob, and told them about Victor's arrival and said there would be a team meeting on Friday morning to discuss an overall plan for the project and how they would each carry out their part of it.

Conventional wisdom has it that curiosity killed the cat. But the next day, Tuesday in the early afternoon, Alex decided to tempt fate anyway and ask Peggy, Jerome's assistant, if he was back or if she had heard from him.

Peggy had a concerned look on her face as she told Alex, "I haven't heard a word from Jerome. In fact, yesterday I received a call from the offices of Mr. Lions in Paris, asking the very same question, 'Where is Jerome?' The woman in Paris said he had a meeting scheduled with Mr. Lions on Monday but never showed up. So I'm getting concerned. He was supposed to be back sometime today."

"What do you think happened to him?" asked Alex.

Peggy said, "I have no idea. I tried calling and emailing, but with no response. I don't really know what to do now. I was thinking of going over to his apartment later today and find out if anyone there has seen him."

Alex thanked her for the information and went back to her office thinking that everything was proceeding just as she'd hoped and expected—so far!

When she first sat down at her desk Wednesday morning, Alex found an email on her screen from the VP of Personnel at Merit stating, "I have the sad duty to inform you about the death of our colleague, Jerome Hall, under unknown circumstances in Paris."

The message went on to express sorrow and condolences to Jerome's family and colleagues, saying they would give more information on the death as soon as the police in Paris had completed their investigation.

That's it, thought Alex. *Sing a song of six pence ... Hopefully, the cook will be the survivor, not the blackbirds!*

Jerome's death was of course the only topic on the office gossip agenda for the day, especially in her department. At coffee breaks and lunch, people were speculating how Jerome died in Paris and what would happen to the position he had held at Merit.

Alex couldn't help noting that no one was expressing any great sorrow at Jerome's death, reaffirming her long-held belief that he was far from being universally loved and admired by his colleagues.

At the coffee room on her floor, Josephine, one of Alex's colleagues, told her in a whisper, "I heard Jerome was found in a private apartment in Paris, strangled to death in some bondage sex game that apparently went off the rails."

Alex's mouth dropped open in a look of astonishment.

"I would never have thought he was that type of person. But then you can really never know another person by their public persona, can you?"

With the knowledge about the nature of Jerome's death now in general circulation, Alex doubted seriously that Merit management would be sending around a second memo with *that* bit of information!

Josephine said, "People are theorizing that Jerome hired a sex worker in Paris to come to him and that the whole thing just went hopelessly wrong, the sex worker vanishing with Jeromes's wallet, phone and other ID."

"Well," replied Alex, "I suppose the Paris police will search for any information that might lead to a suspect. If they don't find any, they'll simply write off the death as an unsolved murder putting it into what must by now be a very large file of such things in Paris."

"You're probably right, Alex. The police there have to be seen as making some kind of effort, especially as the victim is a high-ranking foreign businessman."

"I think so, too," agreed Alex.

"I suspect that a *lot* of high-ranking foreigners come to Paris and rent a lady of the night for their entertainment," responded Josephine. "I doubt the police will turn over every stone before just abandoning the case. Unless of course they happen to run across something that clearly points to a particular suspect."

The pair then went back to their offices, as Alex kept her mental fingers crossed that Josephine was on target with her assessment of the situation.

*

Victor began by throwing out things from his refrigerator and emptying food from the shelves so it wouldn't spoil while he was away for his leave in London. He also took out the trash, tidied-up messes in various corners of the house and, in general, did his best to put the house into the condition he'd like to see it when he came back in several months.

He spent the following morning packing clothes, books and setting up his traveling computer with all the software and data files he might need for the job at Merit. Of course, he could always access his computer files at the Institute from London if need be. But as a man of the old school, Victor felt more comfortable if he had what he needed saved in his own computer, not sitting in an amorphous 'cloud' somewhere.

Victor treated himself to a farewell dinner, consisting of two thick shoulder lamb chops that he cooked on his outdoor grill, along with a double shot of 25-year-old Macallan scotch whisky as an appetizer. The chops were accompanied by grilled vegetables and potatoes, followed by a delicious balsamic panna cotta.

The flight was uneventful, and upon arrival at Heathrow, Victor called Alex as they'd agreed. She told him to take a taxi to his Mayfair flat and she would meet him there at eleven o'clock.

Following a very warm embrace at the entrance to his building, the two of them went up to his flat, which was a nicely-appointed one-bedroom unit directly across Hamilton Place from the Intercontinental Hotel at Park Lane.

"It's only one stop on the Tube from your station at Hyde Park Corner to mine at Knightsbridge," Alex told him. "So we'll be able to see each other quite easily without any logistical problems."

Strangely, though, the way she said this struck him as slightly off-key, as if she was saying that she *expected* him to make use of that connection regularly and that she'd be upset if he didn't. She then noted, "You're living in the poshest area in all of London."

"Pity," he said, "since between my time at the office and the frolicking with you in Knightsbridge, I won't be in his flat long enough to really enjoy it."

Alex smiled and then suggested, "Take a bit of time to get unpacked and get acclimated to your new surroundings, maybe even have a short siesta or a walk. Then we can have dinner together and a chat prior to your formal arrival at Merit tomorrow."

"Perfect, Alex. I'll be looking forward to a nice dinner and a drink with you later."

Before leaving, she proposed they meet for pre-dinner drinks at seven o'clock at the Library Bar, which was only a short walk from Victor's flat and he happily agreed.

The Library Bar turned out to be totally charming, a slice of Merry Olde England—with a heavenly selection of single-malt Scotch whiskies. Unfortunately for Victor, the whisky was a bit too heavenly, and by the time they were ready to eat he was on the edge of starting to slur his words.

He looked over at Alex rather bleary-eyed and said, "I think I've been enjoying this whisky a bit more than I should have. Maybe we can find a restaurant close by and catch a quick dinner there. I then need to get back to my flat and grab some sleep before turning up at Merit in the morning."

In order to respect his condition and the long trip he'd just completed, they had dinner in the Italian restaurant *Amaranto* located in the Four Seasons Park Lane Hotel, just a few steps up the street from Victor's flat.

Over dinner, at which they both chose the Scottish scallops as appetizer, with Victor opting for lobster linguine pasta while Alex went for the artichoke ravioli as her main course, they spoke briefly about how life had been treating them both since they last met. Basically, their conversation focused around how pleased they were about finally being able to officially launch the simulator project in the morning.

Alex also told Victor about Jerome's death in Paris.

“Jerome died under what one might call ‘puzzling circumstances.’ ”

“What was puzzling about them, Alex?”

“According to informed gossip, it seems that he was killed in a sexual bondage encounter that got out of hand, resulting in him being strangled to death.”

“Wow! Although I only met Jerome that one time a month or so ago when I visited Merit to present the simulator,” Victor said, “he didn’t seem the type for those type of games—although who can really say who is the ‘type’?”

Victor wasn’t too upset about Jerome’s death, although he did express his condolences to Alex. She then told him that Jerome’s boss, Michael Zilk, had asked her to step in as official leader of the simulator project, at least until the big bosses at Merit sorted out how to handle the situation on a more permanent organizational basis.

“As a result,” she laughed, “I’m now your boss, Victor. So behave.”

“I’ll be naughty but nice, Alex. Not to worry.” They both chuckled at that double entendre, after which Alex told Victor that he looked like he needed some rest. He concurred and they settled their bill, agreeing to meet at Merit at ten o’clock the next morning.

In the office the next day Alex was outwardly friendly, but rather formal, when the others on the team were around, giving no indication that she’d ever had any private contact with Victor. Before the meeting began, the two of them were alone in his office. Alex came over to Victor, clasped his hand, looked into his eyes, and said in a concerned voice, “How did you sleep last night?”

“Just fine, thank you.”

Victor smiled to himself, but couldn't help but wonder if her behavior was just another example of her trying to regain the momentum in their relationship by playing Ms. Nice, acting as if some of the earlier stress points they'd experienced either had no impact on her or had never even existed.

Curiouser and curiouser, he thought.

After getting reacquainted with Bill and Bob, Victor distributed his plan for how to develop the project, and then, joined by Alex, got down to the details of how they would actually execute his plan. Speaking to the team, he said, 'If there is a single word to describe our mission over the next few months, that word is 'scale.' Every aspect of the existing 'toy' simulator has to be scaled-up in order to make contact with the real world of financial markets and trading."

"Could you be a bit more specific?" asked Bob.

"With pleasure," Victor replied. "In the current simulator, there is only one security being traded and a dozen traders in the market. We need an upgrade of the simulator to many securities being bought and sold, and the trading has to be done by, say, a hundred traders, not just a dozen. Moreover, we have to figure out how to insert derivatives into the simulator, so the traders can trade not only the securities themselves but also buy and sell futures and options contracts on those securities. We also have to create a way to code strategies for trading, so that the traders can shift from one strategy to another. And to make that shift, we have to develop a meta-rule that is in essence a rule for changing rules."

He concluded by saying, "Carrying out this program is not an exercise for the faint of heart. But I'm confident we can make a big enough dent in the problems I've just outlined to keep the Merit management happy and ready to go the next round with us into the actual markets themselves."

With that, he asked each of them to take responsibility for one of the tasks: Bob would work on expanding the number of traders and securities, Bill would look into how to code meaningful trading strategies. And Alex would investigate how to incorporate derivatives into the overall framework. He would oversee each of these subtasks, as well as contribute what he could to integrating them into a single, coherent picture.

After lunch, Michael Zilk's secretary called Victor and asked if he could come up to Michael's office. Victor put aside his work and took the internal stairs up to the next floor to Michael's domain.

"Merit's Advisory Board will be meeting in two week's time," Michael began. "So I wonder if you could make a short presentation to them about the simulator?"

"Of course," said Victor. "I'd be happy to do that."

"Great," said Michael. "The board should know something about how it works, as well as a bit more about what's behind the simulator. And, of course, they'd like to know what Merit might expect from the new version your group is currently creating—and that Merit is paying for."

"If you like, I can prepare a short written explanation of the background to the simulator beforehand, so the Board could read through it before the actual oral presentation at the meeting," said Victor.

"That's an excellent idea," said Zilk. "Please try to do it as soon as you can, so the material can be circulated to the board within the next couple of days." The two then shook hands, ending the meeting.

*

Work on the simulator soon evolved into a daily pattern consisting of a morning meeting of the team, at which each of the players got their marching orders for the day. They then ate lunch together at the Merit canteen, going back to work until around 6 o'clock. At that time, most of the team, including Victor, generally retired to the Horse and Pony Pub up the street to finish off the day with a pint or two of Guinness before heading home.

This pattern was a balm to Victor, as it didn't leave him very much time to think about his social life with Alex, what she was thinking or anything else. Just work, work and more work.

Of course, this didn't mean that Alex and Victor totally avoided each other. Quite to the contrary. They usually met once or twice a week at his flat or hers, where they got reacquainted with each other's minds, spirits and, of course, bodies.

One time at her flat, Alex even reminded Victor of the bondage game they'd played earlier asking him, "Would you like to do it again?"

He said, "Okay—but only if this time I can tie you up!"

At this unexpected role-reversal suggestion, Alex quickly said, "Let me think about that. But right now I have to go to the bathroom to attend to an urgent call from nature."

When she returned the bondage scenario was off the agenda, replaced by a very skimpy, silky negligee. From there matters took their natural course, and the couple spent the next couple of hours coupling in their by now familiar, bondage-free, fashion.

So much for male dominance, thought Victor. *I'm going to have to try harder and be a bit more subtle if I'm to get the upper hand with this lady.*

During one of their after work drinking sessions, Victor's co-worker Bill asked him, "Did you hear about the details of Jerome's death in Paris a few weeks ago?"

"No, I didn't," replied Victor, preferring not to speak about the conversation he'd had with Alex the night of his arrival. "Tell me about it."

Bill then said, "I have an unimpeachable source who told me Jerome was strangled to death in an S&M bondage activity. Apparently, being on the edge of strangulation while having sex makes the orgasms super intense and totally memorable."

Bill went on to remark, "I would never have thought Jerome to be the type to go in for erotic asphyxiation. But, then, who can say?" he shrugged.

As Victor took another sip of his Guinness and thought about Bill's juicy tidbit from the gossip mill, a bell rang somewhere in the back of his mind. The ringing then quickly moved to the frontal cortex with the twin thoughts: Alex's interest in bondage and Jerome's death! He wondered, *Were the two somehow related?* It' was a bit of a stretch, Victor had to admit. But the next thought that came along with it was whether Alex and Jerome had had a sexual tryst with ropes and masks, unbeknownst to anyone in the office?

If this had indeed been the case, then Victor thought Alex would jump right to the top of the list of suspects. He might do some very delicate exploration of this possibility in his interactions with her over the coming days. But for now, back to the bar for a refill before heading home for his usual evening's engagement with his pillow.

An opportunity to meet socially with Alex presented itself the very next day when she came up to him and said, "Friday is just around the corner. Perhaps you'd like to join me for a night out. Maybe we could listen to some live music, go to a film or whatever?"

Victor liked the sound of that 'whatever,' and readily agreed to her invitation.

They decided to revisit Ronnie Scott's Jazz Club, partly because they'd had such a fine time there awhile back, and partly because they were each at least subconsciously aware of what happened at her flat after that earlier evening of eating, drinking and being merry, especially the last part.

After listening to a couple of sets at Ronnie's, Victor leaned over and said, "What about dinner? I was thinking of a return visit to *Shinjuku,* the same Japanese restaurant we went to before. It would be a nice way to complete the second leg of the triangle that we started earlier. What do you think?"

Alex silently nodded her head, confirming that it was indeed time to eat. Then she added the final leg to the triangle:

"From the restaurant, I think we should complete the picture by going back to my flat for a nightcap. Okay?"

Victor couldn't fault Alex's reasoning. He got up and led her out the door and on to the restaurant.

After dinner, on their way to Alex's apartment, Victor reminded himself of his hidden agenda item to explore a bit more of Alex's interest in bondage-style sex games. If his vague suspicion about Alex having been possibly involved in Jerome's death was correct, then he realized it might be rather dangerous for him to volunteer to go through that process again. On the other hand, he had done that very thing before with Alex and survived the experience.

Maybe he'd have to use that card again in order to smoke out any new information she might inadvertently give away. He'd just have to play out the hand and see how the cards fell in real time when they got to her flat. He could then decide what to do.

Victor and Alex were both eager to get to the main event once they reached her flat. To observe the civilities though, Alex said, "What about a snifter of Remy Martin XO cognac to warm up a bit?"

While sitting on the sofa with the cognac in their hands, Alex mentioned, "I'm really happy to have you in town for an extended period, Victor. Your presence dramatically improves my social life. And my private life, too."

Putting down her glass, she went on, "How about if we retire to the 'intimacy room' and further develop our friendship?"

"I think you'll recall our brief discussion of intimacies, bondage-style, last time I was here. In that direction, I recently heard again the office rumor you told me about when I arrived here about how Jerome died in Paris," Victor said. "If this gossip is on the mark, he died of strangulation while engaging in what they call 'erotic asphyxiation'."

Alex stared very intently at him, ignoring her drink, while Victor was recounting this rumor. When he finished, she asked, "What's this erotic asphyxiation all about?"

"It seems," Victor told her, "when the dominatrix or dominator chokes the other person during the sex act in order to cut off blood flow to the brain, it leads to super orgasms—if you survive the experience. Do you know anything about that?"

"No," she said finally. "I don't know anything about this strangling business. Of course, I heard the same rumor regarding Jerome but find it difficult to believe. He never struck me as the bondage type at all, let alone someone who would engage in such kinky sex. What I have heard though is that just like with so-called 'normal' sex, some bondage fans like to record their sessions."

"And how do they do that?" asked Victor.

"Oh, I don't know. Maybe they take photos or home movies. Or perhaps they use an audio recorder. Maybe both. Who can say?" replied Alex. "I think it could be interesting having a record of what happened. Just like with a normal photo album, you could look/listen later and remember the good, old days," she laughed.

"Do you have a recorder yourself for such purposes, Alex?" Victor said with a smile.

"Not yet—but perhaps I should get one. What do you think?" she replied.

Victor didn't really think much of the idea of recording his sexual antics. A quick change of topic seemed to be called for.

"Getting back to Jerome," he said. "As you know I met him only that one time at Merit several weeks ago. I don't recall him saying much that day. But you worked with him for quite a while. Did he ever say anything provocative or come on to you?"

Again, Alex ignored her drink and turned off her flirtatious smile as she focused intently on Victor.

"Jerome often looked at me in a manner that made me feel uncomfortable. But the only time he made any actual physical advance in my direction was at a conference in Bristol when he asked me for a good night kiss."

"What did you do?"

"I simply wrote it off as his being obviously drunk, and managed to easily fend him off. And he didn't repeat this harassment. But so much for Jerome. Now what about Victor and Alex?"

To emphasize that she felt the topic of Jerome was now closed, Alex edged over on the sofa, set her glass and Victor's on the coffee table, and wrapped her arms around him as prelude to a very long, very deep and very sexy down-in-your-throat-style embrace.

Victor got the message and quickly reciprocated her advance in kind, suggesting they retire to the bedroom to consider how to continue this very intriguing, even absorbing, conversation.

And so they did, with no further discussion about bondage, Jerome or anything else other than very up-close-and-personal physical contact of the sort that had now become *de rigueur* for them.

Nevertheless, there was still something about their encounter that nagged at Victor a bit.

As they were lying in bed following their lovemaking, Alex once again had to take a temporary leave of absence to visit the facilities.

While he reflected on the pleasures of the sheets, Victor thought about her remark concerning recording of sexual encounters. While he didn't see any hidden cameras or recorders in the bedroom, he made a note to do a deeper exploration of this space if he were ever there again without Alex in the room.

When Alex returned, Victor said, "I think it's about time for me to leave,"' and began gathering his clothes together. By then the sun was starting to come up and he wanted to get home and cleaned up, both physically and mentally.

*

Victor was now very much focused on the way his roller-coaster relationship with Alex might impact how he would continue the relationship he'd begun in Santa Fe with Natalie. Since he'd been in London, he and Natalie had regularly exchanged very warm, loving emails. In a message a few days ago, Victor raised the possibility of Natalie visiting him here in Europe.

She had written telling him how much she would like to do that, but that it might be difficult for her to get extended time off from her job at the gallery, as this was the busy season for visitors to Santa Fe. She promised to speak with her boss about it and would let Victor know her possibilities.

Victor knew that a visit to London by Natalie would certainly involve some fancy footwork on his part to prevent Alex from knowing about it. However, he seriously missed Natalie and didn't want to have to wait forever to see her again. He hoped she would send him a positive reply in the next day or two, at which time he would try to put all the pieces together to make the trip happen.

With the idea of a visit from Natalie still on his mind, the phone rang and Victor picked it up to find Alex on the line.

In a cheery voice, Alex, cooed about their lovely evening together.

"Ooh, how nice it would be to have an encore tonight. What do you think about that, Victor?"

Victor didn't really want an encore, at least not tonight.

"I'm sorry Alex," he said. "As you know, I didn't get any sleep, and I have to spend the rest of the weekend preparing a presentation for a meeting I'm speaking at soon. So I'm afraid we'll have to take a raincheck on your lovely idea."

He closed the call with a few endearing remarks that seemed to pacify Alex and they agreed they'd see each other again at the office on Monday.

After hanging up, Victor thought that perhaps he should start now putting in place some plausible reason he could give Alex for why he had to be out of London for a few days. The meeting he'd just mentioned to her would be an excellent candidate. Luckily, she didn't ask for any details about that meeting. Victor knew there was always a professional meeting going on somewhere, someplace that he could use as a vehicle to escape Alex's eagle eye.

All he had to do was look on the Internet and assemble a list of such meetings on topics at least vaguely related to his areas of expertise. He would then have a catalogue of times that he could refer to when/if Natalie gave him the green light as to the time she could come and visit him in Europe.

With these thoughts percolating in his mind, Victor went across the street to the Intercon Park Lane Hotel to have lunch and yet once again think through his personal situations with the two women.

As it turned out, Victor's exercise in preparation was not misplaced. On Tuesday, he received a message from Natalie saying that her boss could spare her for only the upcoming week. After that the flood of summer tourists would start arriving in Santa Fe and she would have to be working full-time at the gallery for several weeks.

She wondered whether it was really worth coming to Europe for just one week. In the end, she said she'd leave it up to Victor to decide, hopefully within the next day or two, putting the burden of decision on his shoulders.

Balancing Alex, his job at Merit and his feelings for Natalie was a job for three men and a boy. Not Victor's specialty, at all. After weighing up the pros and cons, not to mention his longer-term life possibilities versus the next few months here in London, Victor finally decided he would tell Natalie to plan to travel from the US to London at the end of the week, arriving late Friday or early Saturday.

He thought they should spend the weekend in London, then go to Venice for a couple of days, which Victor thought would be the perfect complement to London for her quick first trip to Europe.

Then they could take the train from Venice to Trieste, where tourists didn't usually go, but which Victor knew well from his past life in Europe. Moreover, that was the city where he needed to go anyway for the lecture he'd planned to tell Alex about.

He quickly dashed off his reply. Victor told her that if she would send him her preferred flight dates and time to and from the US, he would arrange all travel for her. Of course these were simply details, which could easily be made to vanish by applying a credit card to the matter.

Given the seven-hour time difference between London and Santa Fe, Victor received Natalie's enthusiastic agreement to his plan before he left the office that evening.

The 800-pound gorilla still in the room though was settling with Alex the timing for his absence from London.

Victor's mention of Trieste in his message to Natalie was not by accident. When he was compiling his 'catalogue of escapes' on the weekend, one of the meetings Victor noted was an international symposium on system theory being held *next week* at the International Centre for Theoretical Physics in Trieste.

Victor remembered the ICTP very fondly, as he'd spent several months there a couple of decades ago when the center was expanding its horizons and trying to develop a competence in seeing physics as a system science. Or perhaps it was to see systems as a physical science. He couldn't really remember now. Probably it was a bit of both.

At the time, the ICTP had engaged Victor to put together a series of seminars by renowned system scientists, both to get their ideas on physics and to introduce the physicists to the international systems community.

The ICTP would be the perfect location for Victor to 'hide out' from Alex. As he knew the organizer of the meeting there, it would be no problem getting himself placed on the program. So Victor decided to broach the matter with her at lunch that very day. But he still had to finesse a way to escape from Alex in London during the upcoming weekend when Natalie would be in town.

To solve that, Victor decided to invent a long-time friend, a colleague from the US, who would be going to the Trieste meeting as well, and who had suggested stopping by London on his way to Italy to renew his acquaintance with Victor. Victor's need to entertain this friend would serve nicely to put Alex on the sidelines during that critical period when he'd actually be entertaining his *new* friend, Natalie.

As he left the Merit lunchroom, Victor managed to side-track Alex.

"Can I have a moment of your time, Alex? I have some logistical matters I need to talk with you about."

"Sure, what's up, Victor?"

"I have a presentation to make in Italy next week, and an old colleague of mine from the US is coming to London on his way to the same meeting. I'm going to need to take about ten days off to deal with both of these matters.

Alex said, "No problem. Just prepare an outline for what each of the team members should be doing during your absence."

She then went off to catch the elevator back to her office, leaving Victor somewhat surprised, and rather mystified, that she hadn't expressed any curiosity about his 'friend' or the 'meeting' they would be attending together.

The thought crossed his mind that perhaps Alex believed that their interaction over the past weeks had convinced her that she now had him just where she wanted him, and she didn't want to appear to be a Nosy Parker-type of girlfriend, who needed to know where he was and who he was with every single moment.

Anyway, no use painting the devil on the wall and trying to fix something if it wasn't broken. Just be thankful for small favors and get on with your life had always been Victor's guiding principle. Now was as good a time as any to practice it.

As the week unfolded, Victor had no further discussion with Alex about his upcoming absence.

On Thursday, he saw her and said, "My friend from the USA will arrive in London tomorrow, and I will be touristing around London with him until Sunday. I'll probably leave the office at lunchtime tomorrow and return a week from Monday."

"Sounds fine, Victor," Alex said.

He then gave Alex a copy of his work plan for the team to carry out during his absence, saying they could discuss it the next morning if there were any questions. And that was the end of their conversation.

Of course, Alex was not okay with this at all, and she already had plans to dig deeper during the upcoming weekend into the explanation he'd given to her for his absence.

Alex's suspicions, and they were just that, suspicions, arose from Victor's manner when he told her about the visitor and his need to be gone for a few days. While on the surface it all sounded quite plausible, there was something about his voice and mannerisms when he told her about his plan that somehow seemed just a bit off. She couldn't quite put her finger on exactly what got her antennae vibrating.

But it was definitely something—and she didn't like it.

With this factor whispering into her ear courtesy of her reptilian brain, Alex decided to play detective on the weekend and see what she could see of Victor's actions without his knowing about it.

Thinking through her possibilities for shadowing Victor, Alex quickly dismissed the idea of following him on the street like a spook, hiring a PI to do that job instead of doing it herself, or even more ridiculous means such as trying to insert a homing device into his coat or briefcase.

As Alex laughed at herself over this last fantasy, it suddenly occurred to her that the Intercon Park Lane Hotel was directly across the street from the entrance to Victor's building.

Why not simply book a room on that side of the hotel and use it as an observation post to keep an eye on Victor's comings and goings over the next couple of days? Why not, indeed!

She picked up the phone and called the Park Lane to make a booking for Friday and Saturday evenings. Things were definitely looking better, she thought, as the booking agent at the hotel scanned for a room facing the street, as she'd requested. Her hopes took a nosedive when the agent said he could give her a room only for tonight, but no luck for Saturday. Apparently a big convention group had booked just about every room in the hotel for the weekend, and only tonight was available.

Alex thought she'd just have to do what she could tonight and tomorrow morning and hope for the best.

Check-in time was at 3 o'clock, so she'd just have time to go to her place at lunch time, put an overnight bag together and get to the hotel and check-in. As an afterthought, she threw in a pair of opera-style binoculars just in case the room the hotel gave her was farther away from Victor's front door than she'd remembered. And finally, a wig and sunglasses. Just in case.

She then flagged down a taxi to take her directly to the front entrance of the hotel rather than walking the half-kilometer from her place, where a stroke of bad luck might bring her to Victor's attention if he just happened to be looking her way at the wrong moment.

By 3 o'clock Alex was checked in to her room and unpacking her travel bag. As she hadn't had time for lunch, she called down to room service and ordered a sandwich and a mineral water before setting up her 'observation post' from the window and dining table in her room.

While she didn't have any set time when she expected Victor and his 'old-pal travel-mate' to appear, she thought the best possibilities would be late this afternoon, before they would be leaving for dinner and entertainment, later this evening when they would return (but when it might be difficult to see them in the darkness) or sometime mid-morning tomorrow when they'd be leaving for lunch and a day on the town.

Of course, this all assumed that the travel-mate would come to Victor's flat first, instead of their meeting at either his hotel or at some agreed-upon spot in town.

At least Alex could keep an eye on Victor, and maybe even shadow him if need be by wearing the sunglasses and wig she'd brought along. But she hoped to see the travel-mate and Victor together at least once, perhaps after sharing a drink at Victor's flat before they moved on to other places together.

She jotted these critical times down on a piece of paper and settled in for the duration. Unfortunately for her plan, Alex saw no one even remotely resembling Victor anytime during the afternoon, while in the evening her fears were confirmed about the darkness, as she couldn't really see Victor or anyone else in detail due to the dim street lighting in the neighborhood and the distance between her room and the entrance to Victor's apartment building.

So the success of her experiment would now all hinge upon what happened in the morning. The window of opportunity would be a rather slim one as she had to check-out of the room by 1 o'clock and was not able to get a later check-out as the hotel needed the room for the conventioneers who would be arriving after lunch.

Just before noon Alex caught a glimpse of Victor leaving his building in the company of a tall, rather stylish-looking blonde woman. Alex had her opera glasses zeroed-in on them as they walked down the stairs of the house and onto the sidewalk.

They were not physically holding hands or hugging each other, yet they appeared to be quite comfortable together and seemed to both be laughing at something Victor was saying.

Though this lady *might* be nothing more than one of Victor's neighbors, Alex didn't think that was the way to bet. And whoever she was, she was certainly not Victor's 'colleague' from the States! Wherever that colleague was, if he existed at all, he was not now on the street with Victor.

While she'd hoped her experiment would fail, it didn't. What should she do now with this information?

Fortunately, Alex would have more than a week until she saw Victor again. That was time enough to check on the rest of his story about the meeting in Italy. If the colleague was a fiction, perhaps Victor's whole story was a fiction.

One way she could test that hypothesis would be to track down the details of the purported meeting in Trieste that Victor said he'd be attending by looking it up on the Internet.

She would then call the institute in Trieste, saying she was Victor's assistant and had an urgent message for him. Then she would find out if he was actually registered and in attendance at the meeting.

She could not do that until Monday, at the earliest, though. For now all she could do was check out of the hotel and spend the weekend brooding.

Episode XII

The Trip

London, Venice, Trieste

When Victor's phone rang on Friday morning, he was excited to hear Natalie's voice. She told him she had just left Heathrow in a taxi and should be at his flat in half an hour or so. He said he was already cleaning up the place and couldn't wait to see her.

He reminded her again of the address and described the house so as to ensure she wouldn't by chance ring the wrong doorbell. *What an idiot I'm being,* he thought. *Stop acting like a lovesick schoolboy and start being a mature, lovesick professor.*

Natalie turned up on Victor's doorstep a little after 10 o'clock. Victor welcomed her with a big hug and a kiss thanking her for coming and said how *very* happy he was to see her again. He then almost tripped over her suitcase ushering her into the flat.

Once the door was closed, she gave him a big, New Mexico-sized kiss in return, and began looking around his flat oohing and ahhing at one thing or another, just as she'd done at his house in Santa Fe. It seemed to be her way of telling him she approved of his home environment.

Victor asked, "Are you tired?"

"I had a decent sleep on the flight across the Atlantic, so I feel pretty good at the moment," she said. He smiled at this, thinking she looked more than pretty good, too.

"We can stretch our legs a bit after you unpack," he suggested, "and perhaps have a bite of lunch."

Taking her suitcase into the bedroom, Victor showed her the closet, where she could hang her clothes. After reminding her that they would be in London only two nights before heading to Italy, he went back to the living room and left her in peace—for the moment, anyway.

After a fast shower and quick change out of her travel clothes, Natalie was ready to set out with Victor on her first excursion into life in London.

She asked Victor, "What do you have in mind for this outing?"

"Nothing too strenuous. Maybe a bit of orientation to the local neighborhood, a quick lunch, and then perhaps a walk over to Piccadilly Circus if you're feeling up to it."

Natalie was totally excited about all of that, especially as it was a lovely, sunny day. She told Victor, "I'll put myself in your care."

Strange, he thought, *how nice that statement makes me feel.*

Off they went, down the stairs and into the street.

It was lunchtime for Victor but early breakfast hours for Natalie. He told her he thought they should first get a bit of food into their stomachs before doing any serious touring. They ended up going to a Spanish tapas restaurant named *La Pirata,* not too far away and a place he'd visited a couple of times since he'd been in London.

La Pirata was just around the corner from the restaurant *Amaranto,* where Victor and Alex had dined his first night in town. Coming from the northern New Mexican dining environment of Santa Fe, Natalie thought it would be interesting to explore a bit of classical Spanish food here in Europe, comparing the two.

After a ten-minute walk they arrived at the restaurant and were pleased to see it wasn't too crowded. The maître d́ was able to get them a nice corner table. This was a blessing, Victor thought, since the tables here were quite closely-spaced and things would almost certainly get crowded rather soon. Luckily, their corner table would serve nicely to facilitate saying all the things they had to tell each other without having to shout.

Natalie declined the waiter's wine offering, telling Victor, "I'm not sure how I'd feel after the long trip if I start drinking alcohol right now."

Instead she opted for a glass of sparkling water, leaving the midday wine to him. Victor didn't hesitate, asking for a glass of the house Rioja. They then decided to share an order of Tapas Frias, which was a selection of cold dishes, that included seafood and green and red pepper salads, along with serrano sausage, cured ham and Mediterranean prawns.

After the waiter left, Victor leaned over, clinking his glass with Natalie's in a toast.

"Tell me," he said, "how are things in Santa Fe? Tell me everything!"

"Well Victor, 'everything' is almost nothing, actually. I'm enjoying my life there, my job at the gallery is quite fulfilling, and the overall Santa Fe environment is a very positive change from the one I experienced in Dallas. I think that about covers it."

"Not quite," responded Victor. "You've covered the everyday realities. But what about the 'unrealities?' "

"What kind of unrealities do you have in mind?" she asked.

"The kind that revolve about social life and human interactions. What about those?"

"Oh, I see what you're getting at, Victor. Your 'unrealities' mean my personal and social interactions. Is that it?"

"Bingo!" said Victor. "What about them?"

"OK, it won't take long for me to cover that territory either. First of all, I wouldn't be here with you right now if I were buried in social commitments. As I told you, I'd be staying even longer if my boss at the gallery didn't need me for the holiday crunch of well-heeled, art-buying tourists that will be engulfing Santa Fe in a couple of weeks. I do occasionally meet one of my friends for a drink or even a meal. But I do not have an intimate social life if that's what you're getting at. At least not yet," she said with a wink and a sly smile.

Victor looked rather apologetic at her full disclosure reply and leaned over to hold her hand, trying to convince her that he didn't mean to pry (even though he meant to do *exactly* that).

"Please forgive my gauche behavior, Natalie. I guess I'm a bit out of practice in the interpersonal relations department. I apologize. What you do, when you do it, and with whom you do it is absolutely none of my business. Let's go back to your public life in Santa Fe, not the personal."

"Well, that's not so dramatic, either," she told him. "Mostly I live a typical working woman's life. I get up in the morning, go to work, come home, go shopping, clean my house, so on and so forth.

"Oh, yes, occasionally I might do something very daring like go up to Atalaya Mountain for a walk and a bit of fresh air and some scenery. And one last thing: I spend a lot of time thinking about you, me and us, a topic I hope we can explore in some detail during the coming week."

As the waiter arrived with their tapas, Victor smiled at her.

"Let's eat quickly," he said. "I want to get to that exploration phase as soon as possible."

As the last of the tapas disappeared, Victor asked Natalie if she had any special places she'd like to visit while she was here in London.

"Well, you know I'm now in the art gallery business," she said. "I heard London is one of the world's best places to see great art, both in the museums and in the galleries. So let's try to scratch that itch at least a time or two before we head south to sunny Italy."

"Done," said Victor, calling to the waiter for the check. "It's not too long a walk from here over to Trafalgar Square and the National Gallery. How about that as a starter?"

"Perfect!" Natalie said, getting up from her chair and putting on her coat. "Let's go."

Outside the restaurant, Victor and Natalie began walking toward Piccadilly, hand-in-hand, then turned up Piccadilly toward Piccadilly Circus. They were very comfortable together and Victor asked himself why he was jumping through hoops of fire with Alex when this wonderful woman wanted to be here with him?

He wondered if this time he would finally grow up and take responsibility for his actions, not just enjoy the pleasures that flowed from them?

On the way to the National Gallery, Natalie leaned over and nuzzled into Victor's ear.

"I want to tell you how exotic this seems to me, Victor," she whispered, "being on my way to the National Gallery in London, England. Really, this is a dream come true. I can't thank you enough for your generosity in bringing me over here and showing me around. I promise you, I won't forget it."

Music to Victor's ears—because this was a kind of dream come true for him too, having Natalie beside him in this city that was almost as foreign to him as to her. *Life is good,* he thought.

Within a few minutes, they were at the National Gallery. But before going in, Natalie wanted to look around a bit, get a photo of herself in front of the Nelson Monument in Trafalgar Square and, in short, behave just like a typical American tourist visiting London for the first time.

They got their entry tickets to the Gallery, which to their surprise turned out to be free, and went inside to have a look around. Natalie's eyes were instantly ablaze, as she'd never imagined seeing so many fantastic paintings in one place; from 15th century works by Botticelli and Dürer through 16th-century paintings by Leonardo da Vinci and Michaelangelo, to later artistic masterpieces by Goya, Canaletto, Cézanne and van Gogh.

Natalie told Victor it was so lucky they came on a Friday, as she would have hated to have to leave after just two hours of ogling these masterpieces. While Victor was not nearly such an 'art hound' as her, even his middle-brow interest in art was stirred by what he was seeing.

After more than three hours, they came staggering down the steep steps in front of the Gallery, holding each other to keep from falling and breaking their necks.

"Wow," she said. "That's some introduction to life in Europe. What are you going to show me for an encore, Mr. Safir?"

"I originally thought we would have gone back to my place by now and cleaned up a bit before dinner. I hadn't counted on the display of magnificence at the National Gallery, nor on the time we'd spend there. If you don't mind, let's go directly to dinner. I'm getting hungry. What about you?"

"I couldn't agree more, Victor. Where should we go?"

Victor thought about it for a moment, then had an idea.

"In your youth, did you ever read any of the Sherlock Holmes mystery stories?" he asked.

"Of course," said Natalie. "Who didn't? Why do you ask?"

"Just down the road a couple of blocks is the Sherlock Holmes Pub, which is filled with memorabilia of his adventures, not to mention some quite fine pub food including that English specialty, fish and chips. Besides, they make the perfect gin and tonic. And if you don't like it, they'll replace it for free. What do you say to that?"

"Lead on, maestro. Your hitting all the notes on this tour."

They went over to Northumberland Street and walked into the pub. Luckily, it was still fairly early for a Friday night, so they managed to get seats at the bar and told the bartender they'd both like one of the pub's famous G&Ts, along with a plate of fish and chips for two. While they waited for their drinks and meal, they looked around inside the pub and saw that one whole corner had been decorated just like Sherlock Holmes' sitting room at 221B Baker Street. There was the famous fireplace, Holmes' walking stick, and a replica of Holmes himself standing in his dressing gown with what looked like a bullet hole in his forehead!

"Oh, this is so much fun," Natalie said. "I'm so glad we came to this place instead of a stuffy old restaurant. What a good idea."

By the time they finished their dinners and had each finished off a pint of Abbott Ale to wash it all down, it was pushing 10 o'clock and Natalie was starting to show signs of her long journey. Victor suggested they take a cab back to his flat and get a bit of rest before hitting the streets tomorrow for another full day of playing American tourists abroad. Natalie agreed, thinking to herself that Victor always had the right plan. A little rest right now would go a long way tomorrow.

As the taxi pulled up in front of Victor's apartment building, it was already quite dark outside. Victor was somewhat surprised the driver even found the house number in the dim lighting.

Then he remembered that every London taxi driver has to complete a very extensive course called The Knowledge, which involves negotiating London traffic and finding obscure streets.

Maybe it wasn't so surprising after all that the driver deposited them directly in front of the house. Victor obviously didn't have 'the knowledge'—as he was barely able to see to get his key in the door.

When the couple finally managed to get into Victor's flat, he asked Natalie, "Would you like a nightcap before we retire?"

She thanked him for the offer but declined, saying, "I'm really exhausted and want to just pop into the bathroom right now and get changed for bed."

He nodded and told her he'd have that nightcap for her while she was washing up.

Natalie reappeared about ten minutes later, wearing a very appealing nightgown and slippers. Victor raised his eyebrows and his glass, inviting her to sit next to him on the sofa. When she did, he gave her a hug and said that while he'd like nothing better than to revive their personal connection from Santa Fe, she looked a bit too tired for that right now.

"I'm afraid you're right," she said, nodding her head. "There's nothing I'd like more than a bit of serious hugging and kissing. I hope you'll allow me to give you a raincheck on that until tomorrow morning. I don't think I can be the person you want and deserve right now."

"I understand," Victor told her. "When we reconnect, I want the whole Natalie, not just her shadow. Get some rest. I'll join you in a few minutes and we can at least snuggle a bit before we go to sleep."

*

Victor wasn't surprised to see Natalie deep in slumberland when he awoke around 7 o'clock the next morning. He thought he'd give her another couple of hours' sleep while he had a cup of coffee, read his emails, digested the morning news and, in general, puttered about in the living room while she slept.

To Victor's surprise, Natalie came out of the bedroom under her own steam just before he was going to call her. She came over to his desk, gave him a big hug and grabbed his arm saying, "Now back to bed, Victor. Come on. I need some attention."

As they got back into bed, Natalie took off her nightie while Victor shed his robe. They immediately shared a tender kiss and fell into each other's arms for a physical interaction of the type that only lovers can really experience. Neither of them left any part of the other unattended, as their hands, eyes, lips, tongues and even feet explored each other completely.

"I've been waiting for this moment for a couple of months now," said Victor. "It was sheer agony. My deepest thanks for taking the time to visit me here. Now let me kiss you a bit more and let my more animal nature have its turn."

"How can I resist?" Natalie replied."I certainly don't want to have any angry animals in bed with us. Let's take care of him right now."

With that, Natalie climbed on top of Victor, placing her own more animal aspect where it could caress and soothe his, and the two joined to take loving care of each other to their huge mutual satisfaction and delight. Finally, their animal natures were both sated. Victor and Natalie remained in bed a few minutes longer, stroking each other and wondering where they would be going together—both metaphorically in life and physically today in London.

Finally, Victor said, "We should get up and about since otherwise you won't see anything in London today except the ceiling of this bedroom."

They made their way out of bed, got washed and dressed and shortly before midday were ready to face the big city again.

The *Hard Rock Cafe* was only a couple of blocks away, and they thought this would be a good place to go for a quick lunch, American-style, on their way to at least a half-day of enjoying the sights and sounds of London.

They left Victor's flat and headed out to the sidewalk, unknowingly under the intense gaze of Alex at her perch, watching from across the street. She was obsessively registering Natalie, noting her actions toward Victor as they walked up the street and turned the corner.

At that point, Alex lost sight of them—but silently vowed to find out if Victor was really going to Trieste—or if Trieste was just a cover for a tryst. *That sounds like the kind of pun he'd make up,* she thought, feeling her anger build.

Victor and Natalie spent the rest of the day in a whirlwind of sights, restaurants, museums, shops, even the theatre, squeezing-in as much as possible before they'd leave for Venice the next afternoon.

For Alex, Saturday afternoon it was a time of morbid dwelling over what she had seen out the window of her hotel room Saturday morning. She now knew that the first part of Victor's story regarding his 'old colleague' who would be joining him here in London was total fiction.

She was increasingly gripped by a growing impatience for Monday to arrive, so she could check the second part of Victor's story about the Italian conference.

*

When she got back to her flat, Alex was even surprised with herself by how angry she was with Victor. She kept running over and over in her mind ways to check out the rest of his story about Italy, and she found it difficult to accept that there was nothing she could do about it until Monday.

She certainly didn't feel like sitting around her apartment all weekend. She went downstairs to see if her friend Maerta was home. Perhaps she could go out with her tonight and drink away her annoyance with Victor.

Fortunately, Maerta was there and invited her in for a cup of tea and a chat.

"I came down to see if you were up for a girl's evening on the town tonight," Alex told her.

Maerta's face broke into a big smile at Alex's suggestion. "I'd like nothing more." She mentioned a wine bar in Soho on Cranbourn Street, the *Cork & Bottle,* that she liked. They agreed to meet at 7 o'clock and go down to Maerta's Soho place first, have some wine and a bite to eat. Then they'd move on and see what the cosmos had in store for them in the side streets of Covent Garden, Leicester Square and other London alcoves afterwards.

Located in the heart of the West End, one would have expected the *Cork & Bottle* to be packed. In fact, it wasn't crowded at all. Maybe the location, hidden in a basement below a sex shop, had something to do with that. Whatever the reason, the serious drinking public hadn't seemed to have caught on to it yet. Alex wondered how Maerta knew about this place, but refrained from asking.

As could be expected from the name, the wine selection was extensive. Maerta said her favorite wine here was a chilled sparkling Shiraz. As Alex really didn't have the spirit for getting involved in a wine-tasting party tonight, she agreed with Maerta's choice and they took a table near the back of the room where the waiter brought their drinks.

"It's been awhile since we hit the bars, baby. How are things with you?" Maerta asked.

"Don't ask, Maerta. Events have really shaken me up recently."

"Do you mean events in the love department? Or just plain 'events'?"

"I mean *everything*," Alex responded.

"Oh, oh. Sounds like we're going to need another round immediately if 'everything' is going to be on the table—the prurient parts first, of course. How about your American friend, Victor? Anything cooking in that pot?"

Before Alex could reply, Maerta called the waiter over and asked for menus. She told Alex they had fantastic food at this place, and she was getting pretty hungry. They decided to take a short break to scan the menu and pick out something before Alex answered Maerta's question about Victor. After ordering duck liver pâté and a salmon burger for Alex, Maerta told the waiter she wanted something special. He finally talked her into an order of garlic butter snails to be followed by crab and prawn linguine. And, of course, another round of the lovely Shiraz to wash it all down.

"All right, Alex. Now back to Victor."

Alex then went into her ups, downs, and in-betweens with Victor since she and Maerta had last spoken. Her crescendo was the information from this morning that whatever Victor was doing this weekend, it was not with some mythical old friend from the United States, but very likely with some extremely attractive *new* friend of the female persuasion.

She closed that story by telling Maerta, "I have a call to make early next week to check out the rest of Victor's story. But right now I feel the odds are that his whole story is a myth, and that

Victor will not be going anywhere near that conference in Trieste next week. What do you think about this business, Maerta?"

Maerta said, "The situation doesn't sound good. But at the moment you have just a single piece of evidence, namely, you saw Victor this morning walking out of his flat with a lovely lady."

"Well, that's pretty strong evidence that Victor's so-called 'old colleague' is nowhere near London, isn't it?"

"I'm not so sure," replied Maerta. "What is totally unclear is who, exactly, *is* that lady? And what is her relationship to Victor? After all, she might well be just one of Victor's neighbors from his house."

"Yes, I also thought she might be a neighbor. But my instincts tell me that they were acting a bit too friendly for that. After all, Victor has only been in that flat for less than three months."

"Well, I think Victor is innocent until you can actually prove him guilty. And what you've told me up to now is very far away from a convincing proof. You simply need to get more information. Moreover, Victor's supposed colleague may, in fact, actually be in London. Maybe he decided to stay at a hotel, after all. Or maybe he skipped the stopover in London at the last moment and went directly to Italy. Who can say?"

"Yes, perhaps I'm being a bit too panicky about what I saw this morning. I'll wait until I get feedback from Trieste next week. Then the situation should be clear, or at least clearer."

But Alex was soon to realize that sometimes, more information doesn't always make things more clear.

As they completed their lovely meal, Alex told Maerta, "When we left our building to come here earlier this evening, I was so upset with Victor that I was even considering just picking up some dishy-looking guy at one of these clubs and taking him home for the night."

She went on, “I really needed some heavy-duty comforting after that shock this morning. But now I don’t really want to complicate my life that way. I am very thankful to you Maerta, for putting the whole business into perspective for me.”

“So no ‘toy boy’ for you this evening,” said Maerta. “You can just have a couple more drinks and a good night’s sleep. That should get your head back on track for the coming week.”

Maerta then nodded at Alex, thinking that she was indeed seeing things a bit more realistically now. But she feared what Alex might do if she got knockdown confirmation of Victor’s perfidy in that phone call to Italy. Alex was a pretty high-strung woman, Maerta knew, and a breach-of-trust of that magnitude could set her off in some dangerous directions. She asked Alex to please let her know as soon as she received more information. They could then meet to talk about what, if anything, she might want to do in that eventuality.

*

Monday arrived on schedule, gray skies and all. So did Alex, at least in the sense that she went through her usual rituals and managed to get to the office more-or-less on time. Her thoughts were totally focused on getting in touch with the International Centre for Theoretical Physics in Trieste to find out what she could about Victor and the conference.

First she had to get the information about that conference and, most importantly, the phone number of the Centre. Both were easy problems to solve via the Internet, especially in comparison with solving the overarching ‘Victor problem.’ By lunchtime she was ready to contact Trieste for details.

After lunch, Alex closed her office door and sat down to make the fateful call. The receptionist in Trieste spoke almost perfect

English and understood immediately what she wanted when she said she was Professor Safir's assistant and had an urgent message for him. She asked Alex to wait a moment while she transferred her call to the woman in charge of logistics for the conference.

"Hello, this is Abigail. May I help you?"

Alex was slightly taken aback by 'Abigail,' as she had unimaginatively supposed the person in charge at a meeting in Trieste would be Italian. But then she remembered that it was the *International* Centre for Theoretical Physics, so why not 'Abigail' instead of 'Lucia' or 'Giulia' or 'Giovanna?' Anyway, she posed her question:

"I am Professor Victor Safir's assistant, and I have an urgent message for him. Can you deliver it for me?"

"I'm sorry," said Abigail, "but Professor Safir's presentation is not until Thursday morning. And he is not yet in Trieste. He's scheduled to arrive sometime Wednesday afternoon."

Oh, oh, thought Alex. *So Victor's not a total fraud after all. There is a meeting in Trieste and he is making a presentation. A surprise, and not a very welcome one either, if it meant nailing down his infidelity more difficult. But what if it meant he wasn't unfaithful, at all?*

"Do you happen to have information about where he is staying in Trieste? I'm away from the office speaking to you from my cell phone, and don't have that info readily at hand. I think it was a place called the Savoy or something like that. Perhaps I can call his hotel and leave my message there?"

"Yes I do have his hotel. He asked us to book him at the Savoia Excelsior Palace Hotel, which is right at the waterfront in the center of the city. Wait a moment and I'll get the phone number for you."

A few moments later Abigail was back with the number. Alex wanted to ask if Victor's wife would be staying with him, but she thought this might raise questions in Abigail's mind that she didn't really want anyone else, especially Victor, to know about.

"Thanks very much for this information. Sorry to have bothered you," said Alex as she hung up. Now that she had the name and phone number of Victor's hotel, as well as his day of arrival, she could easily ring the hotel and get the information she wanted about the booking for the room.

Actually, she decided, she didn't really want to wait to get that information, so she called the hotel immediately, again saying she was Professor Safir's assistant and just wanted to confirm his reservation. The desk clerk told her the reservation was set: two nights for *two* people. She thanked him and hung up.

Well, now I'm more confused than ever, thought Alex. *I know there really is a meeting at the ICTP, and that Victor is making one of the presentations on Thursday. I also know that he's booked a hotel room for two people for Wednesday and Thursday nights. While I don't want to put two and two together and come up with five, I think it's pretty safe to say that that second person is not his 'old colleague' from the USA. Rather, the odds now overwhelmingly point to that friend being the attractive blonde lady I saw him with on Saturday. So his story is not total fiction, after all. But it's the worst kind of partial truth: half-fiction, half-truth. The problem is that for me the fiction half is dramatically more hurtful and serious than the half-truth.*

For the next few hours, Alex fretted over what to do next, turning over myriad possibilities, ranging from do nothing to going to Trieste to confront Victor directly about his behavior. In late afternoon, she recalled her conversation with Maerta when she asked Alex to please get in touch with her as soon as she got more clarity on the situation. *I certainly have more clarity now.*

She needed some kind of perspective on this clarity. Hopefully, Maerta could help. She grabbed the phone and called her. "My intuition has become a lot clearer," she said and expressed her wish to talk over her options. The two of them agreed to meet after work at 7 o'clock at their usual pub down the street.

At the appointed hour, Alex was already working on her second drink when Maerta stepped in the door.

"I see the situation has turned serious, baby. Let me get my drink and then you can tell old Maerta all about it."

As Maerta sat down at the table, drink in hand, Alex recounted her phone calls to the ICTP and to Victor's hotel in Trieste.

Alex said, "Victor's story to me is partly true. There is a meeting in Italy and he does have a presentation there on Thursday. That's the good news. The bad news, though, is very, very bad. He definitely felt he had to hide something from me."

"What was that?" asked Maerta.

"He has a hotel reservation for two people. Whoever that second person is, I'm ninety-nine percent sure it is not a man. I'm quite sure it's the blonde woman I saw him with on Saturday morning. She's not his mother either, that's for sure. I can't imagine who else it might be other than the lady I saw on Saturday."

Maerta took another sip of her beer, looking directly at Alex.

"While this new information is not conclusive," said Maerta, "it's a very strong indicator that indeed favors your scenario. I guess you'll just have to wait and confront Victor with these facts when he returns next week."

Maerta's plan didn't appeal to Alex, at all. She felt a burning inside her for more immediate action. This passive approach was not going to do it.

While Maerta prattled on about waiting for Victor's return to London, Alex was revisiting her earlier plan: go to Trieste and confront Ms. X directly. No waiting around here in London she thought, when the answers to all her questions were sitting in Trieste.

"Okay, Maerta, I agree that I have to see who this lady is with my own eyes. It seems to me that at that point I will have to confront Victor directly somehow and either end our relationship on the spot or get him to abandon this other woman. Yes or no, in or out. Those are the choices."

"Well, if you really want to break it off with Victor if you see that he's sleeping with this other woman, then this option is the path with heart. You confront him directly and end it or get him to end with *her*."

Alex was listening carefully to Maerta and hearing what was the rational approach. But an inner voice was telling her she needed to act otherwise.

An idea was already forming in her mind. What she had to do immediately was book a flight to Trieste for Wednesday and find a hotel there for herself very close to the one where Victor was staying. This was her immediate task.

"Okay Maerta, I think I see what I have to do. I really appreciate your wise counsel. Next time the drinks and meal are on me. For now, I want to thank you very much for hearing me out and giving me the benefit of your thoughts on this very stressful situation. See you soon."

With that, Alex headed back to her flat to prepare to go to Trieste.

*

Victor and Natalie checked in to their hotel in Venice, the *Danieli,* one of the finest in town. It was set right on the waterfront, only a five-minute walk from Piazza San Marco, the tourist center of this ultra-touristy town. Somewhere Victor had read that more than thirty million tourists come to Venice each year. Without a doubt, every single one of them visits San Marco.

Victor was an almost habitual visitor to Venice himself, having come here for the first time when he was an ICTP Fellow decades earlier. Since then he'd made it a habit to visit the city with every woman he was seeing, wives and mistresses alike. He strongly believed that there was simply no place like Venice for stirring up the feelings (and the juices) of an intimate, passionate, loving relationship.

After checking in to their room on Sunday afternoon, Victor and Natalie both took a glass of Aperolspritz and went out on the patio to plan their stay in this magical town. They had the better part of three days for holidaying here before they had to catch a train to Trieste on Wednesday afternoon.

Victor asked Natalie, "What do you know about Venice that are 'must see' attractions for us to visit?"

"Never having been here, every place seems magical. But I have heard about or seen in films the Doge's Palace, Harry's Bar, the Rialto Bridge, the Campanile San Marco, and the Bridge of Sighs. And, of course I want to go on a gondola ride, as well as see Venice from the Accademia Bridge. Is that too much?"

Victor laughed and said, "You don't realize what a small town Venice is, physically, as well as in population. What you outline might take a day or so, at most. Keep talking."

"Why don't you talk, Victor? You've been here before. What do you think I *should* see while we're here?"

Victor thought about her question for a couple of minutes.

"I think we should see some things not right here in the center of the town but outside. By that I mean one or two of the islands, like Murano or the beach area at the Lido. Those places are fascinating in their own way, as well as having the big advantage that they're not quite so filled with tourists. So let's write down our 'hit list.' We can start fulfilling it first thing in the morning with a short walk over to Cafe Florian on Piazza San Marco and having a cafe, Italiano-style. It's supposedly the oldest cafe in Europe."

"How old is it?" Natalie asked.

"It was opened in December 1720, so that means it's now nearly 300 years old. I guess in that time they should have learned something about how to make a decent cup of coffee or pour a tolerable glass of grappa," Victor replied.

The next two days were a kaleidoscopic mixture of all things Venetian, including some flooding in Piazza San Marco that forced them to walk across the piazza on wooden boardwalks placed on top of steel supports putting them about two feet above the water.

In Murano, they visited the famous Venetian glass works, where Natalie bought a lovely set of handmade wine glasses to take back to Santa Fe as a remembrance of this trip. When they got back to town, they stopped at Harry's Bar for one of their world-renowned Bellini cocktails.

They concluded with dinner that night at some hole-in-the-wall, family-owned place that Victor knew from previous visits. Natalie thought it was indescribably delicious and was happy to see that it was almost totally devoid of tourists.

Following lunch the next day, they basked in the sun at the Lido for a couple of hours. And so it went for two full days. Finally though, it was Wednesday, time to head to the Stazione Centrale for their midday train to Trieste.

*

In London, Alex was busy making plans for her own hit-and-run trip to Trieste. She fixed up a flight on Wednesday that would get her to her hotel by around 3 o'clock in the afternoon.

Luckily, she managed to get a room at the *My Way B&B*, which was on the very next street behind the Savoia Excelsior Palace, where Victor and his 'traveling partner' were booked.

She would have to figure out how she could keep an eye out for Victor and his lady. This might be tricky because she had no guarantee that the two of them would ever be separated. But she didn't think that was likely for a very good reason.

If Victor's companion in Trieste was indeed the woman she saw with him in London, Alex's hope and belief was that while Victor was doing his thing at the ICTP on Thursday, his lady friend would not be in attendance, but rather, be on her own in the city. In that case, to follow her would be quite easy, since the woman had never seen Alex before. Alex would simply be another tourist enjoying Trieste.

With luck, the lady would go someplace where Alex could confront her. She hadn't yet totally worked out what she would say, but it would have to be pretty direct and confrontational.

Alex wanted this woman to get flustered and have her convey to Victor a sense that somebody was threatening him indirectly through his lady friend. What she did not want was to have a crash-and-burn breakup of her own relationship with Victor—at least not yet. What was important was to have Victor feel under attack, covertly or otherwise.

*

On the short train ride to Trieste, Natalie told Victor that she had never even heard of Trieste before meeting him, and asked him to tell her a bit about this place.

"With pleasure," said Victor as he began his recital. "Trieste is an unexplored gem of a city that while formally in Italy, is not really Italian at all, despite it being the capital city of the Friuli

Venezia Giulia region of northeastern Italy. Its location as a port at the top of the Adriatic Sea, bordered by Slovenia, has made Trieste historically influenced by Austria, Hungary and Italy, and of course Slovenia—and even to a somewhat lesser degree Croatia."

"So how big is this town?" enquired Natalie.

"Trieste has a population of around two-hundred thousand and consists of a medieval old town in the center, where we'll be staying, bordered by a neoclassical Austrian quarter. That section emerged at the time Trieste was the main port of the Austro-Hungarian Empire, which lasted until the end of World War I."

"It sounds just lovely. I hope I can do a bit of exploring while you're busy at your meeting on Thursday," she said.

"That's an excellent idea, darling," replied Victor. "While the ICTP is itself interesting, it would be much better for you to experience the old town—and maybe even a few of its not-so-ancient shops. We're staying at the Savoia Excelsior Palace Hotel, which is right on the waterfront in the very center of town. You'll have lots of sights to see and shops to explore within easy walking distance while I'm doing my job at the ICTP. Besides, the ICTP is not even located in the city itself, but in Miramare. While that's a lovely area just north of the city, it's still pretty barren territory when it comes to walk-around touristing."

"Okay, Victor. While I really do want to see the ICTP—and you—in action, I think our time together here should be in the bed, not at the ICTP auditorium. I'm sure I can see you performing at the podium in many places. But I can't visit the sights of Trieste except in Trieste. And who knows when or if I'll ever be back here again. So I'll leave you to your business tomorrow while I stroll about."

*

By mid-afternoon, Alex was checked in to her hotel and ready to look around the neighborhood. Fortunately, it was a warm, sunny day, so she could put on sunglasses and a hat that did a moderately good job of hiding her face. She knew from her study of photos of Victor's hotel on the Internet, that there was a walking area across the street from the hotel entrance bordered by a parking lot for people going down to the beach. She left the hotel and walked along a side street that led to the waterfront.

With a bit of luck, she thought she might see Victor and his friend arrive, since when she called their hotel a few minutes before leaving her room the desk clerk said that Victor had not yet checked in.

It took just a few minutes to get to a spot across the street from the hotel, where she had a good view of cars and taxis coming and going from the hotel entrance. If Victor hadn't arrived during the time she'd spent walking over here, she felt there was an excellent chance that she would spot the couple when they came from the train station or the airport.

Not more than ten minutes after Alex's arrival, a small Fiat taxi pulled up and Victor came out one side, the lady from London came out the other. *One more uncertainty settled,* thought Alex.

Of course, the possibility still remained that that lady was Victor's neighbor. It didn't really matter. If she was a neighbor, she was a very intimate neighbor. *It's the intimacy that counts here, not her residency or nationality.*

With the first part of her plan now confirmed, Alex turned her attention to the second. How could she meet this lady? For this, Alex would need a bit more luck.

She would have to return to her viewing spot in the morning and hope that the woman was more interested in seeing the sights in the medieval center of Trieste than in seeing how Victor looked at the podium at the ICTP. She also knew from her background research in London that the ICTP was not in Trieste at all, but a bit outside the city. As a result, Alex felt quite confident that the blonde lady would much prefer sightseeing in town than sitting in a lecture room in Miramare.

Alex just had to be ready to follow her when she set out from the hotel the next morning.

For now, Alex could do nothing other than go back to her own hotel, buy some takeout for dinner—to minimize the chance of encountering Victor and the woman at a restaurant—and get some sleep for her early morning stakeout of Victor's hotel.

*

Thursday morning came up partly sunny, which was a relief to Alex, since she didn't want to have to be holding an umbrella while on the lookout for Victor. She knew his talk was scheduled for 10 o'clock and the receptionist at her hotel told her it took about half an hour to get to the ICTP by taxi from here. She was pretty sure Victor would leave his hotel no later than half past eight this morning.

Her plan was to begin waiting across from the hotel at around 8 o'clock, or even a bit earlier. Once she saw Victor leave, presumably without his friend, she would then move inside and take a seat in the lobby. She'd try to get a comfortable chair with a good view of the front exit, but unobtrusive enough not to attract attention from the desk clerk.

She'd then just have to wait until the lady left to begin her own day in town. That would probably be around 10 o'clock. But she was prepared to sit it out until noon if need be. Should the woman not appear by then, Alex would make a call to the room to see if perhaps she had gone out another exit. In that case, she would walk around town, visiting the main tourist sites, in the hope that she would run into her at one of them.

A few minutes after eight, Alex saw Victor alone asking the doorman for a taxi. *One less thing to worry about,* she thought, moving across the street and entering the hotel. The lobby was luxuriously large.

She quickly found the right chair with a view of the entrance and no view of her from the reception. Just perfect.

Shortly after she sat down, a waiter came by and asked if she'd like a drink or something to eat. She ordered a cappucino and a croissant, thinking she'd eat and drink very slowly to secure her position and not arouse any suspicions.

Luckily, the hotel lobby was fairly crowded with lots of people coming and going. As a result, Alex didn't attract any undue attention, other than an extended glance or a raised eyebrow from Italian lotharios looking her over as they passed through the lobby.

There was no sign of Victor's companion during the next hour or so, and Alex was starting to get a bit edgy. She thought she might have to ring Victor's room a little sooner than she'd earlier planned if the lady didn't put in an appearance soon. She'd give her until ten o'clock to come through the lobby, then call the room.

She could hardly wait to confront this woman and put some heavy pressure on her both physically and mentally, so that the woman would cry her eyes out in front of Victor. Hopefully, that would send the right signal to Victor that she was his boss in every area of life and he really should behave!

Alex's luck was in once more that day, as just before 10 o'clock she saw Victor's lady friend making her way through the lobby to the front door of the hotel.

Alex didn't want to lose her, so she quickly dropped some money on the table for her coffee and croissant and followed the lady out the door at a distance of about twenty yards or so.

The sidewalk was only moderately crowded, so unless the woman was expecting to be followed, there was no real reason for Alex to be concerned that she would be spotted. Besides, from the woman's perspective, Alex was simply another sightseer out for a morning stroll through the historical center of Trieste.

She first went to the Piazza Unita d'Italia, a huge public square next to the hotel. It was lined with many important buildings, each of which featured a stunning design and lovely architecture. The Piazza also had many statues and monuments at various points in the square, each offering a spot for Alex to partially conceal herself while observing her quarry.

The lady from London then walked half a block to the Canale Grande, a canal about 200 meters long that allows boats direct access from the Adriatic Sea to the city. The Canale is crossed by three bridges and along the three sides of the Canale there are many restaurants and shops.

From there, she started inland to some of the nearby side streets. As they walked, Alex thought it was amusing, or even providential, that their path took them directly past her own hotel.

At the end of that block, the London lady turned and walked left past a motorcycle shop. Right next door to that shop was a ladies' boutique that caught the woman's attention. As she stoppped to window shop, Alex kept walking, closing the distance between them. Then the lady decided to go in and look around, and stepped inside.

Alex felt this would be as good an opportunity as she would get to corner her and start a conversation—and a confrontation.

The shop was not very crowded, so there was plenty of room for Natalie to browse, picking up one dress after another, feeling different blouses and the like.

She went into one corner of the shop, which left her alone to look at the clothes on offer. At that point, an attractive woman came up to her.

"Nice clothes, don't you think?" Alex said.

Natalie looked over at Alex and didn't seem especially surprised by this comment.

"Yes, I like the style of the clothes here," Natalie replied in a friendly tone. "Italy definitely has the best shops I've seen. And this is only Trieste. It makes one wonder how marvelous the offerings must be at stores in Rome or Milan."

Natalie picked a dress off the rack and held it up to her as she looked in the mirror. Alex's face froze into a kind of vacant stare, focused on Natalie.

Suddenly Alex rushed over to Natalie, trying to grab the dress.

"That's my dress!" Alex screamed. "What do you think you're doing taking that dress?"

Natalie was shocked and didn't know how to react. Her instinct was to hold onto the dress while Alex continued trying to pull it away from her.

For a moment, Alex's grip loosened, leaving Natalie off-balance and she fell against a table displaying sexy ladies underwear and fancy bras.

Then Alex grabbed Natalie, scratching her on the side of her neck.

"You should pay very careful attention to the people you meet," Alex shouted.

With one foot already twisted, Natalie fell down onto the floor and as she did, she lost her grip on the dress. Alex took it and walked back across the room.

"What the hell do you think you're doing, lady?" Natalie yelled at her. "Are you crazy?"

"Not nearly as crazy as you, trying to steal my property," Alex replied. "You're going to regret you ever met me."

"I already regret having met you and am going to report you to the store manager right now," said Natalie, getting back to her feet and seeing the manager making her way back to the room to see what the ruckus was all about.

At that moment, Alex dropped the dress, spun and headed back in Natalie's direction, pushing her again down onto the floor.

Alex spun once more, bolting for the front door, and running outside into the street. She quickly headed back in the direction toward her hotel. She looked back over her shoulder to see if the lady or the manager were following her but saw no sign of anyone.

Her anger now vented on Victor's secret, Alex smiled inwardly, suddently feeling her mission in Trieste was now accomplished. No point hanging around any longer.

She would go back to her hotel right now and check with the airlines to see if she could get a return flight to London today instead of taking the one she was booked on tomorrow.

A few short minutes later, she listened unhappily as the airline told her they could accommodate her only on the flight she'd already booked for the next morning.

This left her with an entire afternoon and evening in Trieste. She didn't want to have an accidental encounter with Victor or *her,* so she decided to stay in the hotel room, read a book that she'd brought along for the flight. Later, she'd call in some takeout food again for her dinner.

In the morning, she'd grab a taxi to the airport and be back in London by lunchtime. After that, all she had to do was wait for Victor's return on Monday and do her best to be cool in the meantime.

*

Natalie was completely shaken as she walked back to her hotel. She was first angry at the woman's tirade in the shop. But the more she went over it in her mind, the more confused and frightened she became.

Why would that woman attack her like that? What did she mean about 'stealing her property?' Natalie knew the dress belonged to the store. She had just been looking at it when that crazy woman grabbed it from her. She just couldn't understand it.

By the time Natalie got back to the hotel, she was really stressed out by the behavior of the disturbed whacko. She couldn't just chalk it up to bad luck to have encountered such a crazed woman. There must be more to it than that.

Victor returned to the hotel just before 6 o'clock, entering the room with a big smile on his face when he saw Natalie sitting on the sofa. He came over and gave her a big hug and a kiss, apologizing for being so late. He then saw the scratch on her neck.

"What happened, Natalie? Why do you have that scratch on your neck?"

"I have to tell you about a *very* strange thing that happened to me this morning in a ladies boutique I was browsing in. As I took a dress off the rack to have a closer look, some crazy woman rushed over to me and tried to grab it out of my hand. I slipped down onto the floor, holding on to the dress, as the woman shouted, 'That's my dress. You have no right to it, or words to that effect. She tried to scratch my eyes, but got my neck instead, while accusing me of 'stealing her property.' Then she took the dress and started walking away."

"Oh my God. What happened then? Did she try to buy it?" asked Victor.

"As I was just getting back onto my feet, she spun around and pushed me back down again, then dropped the dress and rushed out of the shop. This was very scary. I thought the woman was right on the edge of seriously injuring me."

"Are you alright? Have you seen a doctor? Where else are you hurt?" asked Victor, machine-gun style.

"I'm okay, Victor, thank God. My butt hurts a little, that's all." Then she smiled and looked at him. "That might be a little bit your fault."

Victor smiled back. "Sense of humor intact, anyway. Glad for that."

Victor then asked Natalie about the woman."Was this crazy woman an Italian or a foreigner?"

"I guess she was a foreigner, since she spoke to me in English—with a British accent." *Oh, oh,* thought Victor, his vague suspicions growing stronger by the moment. "What did she look like?" he asked.

"Well, she was a bit taller than average, with long brown hair and green eyes. Quite attractive, I would say, at least physically. But why do you ask? Could this be someone you know?"

As Natalie had described the incident, stronger suspicions had begun forming in the back of Victor's mind. But he was afraid to share them.

"Of course not, darling. I'm just curious. You know us scientists. Always curious about everything."

"Well, you know what they say about curiosity, Victor. So I'm glad you're not a cat."

Victor couldn't help but suspect that the woman who attacked Natalie was Alex. He had told her he would be in Trieste, and she could have followed them there so she could check up on him. If true, this gave an entirely new dimension to her psyche that Victor would have to deal with when he got back to London next week.

But of course, it couldn't be. If it was, they were being stalked. They would both be in danger. He'd be morally obliged to share his suspicions with Natalie. They'd have to hole up. No, thought, Victor, his suspicions were really unfounded.

"I'm very glad to see that you were not badly harmed in any way other than that small scratch and a moment's fright. In a ladies' boutique, of all places," Victor said.

"We should forget about this strange incident and try to enjoy the next couple of days," Natalie replied, "and be happy we had the chance to meet at all, given our respective work schedules."

Victor smiled his agreement, suggesting they begin by going down to the hotel bar for a pre-dinner apertif. They could consult the concierge afterwards for a recommendation for a charming restaurant nearby for dinner, preferably one with romantic Italian music to complement the food.

After dinner, a short walk around the harbor and then a return to the room for a bit of rest and recreation, in the opposite order, would then serve well to fill out the night in preparation for their trip back to Venice the next morning.

Natalie could hardly disagree with any part of this plan. They left the room to begin implementing it.

*

On the train back to Venice the next day, Natalie and Victor smiled at each other, held hands, joked about their experiences on this trip and, in general, behaved like two teenagers in love.

At one point, Natalie expressed her unhappiness at their having to part again tomorrow, asking Victor how much longer he had to stay in London to finish his project at Merit.

"It will probably take about three months more," he told her. "Perhaps we can have another European sojourn once the busy season in Santa Fe ends."

"I'll do my best to free up the time. But I still wish you could be in Santa Fe sooner."

As the train neared Venice, Victor was thinking about how he might finish off the Merit project somewhat earlier than planned and return to Santa Fe—away from Alex and close to Natalie. His colleagues at the Institute in Santa Fe were already using video technology allowing them to have face-to-face meetings with their collaborators almost anywhere in the world.

Maybe he could use that same technology as well, perhaps supplemented with emails and voice calls, to continue his work with Merit by 'remote control.'

He was really falling in love with Natalie, and he also didn't want to be separated from her for several more months, especially at this critical juncture in their relationship. He'd have to explore long-distance work possibilities when he got back to London.

He didn't see any insurmountable barrier to implementing such a plan.

Their parting, at the Marco Polo International Airport in Venice, from where Natalie was returning to the United States and Victor to London, left each of them with a small cloud hanging over their thoughts, however. For Natalie, she still wondered a bit about the discomforting encounter with that strange woman at the boutique in Trieste.

Victor was also wondering about that 'strange woman,' even though he'd convinced himself, conveniently, it could not have been Alex in Trieste. But still, he couldn't help but wonder.

No matter. He was falling in love with another woman. He needed to find a way to get disentangled personally and emotionally from Alex, hopefully without destroying his connection with Merit in the process.

As Victor and Natalie kissed goodbye in the airport, however, neither of them were especially concerned about their respective clouds.

Episode XIII

The Departure

London

When Victor returned to Merit on Monday morning, he passed by Alex's office and saw her look up at him through the doorway. Instead of giving him a bright smile and a word of welcome, she immediately looked back down at her keyboard and continued whatever she'd been doing,

Interesting, he thought.

Maybe she really was stalking him, and was in fact the woman who attacked Natalie in Trieste. He'd have to let the day unfold and get a better feel for where she was at.

On his desk, Victor found a note from Alex saying she'd scheduled a team meeting at 10 o'clock this morning in his office. He found this a bit odd, because on previous mornings she had always simply told him about these meetings when he passed by her office. Was this a sign of distance between them, further supporting his feeling that she really had been in Italy? Could she really have been the woman who attacked Natalie?

At the 10 o'clock meeting, Alex was uncustomarily a minute late, avoiding eye contact with Victor as she entered his office. Bill and Bob were already seated, and all three were scheduled to give the usual brief summary of their past week's work on the simulator. Victor was particularly interested in hearing Alex's report; if she was indeed the woman in Trieste, she would not have had much time to work on the project.

The 'boys' reported about the work they had done on expanding the overall size and capabilities of the simulator, while Alex said she'd been pretty busy with meetings at Merit and other sorts of admin items. With a *pro forma* apology, she said work on the simulator had been forced to take a backseat on her priority list last week.

Ah, thought Victor. *One more bit of evidence supporting the hypothesis that Alex had been shadowing him and Natalie in Trieste. And why just in Trieste? Possibly she had somehow been keeping them under surveillance before they left London, as well. Why not?*

"I'm afraid I won't be able to join you all for lunch today," Alex said to the group, referring to their ususal Monday meal together, "as I have another engagement outside the company. I wish you all a pleasant and productive meal." She then left Victor's office, underscoring her seeming wish to distance herself from Victor.

This pattern of interaction between Victor and Alex persisted for the next couple of days: distant, but formal, contact on Alex's part when necessary for work, puzzlement and growing suspicion on Victor's side.

At first, this distance suited Victor fine. He was, after all, falling in love with another woman. But he knew it was still important for his position at Merit not to alienate Alex—at least not until he could further develop the simulator project. The project and the generous consulting fee he was receiving were important to his professional and financial integrity, especially given the rather strident messages he'd been receiving lately from Karin's attorney regarding the need to finalize the terms of the divorce. Mulling these factors over for a few days, he finally concluded that his estrangement from Alex was jeopardizing the work on the simulator. He needed to make a serious effort to normalize relations with her.

On Friday morning, Victor saw Alex at the coffee room on their floor. She was alone, so he decided to broach the subject.

"Good morning, Alex," he said. "I'm glad we ran into each other here today. I'd like to talk with you about what I see as a tension or stress that has arisen between us."

"What kind of 'stress' are you referring to, Victor?"

"The kind that you've been creating between us ever since I returned to London from Italy. You've been cold as an iceberg in Greenland toward me whenever we have to meet, and you've gone out of your way to avoid me when we don't."

"I'm afraid I'm not following you, Victor."

"Given the closeness we had prior to my departure," he said, "I can't help but think something has changed. I'd like to get it out into the open and find out what's bothering you. That's the kind of distance I'm referring to."

Alex was silent for a few moments, then looked straight at him.

"Yes, Victor. I had time last week to seriously think about our relationship, where it stands, where it might go and what we should do to bring it to a place where we both would like it to be. I agree we should sit down and have a civilized discussion of all these matters."

"That sounds fine Alex," Victor replied. "How about meeting for a drink and a meal on Saturday? I'm open to whatever, wherever and whenever would suit you."

"Let me look at my calendar, and I'll get back to you later today with a proposal about when and where to meet."

On that business-like note, they went in opposite directions from the coffee room to their offices to ponder just what the other might have to say when they did finally meet.

Near the end of the day, Alex sent Victor an email suggesting they meet Saturday evening at 7 o'clock at the oddly named *Dinner at Heston Blumenthal,* one of the poshest restaurants in town. It was located within walking distance of both Alex's flat and his own. He wrote back saying he approved very much of her choice and was looking forward to their meal and discussion.

Victor spent that evening pondering what he'd say to Alex when they met in order to get the conversation to turn in the direction he wanted it to go. Truth be told, if Victor could script the ideal scenario it would involve the two of them agreeing to break off their intimate relationship and just be mutually supportive, friendly work colleagues, sharing the goal of completing the simulator project.

That was definitely the path with heart as far as he was concerned. He wanted to gracefully end this intimate relationship with Alex, while at the same time retaining the goodwill and respect of both her and the executives at Merit.

But the path of Alex's heart had a very different trajectory.

*

If nothing else, Victor was pleased with Alex's choice of venue for tonight's meal. He'd wanted to go to Heston Blumenthal's restaurant ever since he'd been in London. But the occasion had never quite come up where it seemed the 'right' place. Tonight was that occasion.

The restaurant had begun in the late '90s, emerging from Blumenthal's fascination with historic gastronomy. He had researched ancient cookbooks from the 14th century to the fantasies of Lewis Carroll in the dishes portrayed in *Alice in Wonderland.* Out of these explorations, the restaurant *Dinner at Heston Blumenthal* had been conceived.

Victor thought he might or might not come away from the restaurant with the deal he wanted from Alex. Without a doubt, though, he would certainly come away with a fantastic meal in his stomach—and an even more 'fantastic' charge on his American Express bill next month! *Ah, well, nothing for nothing in life.*

The maître d́ showed Victor to the perfect table on the side of the dining room by the window. Just right for a great meal and a private conversation. Alex was already sitting there, looking quite devastating in a long, dark blue dress that highlighted her even darker long brown hair.

"Hope I'm not late," said Victor. "Can't really blame it on the traffic, can I, when it's only a few hundred meters from my flat?"

"At most you're only fashionably late, Victor. Very nice to see you again," she answered with a smile and a comforting air kiss as he greeted her and sat down.

"You really picked the perfect place for us to meet. I've been wanting to come here for ages. But I heard reservations are harder to come by than tax deductions. Congratulations—for both of us."

"Well, Victor, I wish I could say it was me," Alex replied. "However, Merit has a lot more clout with Mr. Blumenthal than Ms. Lynne. So here we are. And let me say upfront that the tab is on Merit. A business dinner, you might say."

So, thought Victor, *for the first time I do see 'something for nothing.' Can't complain about that!*

"You look stunning, Alex. Even better than when I saw you for the first time in Tortola. You seem to have discovered the fountain of youth," Victor said, hoping to set a comfortable atmosphere for the meeting.

"You're not looking too bad yourself," replied Alex, giving him an approving look that she held half a second longer than mere formality would require. "I like that dark suit. I don't think I've ever seen you in it before."

"Yes, it's not the type of dress that we academics gravitate toward. We're more the khaki pants, crumpled sports jacket and trainers-types, I'm afraid."

They looked at each other for a moment. Their micro spell was broken when the waiter arrived with menus and asked for their drinks order. Victor chose his favorite G&T, while Alex asked for the waiter's recommendation for a very dry white wine. They then opened their menus and set sail.

"Oh my," exclaimed Victor. "This menu is spectacular. Almost every dish from the starters to the desserts is from the 17th to 19th centuries. And what a choice."

Alex made a few complimentary noises of her own as well, as they made their choices.

"I'll take the Buttered Crab Loaf to start, followed by Spiced Squab Pigeon as a main," Alex said to the waiter.

Victor followed with his selection: "Please bring me an Earl Grey Tea Cured Salmon to start, with a main of Roast Iberico Pork Chops. Perhaps you can advise us on a suitable wine for the occasion?"

All the formalities taken care of, the two could now get down to the not-so-small talk. Victor had a proposal for this, which he stated to Alex:

"You know, I'm really looking forward to this meal and don't want to be distracted from it by discussion of you, me and us. Would it be all right with you if we deferred that conversation until after the meal? Maybe when we're having our cheese and after-dinner drink? For now, how about we just talk about work, life in London or whatever doesn't directly concern our intimate, personal affairs?"

"That's fine, Victor. There's plenty of time for such matters later. Right now, the priority is the meal, not you and me. Let's drink to that."

A few moments later the waiter arrived with their starters and the 'eat-'til-you-drop' session was on.

After nearly two hours of dining, drinking and talking about this, that and nothing in particular, Victor and Alex were finally ready to order their coffee and cognac to finish the meal. As Victor asked for the drinks menu again, Alex leaned across the table and took his hand.

"Now let's talk about us, Victor. As the hostess tonight, let me offer you the floor."

"Thanks, Alex. I'll begin with a return to what I said in the office on Friday. Since I came back from Italy, my impression is that you are in some way disappointed and/or angry with me. I'd like to know why."

Alex stared off into space for a moment or two, somewhere above Victor's head, as she composed her thoughts. Finally, she came back down to earth.

"Yes, Victor. During your absence I had time to reflect upon how our relationship has developed and consider more deeply what, exactly, I want. Up to now, we have enjoyed some very good chemistry together, especially in bed. But a meaningful relationship is more than just good sex. What I really want is some indication of commitment on your part, a commitment that goes beyond just visiting me here in London every now and then."

This was not at all the kind of statement Victor was hoping or even expecting to hear from her. So he had to pause briefly before addressing her concerns. He took a sip of cognac.

"Is treating me as if I were invisible a way of showing me you want a commitment? Do you think that type of behavior makes me eager to be with you in a deeper, more meaningful way? Suppose the situation were reversed and I basically shut you out of my daily life. Do you think you would then be more motivated to make a deeper commitment to me?"

"I see your point, Victor. Perhaps I was too fearful that you only wanted me as a 'sex toy,' and so I put up my defenses against that instead of doing what I could to get closer to you. You have my apologies."

Victor was being given exactly what he wanted: an out. All he had to say was that he wasn't ready at this moment for a serious commitment, and that he hoped they could be friends. But he was also thinking that he had to stay on the right side of Alex for the sake of the simulator project.

The team was small, she was officially its head, and he could not afford to lose this opportunity—and financial support—by alienating her.

Besides, he admitted to himself, *if I'm being perfectly honest, I'm still in the aftermath of the divorce from Karin. Moreover, Alex is so unstable and perhaps even potentially violent that I could never take her seriously as a day-to-day, live-together partner.*

The dishes had been cleared, they had finished their drinks and the waiter was eyeing them for a sign they wanted him to bring the bill. Alex signaled to the waiter for the check.

"Victor, I think we need to go back to my flat to discuss this matter of commitment," she said. "I'm sure you're wondering what kind of commitment I'm looking for, and to be truthful I'm a bit confused about that myself. Let's get out of here, have a bit of a walk and some fresh air, and then resume the conversation. As my place is rather closer than yours, let's go there. Okay?"

"Good idea, Alex. I need a spot of fresh air myself. Let's get our coats and get over to your place where we can have some privacy to continue this discussion."

Given her previous threats of violence, Victor had serious trepidations about going back to her flat again. But like the moth drawn to the flame, his ego and curiosity simply could not resist. Great *This lady is a problem that I know is solvable,* he told himself. *I just cannot give up. As Nietzsche said, 'That which does not kill me makes me strong.'*

"Yes," he said, "let's see if we can't come to some understanding of where we stand and where we're going in our relationship."

Despite her seeming friendliness at dinner and readiness to talk about their relationship, Victor was still suspicious about Alex and needed to get his head around all the factors at play right now.

"I'm very happy to have you back here in London, Victor," said Alex. "We're going to have a good time together working on our project. You'll see. Let's now have a discussion of commitments, and other personal items that seem to be of concern to both of us, and see if we can't find some common ground."

*

While Victor was taking off his jacket and making himself comfortable on the sofa, Alex went into the kitchen to fix drinks.

She had told him when they were walking over that she had a very special, Santa Fe-style, drink in mind and would bring it shortly. In the kitchen, Alex took out a bottle of tequila, some lime juice and Triple Sec. Filling a cocktail shaker with these ingredients, she shook them together and poured the result into salt-rimmed cocktail glasses containing a bit of crushed ice.

Then as a special treat for Victor, she sprinkled half a teaspoon of white powder into his glass and stirred it well. That powder was the recreational drug GHB, which at the dose Alex used would soon make Victor very sleepy, especially combined with the alcohol already in the glass and in his system.

"Here you are, Victor," Alex said, coming out of the kitchen, carrying the two drinks. "A nice Margarita to remind you of Santa Fe days. Drink up as I have enough in the kitchen for a refill if you like it."

Victor was touched by her thoughtfulness in preparing one of his favorite New Mexico drinks and smiled warmly at her as he took a big sip.

"Oh Alex, this tastes very good—although a little on the salty side," he commented. "But perhaps that's only a bit of extra salt on the rim of the glass. Or maybe it's just a new recipe, 'Margarita, Alex-style,' " he joked. He then took another big swallow of the 'special' drink and snuggled over a bit closer to her on the sofa.

"How are you feeling now, Victor?" Alex asked. "Are you getting nice and relaxed for our heart-to-heart chat? I really want us to come to a deep understanding of how we feel about each other. We've known one another long enough now that we can be totally honest and see what kind of commitments we might make to each other."

By now Victor was starting to feel a bit woozy.

"Between the trip last week to Italy, the catching up we had to do at Merit this week, along with the humongous meal we just had at Blumenthal's, not to mention the wine, I guess my system is starting to rebel a bit," he said. "Maybe I should go home and postpone this talk till tomorrow. I hate to do that though, so perhaps it would be enough if I were to just lay back and rest briefly and then we can begin. Okay?"

"That's a good idea, Victor. Why don't you go into the bedroom. I'll help you take off your clothes and get ready for a bit of rest before the action really begins. I have some new wrinkles to show you tonight. Just crawl into the sheets. That's where you're going to end up anyway."

Alex then got up from the sofa, put Victor's empty glass onto the table and took his hands into hers and led him into the bedroom. By that time Victor was very wobbly on his feet, and even needed a bit of help from Alex to get his pants, shoes and socks off, along with his underwear. *What's happened to me?* he wondered. *I feel like I've been drugged!* Collapsing into the bed, he mumbled to her, "Did that margarita have something special in it, Alex?"

"It's just your long trip to Italy catching up with you, Victor," Alex said. "The margarita may have been a bit stronger than you're accustomed to in Santa Fe. Like you said, 'Margarita Alex-style.' "

"Wake me in an hour, okay? I don't want to sleep the evening away and miss all the fun."

Alex looked down at him as he slipped into a slumber. She said softly, "Don't worry, Victor. I definitely will not let you miss the fun. You can just get a little head start in the bed before I begin our festivities."

With that, Alex gently stroked Victor's limp cock, gave him a lover's kiss and left the room to refill her own drink and review her plan for Victor's interrogation. Alex even had a nap herself on the sofa and it was a couple of hours later before she returned to the bedroom, carrying an armful of padded handcuffs and other paraphernalia for what looked to be a serious S&M session.

*

Victor was still in a deep slumber, laying on his back, snoring like a buzz saw. Alex carefully climbed onto the bed and began fastening his hands to the rod at the top of the headboard by means of the smaller pair of padded cuffs. She did the same to his feet, wrapping them in somewhat larger cuffs and fastening them around the bottom part of the bed frame. For the moment, she left his mouth untouched. She wanted him to be able to speak.

She then brought out a shock collar of the sort used to train dogs. Alex wrapped that collar around Victor's upper thigh, making sure the shocking plate touched his genitals. She then firmly attached the collar to Victor's thigh using a few strips of sports tape to secure it.

The fastening completed, Alex retreated to the living room to await Victor's return to the land of the living. Meanwhile, she dug into the back of her cupboard for a couple of pieces of equipment she would need to get Victor into the 'right' frame of mind. This involved disrobing and putting on a sheer, black negligee. She then completed her dominatrix costume with a pair of stiletto high heels matching the color of the negligee.

As she finished her drink in the living room, Alex heard signs of life from the bedroom.

"What the fuck!" shouted Victor as he began shaking the bed frame.

Time to go to work, Alex thought, getting up from the sofa and rejoining Victor.

As Alex walked into the bedroom, she was greeted by an outburst from Victor: "What the hell do you think you're doing, Alex? Why'd you drug me with that Margarita and tie me up like this? I told you last time I was here that I didn't want to play this game again. Untie me right now!"

Alex slowly walked over to the bed and reached beneath it and brought out a small whip of the type jockeys use at the horse races. She stood next to Victor and gently moved the tip of the whip down from his chest to his genitals and back again.

"Don't make me have to use this whip or the electronics attached to your groin to educate you, Victor. I'll release you when the time is right. That will not be until you see your situation realistically. Over the next minutes, maybe even hours, I'm going to teach you lessons that you should have learned earlier but seem not to have yet come to terms with. Think of me as your teacher, and I will regard you as a promising, but rebellious, student who needs disciplining. Then we'll get along fine and the whip and my other educational tools can remain simply as threats to the wise."

Jesus, thought Victor. *From the look of things, this 'conversation' could get very unpleasant and very painful very quickly. I'd better put on my Nice Guy look and personality if I want to get out of here under my own power. What a fool I was to come to her apartment. Idiot!*

"What do you have to tell me," Alex? "What's on your mind that is so dramatic and serious that you had to tie me up like this and set up an extreme interrogation to communicate it to me?"

Alex came over, knelt on the bed, and looked him directly in the eye.

"It's not what I have to tell you. It's what *you* have to tell me. And the first thing you need to understand is that I *control* you, Victor," she said with a borderline insane giggle, enjoying the idea immensely.

"In the future, you must do exactly as I tell you," Alex said. "I already have that power at work. Now I'm assuming it in our personal life, as well. Think of yourself as my pet, a dog, for example. And just like a good pet, you must obey your mistress. Usually that requires some training. And that's what we're going to be doing in this little *tête-a-tête* starting right now. And here's your first lesson in obedience."

Have I fallen into some kind of fantasy world? thought Victor. *What the hell is this lady talking about? Her controlling me? My training in obedience? Has Alex lost her mind? Well, whatever's going on here, it's dangerous. So I'll have to play along with her until I can somehow extricate myself from this bondage and get away from this place.*

"What's this first lesson, Alex?"

"The first lesson is a payback for your disrespecting me, Victor." With that, Alex pushed the button on the shock collar control to give Victor a slightly unpleasant tingle in his lower region. It was enough to cause him to temporarily jerk his hips up off the bed and let out a short expletive of shock and pain.

"That was at the low end of the intensity level, Victor. There's a lot more where that came from if you don't learn well over the next couple of lessons."

"I don't know what you mean by my 'disrespecting' you. I cannot recall any incidents of that sort. But I'm sure you'll tell me, so please let's get on with it."

"I'm still not sure you're in the right frame of mind for this 'conversation,' Victor. But I'll give you the benefit of the doubt for now and tell you directly what I mean. I mean running around with other women while you're claiming to be in a relationship with me. That's what I mean."

Victor's inner self warned him to watch out, as he suspected since Trieste that Alex knew about his time last week with Natalie.

"Perhaps you could be a bit more forthcoming about what you're talking about in regard to my 'running around with other women,' Alex?"

Alex moved closer to the edge of the bed and looked down at Victor with eyes as cold as a wintry blast of Siberian air.

"You still don't seem to want to own up to your actions, Victor. Let me turn up the shock level just a bit and give you something to jolt your memory and lead you to face up to your transgressions."

She put the collar controls in a position so that Victor could see clearly her actions and pushed the button. This time Victor let out a scream as he bucked up from the bed and pulled at the cuffs holding his hands. Finally, Alex released the button and he flopped back down onto the mattress. Breathing heavily, with pain in his eyes, Victor looked at her.

"I guess you're referring to the lady who was visiting me recently from Santa Fe. Is that right?"

"Now you're getting into the spirit of things, Victor. Please tell me about her."

"She's a friend, Alex. And I don't mean an intimate girlfriend. Simply a woman I knew in Santa Fe who was coming to Europe and asked if we might meet. I said yes and she came to London and I showed her around."

"Well, Victor, it seems that your collar and I will have to squeeze every bit of information from you, shock-by-shock, since you still don't appear ready to tell me the whole story voluntarily."

"What do you mean, the 'whole story'? I've told you everything!" he shouted.

"No, Victor, you have *not* told me everything. If what you said were really the whole story, I wonder why you didn't introduce me to this woman. If your contact was purely platonic, you would have had no hesitation in showing me off to her. But you didn't do that, at all. Instead you made up a cock-and-bull story about having a meeting in Italy, along with a mythical colleague from the U.S. who would be coming to London to join you and then travel with you to Trieste. I think you need a bit more electrical energy to jog your memory about this matter."

Alex turned the power intensity dial up another notch and pushed the button again. This time Victor nearly flew off the bed, and would certainly have done so if his hands and feet had not been secured. In any case, the whole bed starting shaking with his convulsions before Alex released the button.

"Did that sharpen your memory, Victor? For your sake I hope it did. Why don't you now give me the real story of last week, not your fantasy version?"

Victor finally had to admit defeat and concede that he would have to come clean with Alex and tell her everything about Natalie. Clearly, Alex had been shadowing Natalie and him since Natalie's arrival in London. And she'd even followed them to Italy. It dawned on him now that Alex was more than a deranged, overly needy girl-like woman.

He had gotten himself too involved with her. Now he was tied up on a bed by a crazy woman who could easily become a much more dangerous threat.

He suddenly thought of Alex's boss, Jerome, found dead in a bed in Paris just two weeks earlier. *How was he going to get himself out of here? Stay calm. Think this through.*

Alex knew that Natalie was more than just a 'casual' friend from Santa Fe. If he were ever to get free from this torture chamber of a bed, the real story between Victor and Natalie would have to come out—but with Victor's true feelings for Natalie concealed as much as possible. Perhaps then Alex would be satisfied and release him.

"Yes, Alex, I met Natalie a few months ago in Santa Fe. She is a recent divorcee, who relocated there from Dallas. We had a good feeling about each other. But I have equally good feelings about you. I've been trying to decide how to resolve these conflicting emotions. Clearly, I'm not very good at juggling this kind of thing. Now you've made it clear how I should proceed. I apologize to you for not telling you honestly about this situation with Natalie. It had not yet moved to the stage where I thought I could do that without hurting you. Anyway, that's how the situation stands."

Victor hoped this would warm Alex up a bit. He couldn't gauge how she was reacting because she had gone into the living room following his confession. Finally, she returned.

"Your story is just what I thought, Victor. I'm pleased you finally told it to me. What I'm not pleased about is the way I had to squeeze it out of you, like a dentist pulling a bad tooth. And make no mistake, your relationship with Natalie is exactly like that bad tooth. You've paid the price for it in pain and suffering tonight. And I'm sure you'll remember this evening in the event you're tempted to think about leaving me anytime in the future. I repeat what I told you earlier. You belong to me. I control you! Don't ever forget that."

"I understand, Alex. I made a mistake and had to pay for it. You've shown me what I should have known all along. There's nothing for nothing in this world."

"Yes, Victor, nothing for nothing. I'm surprised that at your age and with your intellect you didn't learn that lesson long ago. I regret having to teach it to you in such a crude and painful manner. I hope we will not have to do this again."

Victor knew this woman was a dangerous psychopath. Her actions and this crazy talk about 'controlling' him told Victor all he needed to know that she had to have been involved in Jerome's death, as well as the attack on Natalie.

As Victor was pondering what, if anything, he could do, Alex came over to the bed with a soulful look on her face.

"I truly hope you've learned your lesson," she said. "I see that it's already starting to get light outside and I feel the need for a bit of fresh air. I'm going to leave you here on the bed to reflect on what you've learned while I get washed and dressed."

She went to the closet, picked out some casual clothes and took them into the bathroom and closed the door.

Victor let out a silent sigh of relief, thinking that some measure of sanity and positive feeling for him was returning to Alex's mind after her disciplinary-mode went into retreat. He hoped that when she came out of the bathroom she would see him as a broken man ready to comply completely, a change she seemed to believe her torture session would produce.

After all, at some point she'd have to either release him or kill him. Not much in-between. And if she wants to own him, why would she kill him? Simple logic then said she would release him. The only problem with this line of argument was that logic, simple or otherwise, didn't seem to be one of Alex's strong points. All that was really left for Victor was hope, since faith and charity both seemed to be in short supply right now.

At that very moment, Alex was running through the same line of thinking as Victor. She was definitely not going to kill him—at least not yet. Now that she had the information she wanted, there was no real choice but to release him. Given that she had drugged him, tied him up, shocked his genitals and threatened him with a whip, she was worried that his Sicilian nature would almost surely want revenge of some kind when he got free from his bonds.

While that revenge might be taken out by breaking a few things in her flat, she was more concerned that it would be taken out by breaking a few things on her, both physically and emotionally. She didn't want to be present when Victor was freed. But she had a plan for that.

Emerging from the bathroom, dressed for a casual stroll in the park on a halfway sunny Sunday morning, Alex stood at the end of the bed and told Victor what was going to happen.

"I'm going to leave now, Victor. In a moment I'll unlock one of the cuffs on your hands. I will then go to the doorway from the bedroom and throw the key for the other three cuffs onto the bed in a place where you can reach it. You can then free yourself. But before I do that, I want to tell you the ground rules of the game we're playing."

"Of course," replied Victor in a resigned tone. "By all means, tell me the ground rules."

"Basically, there are two rules. First, don't even think of trying to 'get even' with me before you leave by trashing my flat, cutting my clothes, or any other silly revenge-style action. Please recall that *I* control your destiny at Merit. And if push comes to shove, I wouldn't hesitate for a moment to go to Michael Zilk and tell him that you've been sexually harassing me. Or to Merit's Personnel department with the same story."

Victor knew that this statement was pure bombast, and that she had no control that mattered over his situation at Merit.

Nevertheless, thought Victor. *When I get out of this predicament the first thing I'm going to do is draft my resignation letter to Merit. I'll tell Zilk that I simply cannot work with Alex. I'm not too concerned about her sexual harassment threat, since as far as I know she has no real evidence. Better for me to head for Santa Fe than go another round with her.*

She then opened her purse and dug out a small, micro-sized camera that she showed him.

"While you were 'resting', I took a series of photos of you on the bed. Of course, you were not engaging in anything illegal. But it would be quite embarrassing if these photos were ever to be seen by your colleagues in Santa Fe or anywhere else. You would be a laughing-stock in your community and you'd probably have to decamp for Asia or Australia to escape the shame of such a revelation."

Victor could only laugh silently at this threat, since the chances were much greater that circulation of her photos among his colleagues would only enhance his already established reputation as a man of the world, especially with the young women of the world.

He bit his mental lip. Any hint of these thoughts to Alex could prove fatal.

He was thinking that he could do exactly the same to her by exposing her behavior toward him and Natalie. His side of the story would be that she drugged him to obtain the photos and she attacked his girlfriend in a shop in Italy. If he could get ahold of some actual evidence, like an audio tape of the event, he could even accuse her of murdering Jerome. All in all, he felt his case was a lot more damning than anything she could do to him with her photos.

"After I go out the door, please just put on your clothes and leave. The door has a spring-lock, so all you have to do is close it and the flat will be locked," she said. "I'll be back in half an hour and I expect you to be gone by then. If not, I'll engage the police to escort you from the premises."

Then she went on: "The second rule is that when we meet in the office during the coming weeks, you will act towards me in the same way that I will act towards you. That will be friendly, smiling, joking and, in general, the way any two colleagues who know and like each other would act. I will not be distant, and you will not ignore me. Do you get it?"

Given his situation, Victor had little choice but to 'get it.' Alex went to the bed and unlocked the cuff on Victor's right wrist. She then went to the end of the bed, stood there for a moment, before tossing the key to the cuffs onto the bed, within easy reach of Victor's right hand.

"Goodbye, Victor," she said heading for the front door. "I'll see you in the office. Have a nice day."

Good riddance, thought Victor, unlocking the remaining cuffs and stripping off the noxious dog collar. He gently touched the spot where the contact had been.

"Ouch," he said aloud, as the pain shot up his spine. He'd have to take care of that soon.

Right now I just have to get out of here.

As he got out of the bed, Victor was tempted to leave a bit of trash behind in Alex's flat just as a reminder that he was not her 'dog.' But this was not the right time to do that, and he just grabbed his underwear, pants and socks and began getting dressed.

Sitting on the edge of the bed putting on his socks, he wondered about that recorder he saw last time he was in this bed. A quick look up at the closet though showed that the recorder was no longer there. He really wanted the tape on that recorder. It might very well contain evidence of Alex's complicity in Jerome's death in Paris. He began searching her flat.

First, he recalled Alex's earlier statement about putting all the S&M tapes into the drawer with her sexiest panties. It took Victor no time at all to find that drawer. There were several tapes there, each carefully labeled with a number, presumably representing Alex's hostage of the moment, probably also including the tape of Victor's 'last stand.' Presumably, the tape of Jerome's death was either the last one in the drawer or possibly not in this drawer at all.

Looking in other drawers, cupboards, cabinets and closets, Victor found no sign of either the recorder or the possible tape about Jerome. Then he had a bright idea.

It had only been a couple of weeks since Jerome's death in Paris. So if Alex did have the tape and the recorder in Paris, she would have taken them in her traveling bag. Victor went immediately to the closet where she kept that bag, and sure enough there it was: the recorder, a tape still in it. Victor turned on the recorder and what he heard was more than enough to show that this was indeed the tape of her Parisian encounter with Jerome.

A quick glance at his watch told him he had just a few minutes until Alex would be back.

Victor rushed into the kitchen and got a napkin to wipe down the recorder so as to leave no fingerprints, and then he removed the tape but left the recorder. What he would do with the tape was a matter he'd sort out later. Victor looked around the flat to see if he'd forgotten anything.

Only his self-respect, he thought grimly, as he took his jacket down from the closet in the hallway. This game is definitely not over yet, he vowed, acknowledging that his Sicilian nature was certainly not going to sit still for Alex's dog training.

Leaving Alex's flat, Victor slammed the door in a fit of pique to at least make his ego feel better about what had taken place here, if not his higher-level consciousness. He'd salve his consciousness later. Hopefully, the tape he'd taken would provide some ammunition for the next stage of his struggle with Alex. She may have won this battle, but she certainly had not yet won the war.

*

Upon returning to his flat, Victor reflected upon what had happened at Alex's. Ticking off the points of the evening, one-by-one: she had drugged him, tied him up, electrically shocked him, and finally threatened him with loss of his consultancy and what she believed would be a potentially serious public embarrassment. *Not bad for a few hours,* he thought, *but definitely not good enough, either.*

By the time he showered and dressed and was ready for the day, what he now wanted most was to listen to the tape he'd lifted from Alex's recorder to see what, if anything, it might contain that would help him level the playing field for what had now become the game of Victor vs. Alex.

And I will be The Victor, he thought to himself.

Luckily, London was a civilized city with shops of every type open 24/7. It took only a quick walk over to Knightsbridge to find a corner electronics shop open and ready to sell. Most importantly, they were ready to sell a tape machine that accepted precisely the size and type of tape he'd taken from Alex.

Victor sat down on his sofa and loaded Alex's tape into the recorder and pressed the Play button. Almost immediately he heard Alex say, "Let's go to the bedroom," and a man answering, "The bed is definitely the best place to talk."

Victor couldn't be totally sure from the voice whether it was Jerome or not, since he had only met Jerome one time at that meeting at Merit many weeks ago.

But as the tape played on, Alex confirmed that it was indeed Jerome when she said, "Come on, Jerome. Get undressed so I can tie you up."

The rest of the scenario was strikingly similar to what Victor himself had just experienced at her flat, with the exception that there appeared to be no shock collar in the Parisian scenario. Instead, there was a choking sound that matched what he'd heard via the gossip mill at Merit. In total, the taped encounter lasted about half an hour, at which time Victor turned off the recorder and sat back to think about what he'd heard.

To be honest, Victor was rather disappointed to have his suspicions about Alex confirmed in such a detailed fashion. In particular, he felt badly about himself for being stupid enough to let his body chemistry lead him into an intimate relationship with such a person. He realized that this tape offered him exactly the antidote he needed to neutralize any threat Alex might pose to him. In short, revealing the information on the tape would ensure that Alex would not only lose her job, but would be brought to public ridicule and quite likely face a serious jail term for her actions in Paris.

Talk about a delicious twist of fate!

Now he'd have to consider what to actually do with this tape. But he couldn't. Not rationally, anyway, though he didn't realize it. The shocks to his genitals had engaged his reptile brain to the point that he lacked any awareness of that engagement. He was now so caught up in gleeful revenge—beating Alex at her own game—that he studiously avoided the obvious: withholding the tape would make him guilty of obstruction of justice, perhaps even an accessory to her crime. If he then used the tape in an attempt to control her, he'd be guilty of blackmail and extortion in its own right.

But in the heat of the fight-or-flight continuum his life had now become, these messy realities conveniently evaded his consciousness.

The simplest and probably most effective thing to do is ... nothing, at least for the moment. Just keep the tape and if Alex asks about it, say I know nothing. I could always threaten to take it to the police or to Merit later, if circumstances point in that direction. Right now I don't really have to do anything. Simply deny any knowledge of the tape if Alex tries to pressure me and keep the information to myself.

That was how his thoughts were running when he entered the office Monday morning.

When Victor stepped into the elevator to go to his office, who should he see standing next to the button panel but Alex. Even worse luck,there was no one else in the elevator, only the two of them.

"Good morning, Victor," said Alex with a smile on her face, a smile that Victor saw as being more like that of the Cheshire Cat than as anything even vaguely friendly or disarming.

"Hello Alex. Did you have a nice weekend?" he asked.

"Yes, quite fine. Very fine indeed actually," she said playing along with his parry. "I spent it with an old friend from the USA."

"Well, nothing like one of my countrymen or countrywomen to spice up an otherwise dull British weekend. I'm glad you enjoyed it. Oh, here we are at our floor. Perhaps I'll see you later at our team meeting. Should we say ten o'clock in my office, as usual?"

"Perfect," she agreed as the doors to the elevator closed and they walked to their respective offices.

Fortunately for Victor, Alex kept to herself after the meeting and the Monday group lunch, and they did not see each other again for the rest of the day. Victor decided this was a good evening to join the boys at the pub, as he needed a couple of pints to settle his nerves before dinner. This was also a good way to continue avoiding Alex, as the ladies in the office were never part of the after-work pub crawls that the men seemed to enjoy so much.

*

When Victor got to Merit the next morning, there was a note from Michael Zilk's assistant asking if he could come up to meet with Michael that afternoon at 2 o'clock. He called and confirmed the appointment, wondering why Michael wanted to talk with him. Well, he'd find out soon enough.

Michael greeted Victor and asked if he'd like some coffee or tea. Victor declined, saying he'd just come from lunch and was fine. Michael then sat down at the table and said he was glad that Victor was able to come by to see him, explaining that there were developments afoot that would have a major impact on the simulator project.

"What's happening, Michael?" asked Victor. "I still haven't yet gotten myself fully plugged into the grapevine here at Merit. Mostly, I keeping my head down and try to avoid being buried in the details of upgrading the simulator."

"Well, Victor, a lot has been happening lately, much of it at a level that far exceeds my pay grade. Let me tell you what I know."

At this statement, Victor was already beginning to feel a bit uncomfortable because Michael was usually a lot more outgoing and cheery than he appeared today.

"Okay, Michael, fire away. What's on the agenda that us simulation types need to know about?"

"Here it is," Michael said. "A few weeks ago, the upper management of Merit had discussions with the firm MaxFin about their taking over Merit as a subsidiary of their own operation. As you may know, MaxFin is a vastly larger firm than Merit and is able to do things that Merit simply cannot afford to do right now."

"Boy," said Victor, "that's a bit of a surprise."

Michael continued, "They made a very attractive offer for all Merits assets. This offer will give Merit's current shareholders about a 25 percent greater payoff than what our shares are currently trading at on the open market."

"Did this deal go through?" Victor asked. "If so, then it may well benefit the simulator project, since as you say MaxFin has the resources to expand our simulator group to a size commensurate with the needs of what we're now seeing is required to get the job done in a reasonable amount of time."

"All true, Victor—*if* MaxFin were interested in this simulator project. It turns out they're not. And, yes, the deal was signed yesterday. I'm afraid the simulator project will have to be dropped as soon as possible."

Victor was blindsided. He suddenly found himself reeling, trying to recover from the shock.

"I know we have a contract with you for your work on the simulator," Michael continued. "The new firm will honor that contract. Not to worry on that score. Moreover, if you want to stay in London awhile and try to find a new sponsor, you are free to stay in your flat here until the end of next month. I know this must come as a hugely unpleasant surprise to you. I only learned of all this myself a few hours ago."

Victor then asked Michael when the project needed to be wound down. Zilk told him that it should be wrapped up by the end of the current week. That was just a few days from now, barely enough time to write a summary of where they stood with the project at present. In essence, this would be his final report on the simulator.

"If you could just write a few words summarizing where the project is right now and send it to me, I will prepare an official statement regarding your contract and the flat, specifying in writing what I just told you," Zilk said.

"Yes, of course, Michael, I can certainly do that," Victor replied.

"I'm really very sorry about this development Victor, especially as I think the project has huge potential. But what I think is simply not what's at issue here. What's at issue is what MaxFin thinks and they think they'd rather do without it. So there it is."

"And what about the IP for the project?" Victor asked, trying to remember what his intellectual property arrangements had been with Merit, and if there'd been any contingency written into his contract that might cover this development. Would he still be able to profit from future developments with the simulator, or did MaxFin now hold those cards? "Do the intellectual property rights come back to me? Or?"

"I'm glad you mentioned that Victor. I will put in my letter to you that the intellectual property remains with you. That's the least we can do, I think."

"All right, Michael. I appreciate you telling me about this. I'll have to let the team know so we can get everything together for you by the end of the week."

"Please don't tell anyone about this before tomorrow afternoon, Victor. The entire merger will be public knowledge by then. I'm telling you early so you can prepare your own life and plans as soon as possible. The rest of the team are Merit employees and they will be looked after separately as employees, not as consultants."

Instead of walking out of Michael's office with a fistful of cash to expand his group, Victor walked out with a mind full of worries about whether the project could be sold to another sponsor. He also knew there was no point in worrying about that now because it was entirely outside his control. At the moment, Victor's focus needed to be on figuring out his own life.

He thought the best thing he could do right now was take a long walk through Hyde Park and try to fit together all these new pieces in the London puzzle: The end of his project at Merit, his relationship with Alex and, more generally, his future. He needed time to put everything together into a short- and longer-term life plan. He certainly couldn't do that sitting around in his office.

*

As he walked along The Serpentine past The Pond, Victor realized that from a practical point of view Merit's merger and the collapse of the simulator project were more of a blessing to him personally than anything else. He still retained the IP for the project, as well as the money from the contract.

Finally, and most importantly, he could now go back to Santa Fe and to Natalie with a clear conscience that he hadn't abandoned the project.

Victor saw his life plan as being quite straightforward: finish the dangling loose ends of the project report for MaxFin, head for the airport and return to Natalie. No muss, no fuss, all very simple—except for a psychotic killer on the loose whose focus was still on him!

Victor's short-term plan for Alex was quite clear: Organize a meeting with her at a neutral place—not her flat, that's for sure. But a place where he could end their relationship, once and for all. He was thinking that the Club Intercon on the top floor of the Intercontinental Hotel would be a good spot for this meeting because it was a place where they had not met during the course of his stay in London. Besides, it had a panoramic view of the city of London which might serve as a useful distraction from the sobering message he had to deliver to her.

With luck, he thought, she would be reasonable about his decision to abandon London and her and not create a scene. What he expected, though, was that she would explode. He took that as a given. What concerned him most was the nature and confinement of that explosion.

I'd better have this meeting with her the day before I head for the airport, he thought to himself, *giving her as little time as possible to somehow screw up my life before my plane take off for the United States.*

The next day Victor went immediately to Michael Zilk's office and gave the final report on the project to Zilk's assistant. He asked her if perhaps Michael had a quick moment now to see him. She ushered Victor into the office.

"Hello Victor," said Michael. "What a nice surprise to see that you're still talking with me after our rather unhappy discussion yesterday."

"Nothing you could do anything about, Michael. No hard feelings. What I came by for this morning is to give you this final report on the simulator, as we agreed. It didn't take too much time to put it together, since the real action items worth reporting would have been from the second part of the project. But ... well, you know."

"Yes, I do, Victor. I thank you for your promptness in bringing this to me today."

"No problem," said Victor. They shook hands and said they'd 'stay in touch.'

*

Fine. One less thing to do, thought Victor, making his way down to the elevator and back to his office. Now for the packing up of my office items, such as they are. But first, he called Alex and asked if he could have a word with her. She said fine and invited him to her office.

As Victor entered, he saw Alex looking rather pale. He asked if something was wrong, and she motioned for him to take a seat.

"I just heard that Merit is being sold to the firm MaxFin," she said. "It seems that this sale is a *fait accompli,* and one of the consequences is that our project is to be closed down immediately. Did you know anything about this?"

"Yes. I heard it from Michael Zilk yesterday afternoon, but he asked me not to tell anyone until it was officially announced. It's really a shame, as we were making good headway with the simulator."

"Did Michael tell you anything else?"

"Not really. We talked about my contract and the IP for the project. He also asked me to write a brief summary of where it stands. I gave that to him this morning, and will send a copy to you. And I guess that will be that for the project."

Alex looked even a bit worse now, discovering that Victor knew about this closing down of the project even before her, despite the fact that she was at least nominally heading the project. She didn't think that was a good sign at all for her future at Merit.

"Anyway, what did you want to see me about, Victor?"

"Oh, nothing very important. Let it go for now. It can wait."

With that, Victor got up and returned to his own office to pack his things. He would contact Alex later in the day about getting together to tell her his life plans and how they spelled the end of their relationship. Now was certainly not the time and Merit was certainly not the place.

Leaving the office at the end of the day with a bag under his arm containing various items from his office, Victor ran into Alex in the hallway at the door to at the elevator. She asked him about the bag.

"I told Zilk that I would be leaving my office at the end of the week," he said. "The stuff in this bag represents my total accumulation of odds and ends since I took that office three months ago. Not much to show for three months, is it?"

Alex looked at what he was carrying and smiled.

"I'd like to meet you soon," he said. "We can discuss how we're going to handle our own relationship now that I won't be seeing you at Merit any longer. What about a meeting after work tomorrow? Would that suit you? You know, one last drink for the road, and all that?"

"Yes, that sounds better, Victor. Since this is something special, why don't you come to my place and we'll have a wake, with me supplying the meal. I don't really feel up to going to a restaurant right now, anyway. But I can't say I'm in a spirit to prepare a Blumenthal-style meal, either. Okay?"

"I think for this meeting I'd prefer a more neutral place," Victor told her. "What about the Club Intercon at the top of the Intercon Hotel? Tomorrow at, say, 7 o'clock?"

"Yes, that sounds fine, Victor. Better than my place, actually. I haven't been to the Intercon for some time and it would be nice to look out on the entire city while we talk. Besides, it can't hurt if we get a little drunk at such a heavenly place while we bid farewell to our project."

Victor nodded his agreement, wondering what, exactly, she was referring to by 'our project'. If her statements from their last meeting at her flat were any indicator, he didn't think she would be ready to bid farewell to him as easily as to the simulator project. He could hope. He'd find out for sure tomorrow.

*

Alex welcomed Victor to their table at the Club Intercon with big hug and a kiss on the lips to remember.

"Really wonderful to see you, Victor. Even if the circumstances are a bit grim at the moment. Have a seat, have a drink, and let's toast to what might have been."

Victor looked at her for a moment and thought having Alex for a partner was a lot like having an Australian taipan for a pet. It's a fascinating snake, lovely to look at, but you know eventually it's going to bite. And when it does, you're a goner—unless you happen to have a vial of taipan antivenom in your back pocket. Luckily for him, he had that antidote nicely packed into his suitcase at his apartment: the tape linking Alex to Jerome's death. With that comforting thought, he sat down and agreed that the times were rather grim.

"Perhaps the right drink will brighten up those times, at least for the moment," he said, giving his default G&T order to the waiter.

Victor couldn't help noting Alex was in rather a jocular mood tonight, despite the bad news at Merit. As he knew well, that mood could change with a word or even a glance. Unfortunately, what he intended to tell her tonight might prove considerably more downbeat than a simple word or a glance. He hoped he could prevent her reaction from being an emotional catastrophe of nuclear dimensions.

"Well, Victor. Here's your G&T," Alex said, as the waiter brought his drink. "Let me join you in toasting the demise of the stockmarket simulator, at least at Merit. May it find a more congenial home elsewhere."

"Sit here next to me where I can see your smiling face."

"I'm afraid it might not be smiling too much longer, Victor. If the powers at Merit have their way, I fear that I could be on the unemployment line before long."

"Oh, Alex, let's not think about that now. You know the old saying, 'Tonight we must eat, drink and be merry because tomorrow we die.' Things always look bleak when something hits you unexpectedly like this Merit buyout. Almost without exception, that shock event forces you to seriously evaluate your life and see how you can reorganize it in a different mode. Not so miraculously, that new life almost always turns out so much better than the old one that in a few years you look back and say, 'That shock wasn't the worst thing that ever happened to me. It was actually the *best* thing that ever happened to me.' "

"Oh, Victor, you're such a comedian," she laughed.

"Well, black humor, perhaps," he agreed.

They spent the next few minutes talking about this and that, gossip from Merit, speculations about the simulator project being picked up by a new sponsor, and so forth. As the conversation developed, its focus got closer and closer to the overriding issue: What were they going to do about their relationship now that the Merit connection linking them had been severed? What effect was that going to have on their personal lives together?

Finally, Victor suggested they order a bottle of vintage cognac, to which Alex agreed.

The waiter brought out a bottle of vintage Hennessy XO cognac along with two special cognac glasses and set them on the table. He poured a generous level of the amber fluid into each glass, and after the waiter left, Victor and Alex clinked their glasses and sat back to finally address their joint problem.

*

"Do you want to start or should I?" asked Victor.

"You go first. I'm eager to hear your view of things and get some idea of what you plan to do."

Victor looked down at his drink and thought, well, now or never.

"Okay. Here goes. As you know, our project is finished at Merit. That means I'm finished, too. As a result, I plan to return to Santa Fe as soon as I can get everything wrapped up here. Actually, I'm leaving for Santa Fe tomorrow."

Alex looked rather disappointed by this announcement. But she didn't look at all surprised.

"What about me, Victor? How are we going to continue our relationship with you on the other side of the world?"

"I know your situation is a lot more complicated than mine, since you're still an employee of Merit and the management may well have already picked out a slot for you to occupy in the new scheme of things. I guess that means you need to stick around a bit to see what happens. Then you'll have all the information you need in order to make a decision on how to play out your life."

Alex looked intently at him.

"In case you've forgotten our 'discussion' on Saturday, I control you Victor. I don't want you just heading for the airport and leaving me in the lurch here in London."

"I'm sorry, Alex, but I simply don't take seriously your idea that anybody can 'control' or 'own' somebody else. While I don't want to be brutal about it, let me simplify the situation for you."

"By all means, Victor, 'simplify.' "

"We're finished, Alex. Is that simple enough?"

"Why are you ending our relationship, Victor? We've just had a lovely evening and we have certainly enjoyed each other's company a lot over the past several months. Why do you think it has to end? Maybe I could come to Santa Fe with you?"

"No, Alex, you cannot come to Santa Fe with me. Or go anywhere else with me. I don't want to continue seeing you after tonight."

"Would you care to tell me why?" she asked in a rather forceful, almost threatening, voice.

“Since we’re being ‘simple,’ the answer is that you are simply too dangerous for me, Alex.”

“What do you mean ‘dangerous?’ ”

“You’re too unstable, Alex. And while I find you enormously attractive in many ways, I cannot afford the luxury of not knowing when the murderous Alex is going to suddenly appear. That’s what I mean by ‘dangerous.’ ”

“What do you think I’m going to do Victor, murder you?”

“That’s just the point. At any given time, I don’t really *know* what you’re going to do to me. And I only become more concerned, the longer we know and see each other. After all, it only takes one incident going out of control and I’m toast.”

Alex got up from the table and began walking back and forth, mumbling something to herself that Victor couldn’t quite understand. Some of the othre patrons began glancing nervously in their direction. Finally, she stood directly in front of him.

“None of the incidents you are referring to—the hair dryer, the S&M bondage, the ‘interrogation’ were anywhere near a threat to your life, Victor. What are you so afraid of?”

Throwing caution to the wind, Victor decided there was little downside to having a public airing. “That’s easy to say from your side of the street, Alex. But I definitely cannot read your mind. From my perspective each of these incidents was potentially very life-threatening for me. Let me add something here that points even more in this direction.”

“By all means, Victor, tell me more. There’s no holding back here tonight, it seems.”

By this time, much of the room was staring into their own plates—but Victor could feel everyone’s ears upon them. While he had initially felt very hesitant to bring Jerome’s death into this conversation, he now saw nothing for it but to confront her with his facts and conjectures regarding Jerome, public forum or not.

"You'll recall that when we had our first S&M bondage episode at your flat awhile back, I told you that I'd never experienced that before. It left a pretty vivid imprint on my memory. Following Jerome's death, the office gossip had it that he died in Paris from just the same sort of misadventure, an S&M game gone badly wrong. When I heard that tidbit of gossip, the bells started ringing in my head, linking you with Jerome in exactly that kind of sex game.

At the time, I didn't take it very seriously since Jerome died in Paris, while you live in London, and there didn't seem to be any real connection with his death and you—until I discovered that you inherited his job. But even then my suspicions were that these events were purely coincidental."

"Okay, Victor, I get your point. Where are you going with this?"

"The next data point was when we had S&M sex the first time and you happened to mention that recorder under the bed."

"Yes, I remember that conversation. So what?"

Now Victor was up against the wall. He had to either play his trump card or fold his hand. Nothing in-between.

"The 'So What' is that after you left me in your flat on Sunday to untie myself, while you went outside for a brisk morning walk and a coffee and croissant, I searched your flat and found the tape in your machine in your travel bag. I then took it and was able to listen with my own ears what kind of antics were recorded on it."

At this statement, Alex began to stare intently at Victor with her eyes, mouth, and especially her ears wide open.

"You bastard," she shouted. "When I saw the tape was missing, I suspected you immediately. You fucking bastard. You had no right … . I want that tape back, Victor. Right now before you leave London!"

"Well, you know what I heard when I played that tape. And you're not going to get it back. I'm taking it with me when I go to Santa Fe as protection against any more threats or hostile actions against me by you."

At this point, Alex reached down across the table, grabbed her glass and flung the cognac into Victor's face.

With that Alex abruptly turned around and stalked out of the restaurant.

Well, thought Victor. *That was a bit easier than I'd anticipated. Just a drenched sport coat and shirt, but at least drenched with a superior-level liquor.*

The room began to slowly murmur with conversation—he realized it must've gone completely silent during Alex's tirade. He ignored the furtive glances from all directions.

He wondered what she would do next. No use worrying about that now. He had to get his life back in order in Santa Fe and was looking forward to sharing it with Natalie.

As a precautionary measure against Alex turning up at his flat that night, he decided to book a room downstairs at this hotel for the night and make his departure to Heathrow tomorrow morning directly from here, not from his flat. His first order of business was to make that booking on his way out the door, then return to his flat and bring his luggage with the all-important tape over here immediately.

He paid the bill, leaving the waiter a hefty tip, and got out of there.

Victor packed quickly and got back to his room at the Intercon. There, he spent a bit of time writing farewell emails to Bob and Bill, the workers on the project, thanking them for their efforts.

He then composed a somewhat longer message to Natalie, saying he would be arriving in Santa Fe on Monday evening and would tell her the whole story on Tuesday. He closed by saying how much he missed her and expressed his eagerness to hold her close again.

Episode XIV

The End

Santa Fe

Natalie was so eager to see Victor again that she sent him an email, asking for his return flight information to Albuquerque. She told him she'd be there at the airport to greet him.

Victor had not left his car at the airport when he departed for the months-long stay in London, so being picked up like this was a bonus: a beautiful lady waiting to welcome him with open arms *and* private transport for the sixty-mile trip from ABQ back to his home in Santa Fe.

After what he'd just experienced in the battle trenches of the City of London, he couldn't ask for anything more satisfying by way of reward.

When Natalie saw Victor walking up from the arrival gate to the luggage area, she felt a sudden rush of excitement. After a huge hug and kiss, she said, "Wonderful to see you, Victor. On our drive to Santa Fe, you'll have to give me the whole story of why you're back from London already."

"I'm just as excited as you," he said. "It's lovely to see and hold you again."

"I'm so happy your project there got finished so quickly. I thought it would be at least another two or three months before it would end and I'd see you again."

"Well, the story is not especially complicated. An hour's drive should give me more than enough time to sketch the main details. But first, let me go over to the luggage carousel and get my things."

"Perfect. I'll get the car and see you at the exit from the luggage area in a few minutes."

As they entered Interstate 25 for the one-hour drive to Santa Fe, Natalie looked over at Victor, raised her eyebrows and nodded for him to begin the story of why he was now in New Mexico instead of Not-So-Merry Olde England.

Victor told her about Merit being bought out and the new firm not wanting the simulator project. "But the good part," he said, "is the new firm was kind enough to honor my consulting contract and didn't even make me fight with them over the intellectual property rights to the simulator, either. All in all, I came out of the whole situation in pretty good shape."

Natalie smiled and said, "It sounds as if you won the lottery—lots of free money and the right to sell your product to anyone who wants to buy it."

Victor agreed with that analysis, but couldn't really explain to her why he saw this development as being a bit of of a loss as well as a substantial win.

Basically, he and Natalie were using different scales on which to measure the outcome. Hers was simple: hard cash. But his was somewhat more complicated. Basically, it was a disappointment to him that the project was closed down, and the cash only softened, but didn't really come close to eliminating that empty feeling. He really wanted the project to continue so it could be tested on real markets, and the money from his consulting contract could never make up for that.

Of course, he could still try and sell it to another firm, one with a bit more imagination and foresight than MaxFin. So he shouldn't complain. As a big bonus, he got to return to Natalie long before either of them had thought it would be possible.

"What are you going to do now, Victor?" Natalie asked. "On the one hand, you're not due back at the Institute for another three months. But I cannot really imagine you just sitting around your house, puttering about in the garden and marking the days off the calendar until your leave of absence ends."

"I can't either," he said. "I think I'll take a couple of days to unpack my things, sweep up the house a bit and consider that very question. Whatever I do, I promise it will not take me to any more remote time zones where I'd have to be away from you for more than a few days."

"Oh, Victor, those are just the words I wanted to hear," she said, leaning over to give him a tender kiss.

The rest of the drive passed with chit-chat about people they knew in Santa Fe, her job at the gallery and other miscellaneous items helping to bring Victor up-to-date on what had been going on during his absence in London.

By the time they reached Victor's house on the east side of Santa Fe, his eyes were drooping. He was feeling his years and the 14 hours of travel between his hotel in London and his doorstep in Santa Fe. Natalie remarked that he looked very tired, kindly offering to help him carry a couple of bags from the car to his front door. But instead of coming inside, she gave Victor a welcome-back hug, and said she'd call him tomorrow afternoon.

Victor was grateful for Natalie's consideration of his reduced energy level and they parted with a few words about reconnecting tomorrow for dinner.

*

Love me ... I know he loves me. They all love me. From the minute he laid eyes upon me in the dining room in Tortola I had him. I had chosen the perfect dress, the perfect heels, the perfect earrings, and the perfect scent. Just as my mother taught me. It was, she'd said, how she had caught my father in her net. He loved her, and he loved me. Just like I know Victor loves me, even though he left me ...

Sing a song of sixpence
A pocket full of rye
Four and twenty blackbirds
Baked in a pie

*

Entering his house, Victor was pleased to see that his email to the cleaning lady had been received and acted upon, so the house seemed in pretty good order. He didn't even have time to shower or unpack his bags, before heading upstairs to the bedroom, struggling out of his clothes and luxuriating in being able to finally put his head on the pillow and drift off to sleep.

Victor awoke the next morning to the sound of someone opening and then closing his screen door. *Probably the postman,* he thought, *with a package.* He couldn't be bothered to leave the luxury of the pillow and sheets right now, so he turned over and went back to sleep.

A couple of hours later he finally felt rested enough and slipped into his robe and went downstairs to prepare a much-needed cup of strong, dark Italian roast coffee. While the water was coming to a boil, he went to the front door and retrieved the package that had been left for him.

He was surprised to see it was from Natalie!

Opening the box, his heart skipped a beat when he saw it was a set of exquisite-looking whisky glasses, along with a loving note saying she'd bought these in Trieste and stashed them away as a welcome back to Santa Fe present for him.

She must have packed the box last night and dropped it off on her way to the gallery this morning, Victor realized. He was grateful to be home. For a lot of reasons.

*

I must do something to win him back. I must think of the perfect gift. Victor is a man who likes things, and I must buy him an exquisite gift that will show him how much I mean to him and that will show him how much I mean to him ... He is probably with that woman he loves. The woman he also loves. I followed her in Trieste as she was looking for a gift for him—a gift for him because he likes things—and she was buying him an exquisite gift that would show him how much she means to him and how much she means to him ... Yes, and with my gift I will take it to him ... He will receive my gift in the same way Jerome did in Paris ...

When the pie was opened
The birds began to sing
Wasn't that a dainty dish
To set before the king

*

After a bit of re-energizing from the coffee, Victor had a shower, got dressed and unpacked his things from London. He then sat down to put together his plan for re-entry into life, Santa Fe-style.

The first item on that list was to arrange an appointment with the Institute Director, John Casey, to sort out details surrounding the end of his leave-of-absence. The Institute was not paying him during that leave, so they had almost surely allocated his salary to someone or something else.

It could even be that his office too was now being used by a short-term visitor or a post-doc. Victor definitely wanted to get back to his old life at the Institute as quickly as possible. He needed to settle the best—and quickest—way to do this with Casey.

Luckily, when he called Casey's office, his assistant said Casey had an empty slot on his appointment calendar at the end of the day today. If Victor could come by around 5 o'clock, they could meet then.

Perfect, thought Victor, until he looked at his watch and saw that it was already nearly 3 o'clock! *Wow, how time flies or drags when you're jet-lagged.* He had a moment to call Natalie and thank her for the lovely whisky glasses. "I promise you I will start using those glasses this very evening. And on that note, what about meeting me for an early dinner tonight somewhere nice and romantic?"

"Oh, Victor, you always have such great ideas. Let's meet at *Geronimo's* at half past seven. Would that work for you?"

"Perfect," he said, heading out the door to his appointment with a spring in his step.

*

I want to see you so much, Victor. I have a lovely gift that will bring you back to me ... back to me ... You will soon see that I am the woman for you, not the lady in Santa Fe. Your heart belongs to me ...

*

They enjoyed a leisurely dinner at *Geronimo,* catching up with Natalie's plans for her work at the gallery, various happenings with mutual friends in Santa Fe like Stephanie, and other items of common concern. They also talked a bit about taking a short, more leisurely, trip back to Taos, as they both thought their earlier visit was a bit too hit-and-run.

As they were having their post-dinner cake and coffee, Natalie asked, "Have you decided what you're going to do now that you're back in Santa Fe?"

Looking at his watch, Victor stated: "That question was answered just about two hours ago."

"And?"

"Prior to coming here to join you for dinner, I met with John Casey, the Director of the Institute. I told Casey that I would like to change my leave from six months to three and now return to the Institute. I said I wouldn't need any financial support from the Institute until the normal leave expired. But I would like to be able to come to the Institute regularly, have my office back and, in general, join back into all the Institute activities."

"If he agreed with this plan, you're in heaven, Victor," replied Natalie. "Did he agree?"

"In fact, he did! Now I'm in heaven—with you and with the Institute. I think that calls for a celebratory drink, don't you?"

"Absolutely. But I think we should go back to your house and use those whisky glasses I gave you."

"The best idea I've heard since I returned to Santa Fe," replied Victor.

And off they went, back up the hill to celebrate Victor's return in style.

*

Over the next few weeks, as Victor and Natalie were busy getting cozy and reacquainted, life dealt Alex a very different hand.

About a month after the Merit takeover, Michael Zilk called her to his office for what he termed a chat. The result of that chat was that Alex walked out the door unemployed.

When she got back to her flat that evening after receiving her walking papers from Merit, Alex poured herself a good-sized glass of wine and sat down to consider her life. She had lost her lover, her job and now she was about to lose her home in London. And all in just a few days.

Her first thought was Victor.

I love Victor for a lot of reasons. But I'm also very angry at him for abandoning me here In London and for stealing that tape from me. I want to get him back and get back that tape, too. I even liked the looks of his lady friend, Natalie. Maybe all three of us could be together one day.

Then came the end of the third glass of wine, which brought forth strong, negative feelings as she began thinking about how badly she had been treated by Victor.

All the shit I've swallowed over the past few weeks after his disappearance to Santa Fe. After all I did for him. I was the one who got him that project. I was the one who took him into my bed, day after night for months, told him I loved him, treated him like a king. Then he simply up and left me for that lady in Santa Fe. Someone he barely even knew. If I ever want to feel secure again, I must get that tape of my encounter with Jerome back from Victor.

*

Finally, Alex found herself at the place she was longing so desperately to be—now they could be together. All of them together.

Oh! What a lovely house in this charming district. I would love to live here. It seems more like being in Spain three hundred years ago than in the USA in the 21st century. Maybe all three of us can live here together.

First though, I have to deal with that tape!

The king was in his counting house
Counting out his money
The queen was in the parlour
Eating bread and honey

She drove by yet again very late one night. No one was around. The lights were all off in Victor's house. Leaving her car down the street, she quietly walked up to his house and left the street to reconnoiter along the sides and back of the house.

I need to get a good idea of how the house is organized.

She looked in the windows to the living room area and saw how the furniture was arranged and the relationship of the living area to the kitchen. She gathered that the bedrooms were upstairs, reached by the stairway that she saw at the edge of the kitchen.

Now I can start making my plan to confront Victor and try to win him back. If that doesn't work, I'll strong-arm him into returning the tape. But I hope he–and Natalie, too—will welcome me into their family. How delightful that would be.

The maid was in the garden
Hanging out the clothes
When down came the blackbird
And pecked off her nose

*

Next door to Victor's house was an empty lot that many visitors coming to see people in the neighborhood used as a place to park their car, since the street was pretty narrow without much on-street parking available.

Alex decided the best time to confront Victor was after dark, when she could park next door to his place and not be seen, or at least not be recognized, by anyone happening to be looking out on to the street at the time.

Moreover, by pulling into the lot she could also see whether Victor's car was in his driveway, suggesting he was likely to be home.

Getting out of her car, she walked on the unpaved street to the path leading to his front door. She was wearing trainers so as not to make any extra noise on her way to his door.

Luckily, the screen door was not fastened and the evening was mild, so Victor had left the front door open to get a cooling breeze as he enjoyed a drink in the living room while Natalie was in the kitchen preparing one for herself.

Alex pulled out her gun and stepped quietly into the entrance hall.

She heard Victor call out, "What about joining me here in the living room, Natalie? I'm missing you."

Alex began to silently move in his direction, but accidentally brushed the edge of a table on her way, causing a magazine to fall onto the floor.

What was that? thought Victor, as he got up and moved into the hallway, where he saw Alex standing there pointing a gun at him.

She motioned him to step back a few paces into the living room.

"I won't bore you with the details of what happened to me in London after you left Victor, other than to say I am now a free agent. But I came here to Santa Fe to repay you for your 'kindness' in abandoning me in London. Maybe you'd like to also return my property you stole in London."

"Ah, yes, the tape of you and Jerome," said Victor.

"You were always smart, Victor. Give it to me and I won't have to use this gun. I don't want to have to kill you to keep that tape from ever being used against me. But I will most definitely do that if you don't return it *right now!*"

"I don't have it any longer, Alex. I threw it into a trash can before I left London. You have nothing to worry about, at least from the point of view of that tape."

"Ha! Ha! Very funny, Victor. Hard for me to believe you'd just dump the tape when it is the only piece of evidence linking me to Jerome's death. Now *get* that tape and give it to me."

At just that moment, Alex and Victor heard a voice from the kitchen saying, "What's that? Hold on a minute Victor, I'll be there shortly with my drink."

"Who's that?" said Alex.

"It's nobody. Leave her out of this."

It doesn't sound like 'nobody' to me. In fact, it sounds a lot *like somebody named Natalie. How nice. Just the person to round out the trio I've been dreaming about.*

Sing a song of sixpence
A pocket full of rye

*

At that moment, Natalie came into the living room with a drink in her hand. Seeing Alex with a gun pointed directly at Victor, her grip involuntarily loosened. She dropped the glass and it shattered.

Before Natalie could recover from her shock, Alex had moved closer, twitching the gun in the direction of Victor.

"Nice of you to join the party. Move over there next to Victor," Alex said.

Natalie moved closer to Victor, looking curiously at Alex, somehow seeming to recognize her but not quite able to pinpoint . . . .

Then it hit her: Trieste!

"*You!*" shouted Natalie. "You are the woman from the dress shop in Trieste. What the hell are you doing here?"

"Calm down," said Victor. "This woman is here because she thinks I have something important that belongs to her and she's come to get it back."

Looking back to Alex, Victor suggested that she just turn around and walk calmly back out the door.

Alex was having none of that and moved closer to Victor, then suddenly turned and grabbed Natalie and held the gun to her head, threatening to shoot her if he didn't produce the tape.

Victor had no option but to agree. Recalling that he had a couple of old cassette tapes in his office upstairs, he'd bring one of them down for her, pretending it was the tape from Paris. He told her, "It's upstairs. I'll go get it."

Alex then said, "Leave your cell phone on the table here before you go upstairs. And if I hear anything like a land-line phone call to the police, I'll shoot her immediately. Do you understand?"

Nodding his head, Victor took his cell phone from his pocket and placed it on the table. Then he went to get the tape.

When he came back he casually tossed the false tape in Alex's direction, the cassette falling onto the floor. Her attention was distracted for a moment as she looked down at the tape. Since one hand held the gun that she could not afford to release, Alex momentarily let go of Natalie with her other hand to use it to reach down and pick up the tape. At that moment, Natalie twisted away from Alex and threw an elbow into her face in an effort to get control of the hand holding the gun. That pushed Alex's arm up and the gun went off, wounding Victor in the upper arm.

Four and twenty blackbirds
Baked in a pie

Amidst much screaming and shouting, Natalie pushed Alex back against the coffee table, a square-sided hardwood table on metal legs. Alex slipped on the carpet beneath the table and fell against the hard corner hitting the back of her head right where her neck and skull came together. She immediately dropped the gun, rolled over and was silent.

Natalie rushed over to Victor, "Are you all right?" she asked. "What's happened to your arm? It's bleeding. I have to get a cloth to stop the flow."

Natalie then ran into the bathroom, while Victor looked carefully at Alex. She was totally silent, unmoving.

He thought she must be unconscious from the blow to her head from the table. At least she was temporarily out of action, which was what counted most at the moment.

As Victor stared down at Alex, Natalie returned with a cloth and asked:

"Can you feel her pulse, Victor?"

Victor grabbed Alex's wrist and quickly checked.

"Not really," he replied. "Maybe she's dead."

"Oh, my god, Victor. That would be terrible. What can we do? Oh, dear! The blood is now dripping down from your shirt on to the floor. You need to get into the bathroom *now.* I have to bandage that wound."

"We've got to call the police," said Victor. "Could you grab the phone, Natalie, and do that please?"

Natalie looked over at Alex and said, "Dead or not, she seems totally out of it. I don't think she's going anywhere. We have to take care of your arm immediately. We can call the police afterwards."

In the bathroom Natalie got out a towel and a box of bandages and told Victor to take off his shirt. They could then both see that the bullet had just grazed Victor's arm, so it was only a minor flesh wound. The bleeding should be easy to stop.

Natalie immediately washed the wound and wrapped the towel around it, bandaging it with some sports tape from the bathroom cupboard.

As she finished the bandaging on Victor's arm, Natalie thought she saw something moving in the mirror above the sink. Turning to the bathroom doorway, she screamed when she saw Alex standing there wide-eyed pointing the gun.

Sing a song of sixpence
A pocket full of rye

*

"I'm going shoot both of you," said Alex in a robot-like tone, with a smile on her face.

How delicious it would be to kill them both. If I can't have Victor, then nobody can.

Just before Alex pulled the trigger, Natalie dove to her right and pushed Victor down with her. The bullet just missed them, shattering the bathroom mirror into hundreds of tiny shards instead.

Before Alex could get off another shot, Natalie rushed her and they both fell onto the floor, the gun scooting back into the living room. Each of the women were digging in with their fingernails, clawing at each other, while Alex tried to bite Natalie to get free.

Finally, Alex's greater height and weight took their toll, and she rolled over onto Natalie, jumped up and grabbed the gun.

By then Victor had come out of the bathroom and managed to tackle Alex from behind, taking them both onto the floor. He twisted Alex's arm and sent the gun scooting across the floor again. In her efforts to get loose, Alex managed to turn over but found Victor sitting on top of her, reaching with both hands for her throat.

Squeezing harder and harder on Alex's throat, Victor put his fingers on the carotid artery on both sides of her neck, slowing down the blood flow to her brain. Alex struggled wildly, scratching, bucking and flailing, attempting to break Victor's hold on her throat and throw him off. But Victor was now in a manic state, his adrenalin flow giving him the added strength he needed to tighten his stranglehold on Alex's throat. He bore down hard.

Her face turning purple, then blue, Alex's eyes began rolling back in her head, as her bucking became weak and the flailing of her arms more flaccid. Suddenly, her arms fell to the floor and her eyes rolled forward, now staring directly into Victor's. But Victor was still holding on to her throat and squeezing it until Natalie came up behind him, saying,"She's no longer breathing, Victor. You can let go of her now."

Victor finally loosened his grip and fell over onto his back on the floor, gasping for air himself.

After a few moments he sat up and said, "You can call the police now, Natalie."

ACKNOWLEDGMENTS

One of the biggest misunderstandings readers have about books, especially fiction, is that somehow the book springs full-borne from the author's mind. Not one novel in a million has this history. The remaining 99+ percent come about from the author's interaction with a multitude of friends, relatives, colleagues and other such 'high life', who offer many and varied opinions, suggestions, time and energy into helping the author shape the words people actually read. *Prey for Me* is no exception to this iron rule.

As a result, I am now in the position of performing the single most pleasant task associated with writing a book: Thanking all the people who supported me in a vast number of different ways to getting the words you read onto the page.

First, let me thank in no particular order people who read one of the seven or more drafts of the book, in part or in full, and offered their suggestions. In this connection, I thank Trudy Draper, Zac Bharucha, George Leitmann, Aviott John, Josephine Liu, Joe Tabacco, Joleen Rocque-Frank, Dan Yost, Olga Protassova and Albert Frantz.

Friends engaged in various aspects of publishing also contributed mightily to this book. For their more professional input, I want to tip my hat to David Berlinski, Paul Makin, Peter Hubbard and Marc Elsberg.

Colleagues who worked directly to get the words you have read on to the page and/or who contributed their talents in other ways were Roger Jones, who offered numerous ideas for the book and its promotion, Mumtaz Mustafa, who created the cover, and Martina-Gleissenebner-Teskey, who directed, produced and filmed the videos used in promoting the book. .

Next to last, but very far from least, it's a pleasure to thank profusely Marc de Celle, my proof-reader, copy editor and general advisor on matters of getting the right words inserted into the right places.

Finally, a big round of applause and a bow of appreciation to my editorial advisor, Henry Ferris, who taught me the difference between writing fiction and non-fiction. Thanks, Henry, for making sure I stayed on the fiction side. I couldn't believe how huge the difference is between the worlds of non-fiction and fiction. Henry showed me that the two have almost nothing in common other than that they both use words. Now I'm a believer!

CPSIA information can be obtained
at www.ICGtesting.com
Printed in the USA
LVHW051157100920
665517LV00001B/84